AFTER THE
EXECUTION

AFTER THE EXECUTION

James Raven

ROBERT HALE · LONDON

ISBN 978-0-7198-0920-0

Robert Hale Limited
Clerkenwell House
Clerkenwell Green
London EC1R 0HT

www.halebooks.com

2 4 6 8 10 9 7 5 3

Typeset in Palatino
Printed in the UK by Berforts Information Press Ltd

Author's note

THE INFAMOUS 'WALLS' prison in Huntsville, Texas is where hundreds of death row inmates have been executed by lethal injection. I was in Huntsville in 2007 as a journalist researching an article about capital punishment in America.

I spoke to a former prison official who made an astonishing claim about what really happens to some of the inmates who enter execution chambers in the United States.

His shocking claims inspired me to write this book.

James Raven – 2012

PROLOGUE

THERE WERE FOUR bodies in the alleyway. They were lying next to each other, fully clothed and drenched in blood.

They'd all been shot – two in the head, one in the chest, one in the back. From the look of them they were all young Hispanic men.

They had dark hair and olive skin. Some of their bare arms were covered in intricate tattoos. One of them was wearing shorts and his left leg was bent at an impossible angle beneath him.

The sheer scale of the crime had prompted the cops to send out an alert to all the other law enforcement agencies in the city of San Antonio.

That was why Aaron Vance had left his warm bed and rushed straight across town to the scene. He'd arrived five minutes ago and had been put in the picture by one of the uniforms. As the Special Agent in Charge of the FBI's local field office Vance knew that the killings were going to send a shockwave all the way to Washington.

As he stood in the mouth of the alley, surveying the gory scene, he could feel a tight ball of tension forming in the pit of his stomach. The contorted bodies were about fifteen feet away and they seemed to come to life whenever a police camera flashed.

Murders were not uncommon in San Antonio, the second largest city in Texas. In fact, in the four years he'd been based here there had been a huge increase in the number of homicides, especially those involving drugs. But nothing like this. This was the kind of bloodbath that happened across the border in Mexico where the cartels ran amok. Not in the tourist mecca of San Antonio.

The alley was in the heart of the city, a stone's throw from the famous River Walk and close to one of America's most treasured sites

– the Alamo. Both were major tourist attractions. The River Walk with its myriad restaurants, bars and hotels. And the Alamo mission where, in 1836, a band of brave volunteers sacrificed their lives fighting for Texan independence.

The cops had yet to confirm whether the men had been gunned down in the alley or if they'd been slaughtered elsewhere and dumped here. But whatever the outcome of the forensic examination the repercussions were going to be enormous. An outraged media would use it as more evidence that the authorities were no longer in control of the streets. They'd demand tougher action to combat the crime wave that was raging across this and every other city in Texas.

Vance was in no doubt that these were gang-related killings. The four men had been executed. And he suspected that those responsible were members of the notorious Texas Syndicate – recently described by the Justice Department as the most dangerous gang in American history. They'd been particularly active this past year, racking up a shameful body count during territorial disputes with other gangs.

The Syndicate was founded inside a prison in the 1970s. Since then it had been recruiting Mexicans in prisons across the state and latest estimates put their numbers at eight thousand, with twice as many on the outside. The gang controlled many of the street operations across Texas, including drug trafficking, murder, extortion, prostitution, robbery and loan-sharking.

Their illegal activities were netting them tens of millions of dollars every year and although the Bureau had managed to jail scores of them for racketeering and other offences, the gang just kept getting bigger and more powerful.

'Well if it isn't my favourite federal agent.'

Vance turned towards the voice. It belonged to a silver-haired detective named Chris Koppel. He was of average height, thick through the neck and shoulders, with a face as rumpled as his blue suit.

'Hi, Chris,' Vance said. 'This looks bad.'

Koppel nodded. 'It'll cause a shit-storm for sure. We'll all come under pressure to ratchet up our operations.'

Koppel plucked a bottle of water from his jacket pocket and swigged from it. It was a humid night and he was sweating.

'It looks like a Syndicate hit,' Vance said.

Koppel swayed on the balls of his feet. 'That's what I figure. Those bastards are taking things to a new level. How the hell are we supposed to stop them?'

It was a good question, and one they had all been asking themselves for some time. The rapid growth of the Texas Syndicate – along with other organized gangs – had become a matter of grave concern. But drastic cuts to law enforcement budgets meant they had fewer officers and resources to cope with the problem.

'Who's running the show?' Vance asked.

'Lieutenant Fernandez. He's over there with the medical examiner.'

'Are there witnesses?'

Koppel shook his head. 'Not so far, but it's early days. We might get lucky.'

'Who found them?'

'Some wino looking for a quiet place to bed down for the night. He got the shock of his life.'

The alley ran between the rear of an empty department store and a warehouse. It was just about wide enough to accommodate a medium-size truck. Vance stared at the bodies and felt a flash of heat in his chest. The dead men were spread across the alley. Two of them were lying on their backs, one was face up and the fourth was on his side.

'They took two bullets each,' Koppel said. 'I reckon they were wasted somewhere else and their bodies were offloaded here in the alley earlier this evening.'

'What about street cameras?' Vance asked.

'They're being checked. But whoever did this would have used a vehicle that can't be traced back to them.'

Koppel was called away by another detective so Vance lit a cigarette while he waited to speak to Fernandez. It was already clear to him that he would be heavily involved in this case. It was almost certainly linked to organized crime and therefore within the Bureau's jurisdiction.

He inhaled deeply and sent smoke towards a cloudless sky that was crammed with needles of frozen light.

Just then, his cellphone rang. He took it from his pocket and glanced at the small screen. The caller's name was withheld. He answered it anyway.

'Vance here.'

'Is that Special Agent Vance of the FBI?' It was a male voice. Deep and husky.

'That's right. Who is this?'

The guy cleared his throat. It sounded like a nervous gesture.

'At this stage I intend to remain anonymous,' he said. 'My identity will be revealed to you when we meet.'

'Is that right?' Vance said. 'So what makes you so sure that we're going to meet?'

'Because I know you'll be desperate to find out who I am when you hear what I have to tell you.'

The FBI agent's ears pricked up. He said, 'Mind my asking how you got this number?'

'I have access to all kinds of useful information, Mr Vance. That's how I know that right now you're at the scene of a multiple homicide in the city centre.'

Vance looked around. There were people about, mostly cops and crime scene investigators. At the entrance to the alley a small crowd had gathered beyond the police tape. He didn't spot anyone looking at him.

'OK, fella,' he said. 'You've got my attention. What do you want to tell me?'

The guy paused, maybe for effect, and then said, 'The four dead men in the alley are members of the Texas Syndicate. They were rounded up earlier this evening and then shot out at the quarry near the airport.'

Vance raised his brow and blew smoke from the side of his mouth.

'Well I appreciate you telling me that,' he said. 'I'll pass it on right away to the detective in charge.'

'That's not all, Mr Vance. The men are all police informants. That's why they were dumped in the alley. The gang want to show you who's running this city. And they want to send out a message to their own people who might be thinking of turning against them.'

Vance experienced a spot of dread in his stomach. If what the guy was telling him was true then a terrifying new phase in the war with the Texas Syndicate had begun.

'I know who carried out the killings and I know who sanctioned them,' the man continued. 'And I know a lot more besides. Such as the names of the people inside the San Antonio police department and legislature who are on their payroll. Plus, how they launder their cash, where they get their drug supplies and just about everything else you've been trying to find out about their organization for years.'

This guy had to be kidding, Vance thought. Only high-ranking members of the gang would be privy to that kind of information, and those guys rarely snitched.

'I don't get it,' Vance said. 'If you know all this shit then why are you telling me?'

'Because you're the FBI's head honcho in this town,' he said. 'And you're in a position to cut a deal between the Bureau and me.'

'What kind of deal?'

'One that will finally deliver a hammer blow to the Syndicate's operations and to their leadership structure. It'll set them back years and save countless lives. I'm at the heart of the organization and I know everything. All of the information I have is supported by documents that will stand up in court. It'll more than justify what you have to do to get your hands on it.'

Vance could feel the adrenaline start to move through his veins. Could this guy really be on the level?

'So what exactly do we have to do in return for this information?' Vance asked.

'Just one simple thing,' the guy said.

He went on to spell out his extraordinary demand, which caused Vance's heart to kick up a notch.

The FBI agent drew in a rapid breath and said, 'The powers-that-be will never go for it.'

'Then it's up to you to convince them, Mr Vance. If not, you can kiss goodbye to the opportunity of a lifetime.'

Vance's thoughts raced wildly. He blew out a stream of smoke that settled in blue-grey clouds above his head.

'How can I be sure that you're not just bullshitting me?' he said.

The guy issued an audible sigh. 'OK, I'll give you a little nugget for free. One of the people on the Syndicate's payroll is a detective Dennis Cross who works in the San Antonio police department. Check out his bank accounts. He receives a fixed amount each month of two thousand dollars. Get him to try explaining where it comes from.'

Vance dropped his cigarette and pummelled it into the ground with the heel of his shoe.

'I'll check it out,' he said. 'How can I reach you?'

'You can't,' the guy said. 'I'll call *you* in a couple of days. Give you time to talk to your bosses. Once I know the Bureau's keen we'll have a face-to-face and start the process.'

'You better not be wasting my time,' Vance said.

'I'm not. You'll see. Just agree to my terms and what you'll get in return will blow your fucking mind.'

With that, the guy suddenly hung up. Vance felt his lungs itch for tobacco so he lit up another cigarette. His pulse was racing. After a minute he bounded over to Lieutenant Fernandez and asked him if the victims had been identified. The detective took him to one side and told him that he'd known each of them personally because they'd been police informants who'd been working for the Texas Syndicate.

Vance felt a kernel of excitement take root in his chest.

'I just got an anonymous tip-off,' he told Fernandez. 'The caller said these guys were shot out at the quarry near the airport.'

Fernandez gave Vance a surprised look. 'Who the hell would know that?'

Vance shrugged. 'Someone on the inside I guess. You'd better check it out.'

He decided not to ask Fernandez if he knew a detective Dennis Cross because he didn't want to spark his interest. Instead he stepped away and called the police department's main switchboard. Sure enough, Detective Cross existed and he'd be on duty the following morning.

Vance then put in a call to his section chief in Washington. He passed on every detail of his conversation with the mystery caller and said he wanted the go-ahead to act on it.

'Sounds interesting,' he was told. 'I'll get back to you with an answer as soon as I can.'

Vance pocketed his cellphone and realized that his heart was in a sprint. He was glad he'd set the wheels in motion. His intuition told him that Detective Cross would turn out to be a crooked cop. And that the Bureau would stop at nothing to get their hands on every other piece of information in the mystery man's possession.

Even if it meant crossing the line to do a deal with the devil.

1

EIGHT WEEKS LATER

IT WAS 7 a.m. on the Monday before Thanksgiving. I was lying on my bed staring up at the ceiling. My eyes were heavy and my joints were stiff.

I hadn't slept all night and I'd hardly moved a muscle. But then I had a lot on my mind. Today I was going to die. It would happen in eleven hours from now and by this time tomorrow I'd be six feet under. There would be no fanfare. No poignant eulogy. The end for me was going to be swift, efficient and merciless.

I'd been thinking about this day for almost a decade, wondering how I would cope and what it would feel like as the time of my death approached. Now that it was here I felt strangely numb. Maybe that was because the faint glimmer of hope that had sustained me had finally been extinguished and I had no choice but to accept my fate. All I could do was die with some dignity.

It would be the end of a life only half-lived. But for a lot of people it would be a cause for celebration. In their eyes my death was long overdue. They wanted me to rot in hell for what had happened. Even now, after all this time, the name Lee Jordan still provoked angry sentiment.

It should have been so very different, of course. Before it all went wrong the future had looked bright and promising. I was twenty-eight then and had been married to Marissa for a year. We were trying for a baby. If we'd had a boy we were going to name him Antonio after my much-loved late grandfather. A girl would have been called Julie after Marissa's mother.

We lived in a two-bed rented apartment on the outskirts of Houston. We were saving to buy a house and I had a steady job with a construction company, building homes and shopping malls. But then the icy winds of recession swept across the country and Texas was battered along with every other state.

I lost my job. Then both my parents died within months of each other of unconnected illnesses. Shortly after, Marissa suffered a miscarriage. Life became tough and miserable. Like most other couples we struggled to cope. We had enough money to cover rental payments on the apartment for two months and no idea what would happen to us after that. Our hopes and dreams were disintegrating like ash in the wind.

Out of desperation I allowed my old friend Sean Bates to talk me into some acts of criminality. I saw it as a way to put food on the table and stave off eviction. A way to provide for my wife.

Sean was a young African-American. He used to call me his 'white honky pal'. As boys we lived on the same street and went to the same high school. We shared the same girls and the same soggy joints. He had always operated on the wrong side of the law, but as a petty thief he was at least managing to keep his head above water – which was more than could be said for a lot of other people.

It was small fry stuff to begin with. We stole some cars and carried out a few burglaries. Marissa didn't like it one bit, but she didn't try to stop me. The cash eased her conscience and calmed her fears. And it ensured we kept a roof over our heads when many others lost theirs.

But then, emboldened by our run of success, Sean decided it was time to raise our game. He produced a couple of handguns and persuaded me to embark on a series of 'home invasions' in the affluent neighbourhoods south of Houston. He assured me it would be easy and like a fool I took him at his word. But it was a big mistake. I should have trusted my instinct to say no.

Our first target was a large detached house next to a golf course. It was a sumptuous place with its own swimming pool and several acres of grounds. We struck at nine in the evening when the owner and his wife were relaxing after dinner. The aim was to kick open the back door and barge right in. But the door proved more difficult to get open than we expected. The delay gave the guy time to find his gun and use it as we rushed into the living room.

Two people were killed in the bloodbath that followed. I managed to get away, but I was arrested three days later and charged with murder.

That was how I ended up on death row. And it was why today was going to be my last.

The execution was scheduled to take place at 6 p.m. I figured the time would fly past, unlike the last nine years, eleven months and twelve days – a lost decade cooped up in a cell just ten feet by six. No TV. No physical contact with anyone other than the guards. Just a bed, a small window, a combo washbasin and toilet, a few books, and an old radio with poor reception.

The cell was cold and claustrophobic. Barely enough room for push-ups, sit-ups and squats. I'd seen better accommodation in a zoo. The one small window to the outside world was never cleaned so it was thick with grime.

The State of Texas doesn't believe in making condemned prisoners comfortable. They keep us in solitary confinement in a special segre-gation area of the Alan B. Polunsky Unit near Livingston. And they leave us alone for up to twenty three hours a day, with only an hour's recreation in a caged courtyard. Nothing to do except read and think. Just mind-numbing boredom. All part of a routine designed to break the spirit.

It's why some inmates go crazy. It's no secret that prolonged isola-tion can lead to severe mental illness. Somehow I'd managed to stay sane, despite the sheer monotony and the emotional deprivation. At least that was according to the prison shrinks who had been monitoring me since I arrived. They described me as strong and resilient. They said I'd found a place within myself to hide, whatever that meant.

Until now I'd never given up hope of getting out, but the countless appeals had gone nowhere and my lawyer had failed to drum up sym-pathy in the outside world. For him it was an uphill battle. A month ago his latest request for clemency had been rejected. But then the case against me had been overwhelming from the start, which was why the jury had taken less than an hour to convict me of murder.

So today, society was going to exact revenge. I was going to pay the ultimate price. They were going to kill me over in the town of Huntsville, sixty miles away. Huntsville is known as the prison capital of the USA because it has no less than five jails, including the State's execution chamber, which is housed in the notorious Huntsville Unit, more commonly known as 'the Walls'.

It's a strange set-up. All male death row inmates reside at Polunsky. But their exit from the world takes place at the Walls. So this afternoon I'd be taken there in a van and put in a holding cell until 6 p.m. when I'd be escorted into the death chamber and given a lethal injection. It was a tried and tested method of capital punishment and Texas was top of the league when it came to numbers. Already this year fifteen men and three women had been executed.

It's a wild concept to think that you're going to be put to sleep like a dog. At first your mind is totally consumed by your impending fate. Gradually you find a way to push it into the background so that you can embrace the primal part of the human spirit that wants to keep on living. But the fear and dread is always there below the surface, like some creature waiting to drag you back to reality.

I was trying hard to focus on the positive side of things. And believe it or not there was a positive side. During my incarceration I'd found comfort in a dog-eared copy of the Bible. I now believed in God and Jesus and all the other stuff that I'd previously dismissed as claptrap.

So it followed that I also believed in the hereafter – and that my darling wife would be waiting for me when I got there.

Marissa had died seven years ago in a fire. They said it was a tragic accident. She apparently fell asleep in her apartment after a heavy drinking session and dropped a lit cigarette onto a pile of newspapers. According to the medical examiner she would have succumbed to smoke and fumes within minutes.

We were still married at the time because Marissa had refused to divorce me. She'd always known I was no murderer and she'd clung to the hope that I would eventually be exonerated. She'd been coming to see me once a month and told me on each occasion that she loved me and had forgiven me for screwing up our lives. But I could tell that the strain was getting to her. Her face became gaunt and pasty and I knew she was drinking even though she denied it.

The guilt I felt back then was bad enough, but after she died it became unbearable. That's when I sought refuge in the Bible that Marissa had given to me only six months before she died.

'I know you're not religious, Lee,' she'd said. 'But it will help you get through this ordeal. I promise. Just open your heart to it.'

Marissa had been a committed Christian and I'd mocked her for it when we were together. But she'd been right. It was the first time I'd read the Holy Book and what I learned from its pages helped me to deal with all the grief and despair. And it had dulled the fear of death. But it didn't stop me from missing her. And it didn't dilute the guilt that still hung around my neck like a heavy weight. After Marissa died the only people to visit me were my sister Emily and my lawyer Marcus Zimmerman.

Emily had been making the three-hour journey from her home near Austin about every two months. She was all the family I had now and thankfully she still believed in me. But her life had been blighted by what had happened. Her marriage broke down and she was forced to move away from Houston because she was being constantly harassed by the media and some members of the public. She was now single and living alone in a house at Mountain City, south of Austin.

It was Emily who had talked Marcus Zimmerman into taking on my case two years ago. He was a well-respected lawyer working for the Texas Defence Group, a non-profit firm that represents death row prisoners. My original lawyer had been appointed by the court and was incompetent and inexperienced.

Zimmerman was supposedly in a different league. He had managed to overturn twelve death sentences. But he was ever the realist and had cautioned me against optimism. When I last saw him he'd said, 'The odds are stacked firmly against you, Lee. But I'll do my best. Just hang on in there.'

I didn't want to die, but the alternative did not appeal to me either – life without parole in this hell hole. The buildings were dilapidated, the cells grim and run down. The prison regime was set up to dehumanize and humiliate the inmates and living conditions were desolate.

But as Zimmerman had frequently pointed out: *Keep on breathing and there's always the chance that one day you'll eventually get out.*

2

TEXAS CONGRESSMAN GIDEON Crane had only been awake for half an hour, but he was already exhausted. He had the woman who was lying next to him to thank for that. Morning sex was Beth Abbot's favourite kind. It made her wild and wet with passion. As soon as she opened her eyes she was up for it.

This morning she was on him the moment he began to stir, running the tips of her fingers across his chest. Her touch was electrifying, and as always she'd shown a degree of enthusiasm that put his second wife Pauline to shame. Beth was thirty five, ten years younger than Pauline, and her libido was still firing on all cylinders.

Pauline had stopped wanting sex with him a year ago, a couple of months before she took a non-fatal overdose of sleeping pills. Even after she was put on anti-depressants she was never in the mood. There was always a ready excuse. The curse of the menopause. She was too tired. She had a goddamn headache. But that suited him fine because Beth satisfied all his needs in that department now. She was the one who rocked his boat – the one he wanted to spend the rest of his life with.

Their love-making this morning had been fast and furious. She'd ridden him into the mattress. Then she'd got him to mount her from behind. And when she'd finally come he was pretty sure that her scream must have been heard by every guest in the hotel.

Now he was lying back against the pillows, breathing hard and thinking that sex with Beth was better for his fifty-three-year-old body than any physical work-out in the gym.

'That was just sublime,' Beth said as she rolled on her side to look at him. 'It was even better than the performance you put in last night.'

He furrowed his brow at her. 'We didn't have sex last night.'

She laughed. 'I'm talking about the debate, silly. You were absolutely terrific.'

She was referring to the latest televised debate between him and the four other candidates seeking the Republican Presidential nomination. He was pleased with the way it had gone and there was no doubt in his mind that he had come out on top. The studio audience had responded well to his campaign pitch, which was focused on the preservation of social values and the need to crack down on filthy rich tax dodgers.

'It'll give us a boost in the polls,' Beth said. 'I guarantee it.'

'We'll see,' he said. 'Switch on the TV and let's check out the reaction.'

She sat up and grabbed the remote from the bedside table, flicked on the TV and channel-hopped to Fox News. They were reporting on yet more gang-related murders in Texas. A man and a woman had been shot dead outside a nightclub in Austin. An FBI spokesman pointed the finger at the Texas Syndicate, who had been responsible for a spate of gruesome murders in recent months.

'We should react to this,' Beth said, suddenly all business-like. 'We'll condemn the killings and trash law enforcement spending cuts. What do you think?'

'I think it's a great idea,' he said.

'I'll write it up as soon as I've showered then.'

The texture of her voice was rough and rasping. For him it was part of her appeal. She sounded as sexy as she looked. When she'd started working for him just over a year ago he knew he wouldn't be able to resist her charms. She was pretty, intelligent, ambitious and selfish enough not to ever want children. Great qualities all wrapped up in one delicious package.

He was looking forward to the day when they could finally be together and their relationship made public. He didn't like pretending that she was just his press secretary and that his marriage to Pauline was anything but a sham.

'I need to pee,' Beth said, dropping the remote and sliding off the bed.

Crane watched as she padded naked to the bathroom, her long auburn hair falling about her shoulders. She moved with a sinewy grace that he found captivating. She had the face and body of a much younger woman and every part of her was natural. No Botox or collagen fillers. No silicone implants. It was all beautifully real.

He felt a stirring between his thighs and wondered if he had time for some more action. He checked the bedside clock. It was 8 a.m. He was due to fly to Houston at ten. Before that he had to do a couple of interviews. Then he had to get from New Orleans city centre to Armstrong International Airport. He shook his head and heaved a heavy sigh. More sex was out of the question. It would take him at least forty minutes to revive his manhood – too long by far if he was to stick to his schedule. It was a shame, but today of all days he couldn't afford to fall behind.

'You look good,' Beth said as she emerged from the bathroom and gestured towards the TV.

The Fox newscaster was now talking over a clip from last night's debate. Crane was one of five candidates standing behind lecterns in an over-lit studio. Four men and one woman. He was in the middle, head and shoulders above the others. And Beth was right. He did look pretty good. The dark blue suit went well with his grey hair and healthy tan. It made him look leaner than he actually was. And younger.

'You're coming across as very presidential,' Beth said as she threw herself onto the bed next to him. 'Keep it up and you'll be ahead of the field in no time.'

After the clip, various pundits were asked for their reaction to the debate. To Crane's delight he was declared the outright winner. He was described as articulate, decisive, confident and well briefed. One said that his rhetoric and demeanour would appeal to middle-class Americans.

The response was better than he had dared hope for. The debate had almost certainly reinforced his position as the early-stage front-runner. But he wouldn't be complacent. There was a long way to go. More debates in more cities. If the party finally chose him as their candidate to go up against the Democrat who currently occupied the White House then he would have an even tougher fight on his hands.

On screen the newscaster suddenly adopted an altogether more sombre tone as he looked into the camera. Crane knew what was coming next and he felt the blood stiffen in his veins.

'Gideon Crane is also in the news today for a different reason,' the newscaster said. 'The man who murdered the congressman's first wife will be executed at six o'clock this evening at Huntsville in Texas. Thirty-eight year old Lee Jordan has been on death row for almost ten years. He was convicted of gunning down Kimberley Crane during a bungled raid on the *couple's home near Houston.'*

A photo of Jordan appeared on the screen. It was the same one that had been shown a thousand times before. It had been taken after his arrest and in it he looked pale and haggard. His thick dark hair was dishevelled and his eyes were large and vacant. He had a narrow face and slightly crooked nose.

Crane bit into his bottom lip and tried to supress a huge surge of emotion. But his heart lurched and his breath caught in his throat. Beth reached out and put an arm around him.

'Take it easy, hon,' she said. 'After he chokes you won't have to keep seeing his ugly mug.'

Crane was glad that the day had finally arrived. Lee fucking Jordan had haunted him for a decade. Even now he had frequent flashbacks to the night Jordan and his accomplice Sean Bates burst into the house. He and Kimberley were watching a movie when the pair appeared at the back door and tried to force it open. Crane managed to arm himself with his own pistol just as they came crashing inside wielding revolvers and wearing ski masks. He got off a single shot that struck Bates in the head, killing him instantly.

But Jordan was on him before he could pull the trigger again. There was a brief struggle during which he managed to rip off Jordan's mask and get a look at his face. But then the bastard smashed the butt of his gun against his head, rendering him unconscious. When he came to fifteen minutes later Jordan was gone and Kimberley was lying on the floor in the hall covered in blood.

The cops had no trouble tracking Jordan down and building a case against him. The fool had fled in such a panic that he'd dropped his gun which was covered in his fingerprints. It was more than enough to get him convicted despite him insisting that he was innocent.

'Are you OK?' Beth asked.

Crane closed his eyes and clenched his jaw. The air suddenly felt heavy around him. He took a deep, ragged breath and nodded slowly.

'I'm fine,' he said.

Then he opened his eyes and blinked away those hideous memories. He looked at Beth and a sardonic smile twisted his lips.

'In fact I'm better than fine,' he said. 'I've been waiting for this day for a long time and I intend to make the most of it. After I see that bastard die I'm going home to crack open a bottle of champagne.'

'I wish I could be with you,' Beth said.

He reached out, took her hand. 'One day, sweetheart. We just have to play the long game now. Any whiff of scandal or divorce will derail the campaign and ruin my chances. You know that. So be patient and we'll be together before you know it.'

He pulled her to him and held her tight. Her warm, soft body banished the dark thoughts that had gathered in his mind. He had every reason to be upbeat and positive. Not only was he in love again, but he also had a good chance of becoming the next president of the United States.

And to cap it all he would soon witness Lee Jordan taking his final breath.

3

I WAS GIVEN breakfast at 8.30 – much later than usual because it was my last day. The tray was slipped through the little metal opening in the door. But I had no appetite so I didn't eat it. I drank the coffee though, which was lukewarm and stewed, and tried to shut out the prison noise. It was always worse in the mornings. Shouting, screaming, crying, howling – a grating cacophony of protest and suffering that was a form of torture in itself.

After breakfast I was cuffed and my legs were shackled. I hobbled in truncated steps to the shower area, a guard on either side of me. There were another three hundred inmates on death row and a few of them called out to me through the little grills in their doors as I shuffled along the corridor.

'Way to go, Jordan. Keep smiling.'

'Show the fuckers you're not scared, man.'

'See you in hell, asshole.'

Showering, as always, was an unpleasant experience. The water was cold and discoloured, but I was used to it so I didn't make a fuss. After drying myself off with a damp towel I slipped back into my prison-issue white jumpsuit and was marched back to my cell.

I sat on the bed and tried not to acknowledge the fear and sense of panic that was growing inside me. I could hear the guy singing in the next cell. His name was Michael Ortiz and he was one of about forty inmates who had been on death row for over twenty years. Once a formidable member of a street gang, he was now a mental wreck whose idea of fun was to spread faeces over the walls of his cell.

I didn't want to end up like him. And I knew I would if I had to put up with the pain and drudgery of life in this tiny cement box for much longer. But that didn't make the prospect of dying any less scary. Humans are hard-wired to survive. It's a basic instinct in all of us. No matter how bad things get most people find it impossible to let go. We hang on by a thread to the belief that something will happen to make things better.

But we're usually disappointed.

At ten o'clock I was told that my sister had arrived to see me. I'd been expecting her and was looking forward to the visit.

It was our last chance to say goodbye to each other. We'd agreed long ago that she should not witness the execution. I didn't want her to see me die. It would be too upsetting and traumatic. I also didn't want her to claim my body afterwards or pay for a funeral. The state might as well bury me in the prison cemetery.

I was taken to the visitation area, a bleak, unfriendly place. She was already there, sitting in a small cubicle on the other side of a Plexiglass window.

'How are you doing?' I asked.

She gave a small, tentative smile. 'I've been better.'

She looked defeated, emaciated, a shell of the woman she once was. Her face was drawn and sallow and there were dark circles under her eyes.

She was three years younger than me. Thirty-five. But the last ten years had taken a brutal toll. As I sat there looking at her I felt an overwhelming wave of guilt barrel through me.

'Zimmerman called me on the way here,' she said, her voice sounding dry and cracked. 'He wants you to know that he's going to ask the governor to grant a stay of execution. And he's filing an emergency appeal with the Supreme Court.'

I nodded, felt my eyes begin to sting.

'To be honest I'm not sure it's what I want,' I said.

'I told him that,' she said. 'But unless you ask him not to he'll go ahead and do it.'

I felt a knot rise in my stomach. I loved my sister and I knew that as long as I was alive she couldn't move on. I'd be a never-ending burden to her. A constant reminder of how and why her own life had been so cruelly trashed.

I wanted desperately to reach out and touch her. To stroke her hair and hold her against me like I used to when we were kids and she was upset. We were always close, partly because our father was a drunk and a bully and our mother was too weak to stand up to him. So I looked out for her. Made sure nobody messed with her.

Right now there was a lot I wanted to say to Emily, but suddenly I couldn't find the words. Maybe that was just as well. She didn't want to hear yet again how sorry I was about everything. How much I regretted going to the Crane house that night. And how stupid I was to follow Sean's lead.

Thankfully she was the one who broke what turned into a long, drawn-out silence.

'This is so unfair,' she said. 'You don't deserve to die.'

Emily had never asked if I killed Kimberley Crane. She didn't have to. She just knew that I didn't. I was a bad boy back then and I did some bad things. But shooting that woman wasn't one of them. I didn't even know she was dead until I heard it on the news.

Emily leaned forward and put the tips of her fingers against the glass. I reached out, touched the window, tried to imagine that our fingers were interlocking. I could see the tears gathering in her eyes now. She was struggling to hold it together. She was also finding it hard to know what to say.

I knew she'd been dreading this last, long goodbye, but there was really no way I could make it easier for her. I tried, though. I mentioned some of the good times. Like when I used to take her fishing. And when she was a bridesmaid at my wedding. I also told her I was looking forward to seeing Marissa and our dead mother.

'Is there a message you want me to pass on to Monty?' I said.

This made her smile for the first time. Monty had been Emily's pet Labrador. She was fourteen when he died and she was heartbroken. Cried for weeks.

'Tell him I hope he's behaving himself,' she said. 'Though I don't imagine for one minute that he is. That animal was beyond bad.'

That's when the floodgates opened and she broke down. Her shoulders heaved and the tears gushed out. I started crying too then and it felt like my chest would explode. It all came out of me in one great wave of despair. The guilt. The shame. The anger. The sadness.

It took several minutes for the both of us to calm down. After we'd dried our eyes, I said, 'I've come to a decision, sis. I'm going to tell Zimmerman that I don't want him to do anything more. It's time to bring this nightmare to an end.'

She said nothing, just nodded. I think she knew it was the best thing for both of us.

'I want you to go home now,' I said. 'Get on with your life, and think about the good times. I'm not the only guy to have been dealt a shit hand and I won't be the last. So don't waste your time grieving. It'll piss me off.'

Before she left she blew me a kiss and told me that she would pray for me.

And I told her that I loved her and that I was so very sorry for what had happened.

4

THE FLIGHT TO Houston in the campaign's chartered jet took just over an hour. Congressman Crane travelled with his six-strong personal entourage which included his three assistants, his key strategist, a security officer, an official photographer and his press secretary, Beth Abbot.

Running for the Republican Presidential nomination was an expensive business. He'd had to raise millions of dollars. Much of it would be spent on TV ads ahead of the usual series of primary elections and caucuses after Christmas.

He was convinced that his dream of being President was close to becoming a reality. But he knew it was not going to be easy. The negative campaigning would soon begin. The gloves would come off and the candidates would try to destroy each other by exploiting any weaknesses. That was why he could not afford to be exposed as an adulterer. His opponents would seize on it with relish and it would not play well with his Bible-thumping conservative supporters.

So far he and Beth had managed to keep their affair under wraps. He was sure that no one knew or suspected. Not even the rest of the team.

They wouldn't be alone now until after Thanksgiving. He'd promised Pauline he'd be home for the holiday weekend. She wanted to make it special this year as it fell only a few days after Lee Jordan's execution.

At the time of Kimberley's death Pauline was Crane's mistress. They'd been seeing each other for seven months. To her credit Pauline had remained patient and understanding after Kimberley was put in the ground. She couldn't help but feel guilt-stricken.

She helped him through the shock and the grief. Back then he was a successful hedge fund manager on the verge of entering politics and Pauline was his PA. So people expected her to be by his side. And it surprised no one when they married a year later – eighteen months before he was elected to Congress.

Crane wasn't proud of the fact that he was on the same illicit merry-go-round with Beth. But then he had always found it hard to remain faithful. Only now was he determined to change his ways and be a good, loyal husband – but not until he was married to Beth.

The team went their separate ways at the airport. Crane had a car waiting to take him home. Beth went with the others to get taxis. She had an apartment in the city centre and as Crane watched her walk away he felt his heart sink.

His wife was waiting for him when he got home, watching from the living room window as the car pulled onto the gravel driveway. Their house was only a few miles from the one he had shared with Kimberley. It was next to a lake in a posh, gated community. Five bedrooms, a games room and a pool.

Pauline opened the front door looking smart and refined in white pressed shorts and a thin cashmere sweater. Crane kissed her on both cheeks and she responded by putting her arms around him and giving him a gentle squeeze.

'I've missed you,' she said.

'I've missed you too.'

He dropped his briefcase in the hall and Pauline led him by the hand into the kitchen where she handed him a glass filled with his favourite cocktail – a Margarita.

At least she's trying, he thought. Since she'd started seeing the new shrink she'd seemed less depressed. At times she even reminded him of the vivacious woman he'd married; the one who'd been so full of life before she learned she could never have children.

She stepped back and smiled at him and her brilliant white teeth positively glowed. He had to admit that she was still in good shape. She had radiant eyes the colour of parched stone and cosmetic surgery had smoothed out the wrinkles around them. Her honey brown hair had a glassy sheen, like the kernel of a nut, and was cut short and manageable. She still had a great figure, and hours spent working out ensured her ample breasts continued to defy gravity.

'I've prepared a nice lunch,' she said. 'I thought we might have it by the pool. And you can tell me all about New Orleans. I watched the debate and you were sensational.'

He looked at his watch.

'Don't worry,' she said. 'We've got plenty of time. The car is picking us up at four. It'll take just over an hour to reach Huntsville so we'll be there well before the execution is due to begin.'

He furrowed his brow at her. 'Are you sure you want to come? You don't have to. I'll be fine.'

'I want to be there,' she said firmly. 'I need closure just as much as you do.'

It was a beautiful day and typical of November. The sun was high and bright and its reflection sparkled on the surface of the lake. Back in the summer it would have been too hot and humid to eat outside, but now it was pleasantly warm.

Crane had taken off his jacket and was sitting at the patio table in his shirtsleeves. Pauline had served up a lunch of cold chicken with a crisp, tasty salad and lots of hot crusty bread. Now she was sitting back in her chair puffing on a cigarette, a nimbus of smoke swirling around her head.

'That was wonderful, honey,' he said. 'I skipped breakfast in the hotel so I was famished.'

'Would you like some coffee?' she asked him.

'Good idea,' he said. 'I'll make it.'

He was about to get up when his cellphone rang. He picked it up from the table. It was his long-time friend Josh Napier, who also happened to be the governor of Texas.

'Hi there, Gideon,' the governor said. 'Are you back in Houston?'

'I am. Arrived a couple of hours ago. I wondered when I would hear from you.'

'I told you I'd call as soon as I had some news and I've only just got it,' the governor said.

Crane and Napier had met and got to know each other whilst working on Wall Street years earlier. They had a lot in common, from their right-wing stance on most political issues to their inability to maintain a monogamous relationship. Napier had screwed up three marriages to date.

'Well, come on,' Crane said. 'Don't keep me in suspense.'

The governor gave a little cough and said, 'I just heard from Jordan's lawyer.'

'You mean that prick, Zimmerman?'

'The very same.'

'Well you knew he'd apply for a stay of execution at some point today. You told me you'd refuse to grant it.'

'That's just the point,' the governor said. 'I won't have to refuse it. Zimmerman wanted me to know that Jordan had called him from the Polunsky Unit to tell him not to pursue a stay. He's finally accepting his fate. He wants to die.'

Crane felt his breath become shallow in his chest. He was aware that Pauline was staring at him, a worried expression on her face. He gave her the thumbs-up sign to let her know that everything was OK. She nodded, relieved, and signalled that she would go and make the coffee.

'There's something I need to ask you, Gideon,' the governor said.

'Oh?'

'I've just been leaned on by the FBI about this case. That's never happened before. I want to know if they're pushing their weight around on your behalf.'

Crane frowned. 'Absolutely not. I've had no contact with them.'

'Then have you ever heard of an agent named Aaron Vance?'

'No I haven't. Why?'

'Well this is strictly between us,' the governor said. 'And I'm only telling you because we go back a long way.'

'So what is it?'

The governor hesitated, then said, 'This agent Vance came to see me early this morning. He made it clear that the FBI did not want to see Jordan live beyond today. He wanted a guarantee that I would reject any last-minute appeal to delay the execution.'

'Why would he do that?'

'He said he couldn't reveal the reason.'

'So what did you tell him?'

'I should have told him to go get fucked.'

'But you didn't.'

'No.'

'Why not?'

'Because the Bureau knows things about me that I wouldn't want to become public knowledge. Things that happened a long time ago.'

'And this guy Vance used that as a threat against you?'

'He was too shrewd to say it outright, but I got his drift.'

Crane wasn't really sure how to react. On the one hand he felt like tracking down this agent Vance so that he could shake his hand. On the other his curiosity was aroused and he wanted to know why the Feds were so desperate to see Lee Jordan put to death.

'There's no need to worry about it, Josh,' he said after a beat. 'It seems to me the issue has resolved itself.'

'That's not the point. What the Bureau has done isn't right. Those guys have stepped over the line.'

'Come on, Josh. The FBI and the CIA have been stepping over the line like forever.'

'So have you got any idea why they're so desperate to ensure that the execution goes ahead as planned?'

Crane thought about it for a few moments and said, 'I don't know and I don't really give a damn. I'm just glad they're not trying to save the bastard.'

5

MY DAYS ON death row came to an end at twelve thirty in the afternoon. That's when the guards came to get me. They attached a belly chain and leg irons. I was then marched out of my cell for the last time. Never to return.

It was a strange feeling. The emotions in my chest started to build. I had to force myself to remain calm. I'd seen other guys lose it at this point. They'd had to be dragged out kicking and screaming. But I was determined to hold it together. I didn't want to give the guards the satisfaction of seeing me crumble.

They put me into a white van that was part of a three-vehicle convoy. I was placed in a dog cage with a guard on either side. One was armed with a rifle, the other with a pistol. I was warned that if someone tried to stop the vehicle to set me free I'd be killed first. As we drove away from the Polunsky Unit I began to feel woozy and light-headed.

My date with death was only five and a half hours away. This was the last journey I'd ever make. It would take only about forty five minutes. Barely enough time to appreciate what a beautiful day it was. The sun was shining and the fields and woods of East Texas looked magnificent. But my thoughts were scattered and I found it hard to concentrate. The blood was pounding in my ears and my mind was cartwheeling. A crushing trepidation pressed in on me with cold insistence.

Our destination was Huntsville. Of the 35,000 or so residents one in three is an inmate.

We arrived just before 1.30 p.m. at the Walls. It's the oldest prison in Texas, a large imposing building that takes up almost two blocks in the centre of town.

There was a small group of protesters outside the entrance, members of the Texas Coalition Against the Death Penalty. Some carried banners. One banner read: 'Stop the Killing.' Another read: 'This is legalized murder.'

A couple of cops were on hand to stop the protesters blocking the van and as we drove into the prison compound I felt a corkscrew turn in my gut.

This is it, I thought. *My final destination.*

Five minutes later I was being escorted into the building through a rear door. Once inside I was strip-searched, fingerprinted, given a change of clothes and told that I would not be granted a last meal of choice. That time-honoured tradition had been stopped because in the past some inmates had abused the privilege.

Then I was led through the prison to the death house, a low, non-descript brick building that had been built in 1952 with inmate labour. The tiny holding cell they put me in was only about thirty feet from the death chamber. I couldn't see inside the chamber because the door was closed, but the sight of it flooded me with apprehension.

When the cell door was slammed shut behind me I sat on the bed, clutching the only things I'd been allowed to bring with me – a photo of Marissa and the Bible she gave me.

I closed my eyes, but I couldn't empty my mind or stop my heart from thumping out of control. I was scared. A cold sensation settled in my belly and I felt the cloying grip of nausea in my throat.

I didn't move for almost an hour. I felt like a zombie on ketamine. My thoughts moved like thick muddy waters. My stomach started tying itself in a thousand painful knots.

Oh God how do I get through the next few hours?

Eventually the warden came to see me. A slightly cadaverous man of about fifty with graveyard looks. His fish-grey eyes were small and deep-set. He stood outside the cell and spoke to me through the bars. His voice was rough and clipped.

'I want to explain what's going to happen later,' he said. 'There's a strict procedure that we have to follow here in the death house.'

He explained that there would be people in the victim's witness room, people who had been close to Kimberley Crane, including her husband, the congressman.

'Other witnesses will include a county judge and a member of the

Board of Directors of the Department of Corrections,' he said. 'Plus, members of the media.'

He then went on to tell me what I already knew – that I would be put to death using a cocktail of three drugs injected through an IV line into my arm in a precise sequence. The first was sodium thiopental – a fast-acting anaesthetic that would put me to sleep in seconds. The second was pancuronium bromide – a powerful muscle relaxant that would cause complete paralysis. The third – potassium chloride – was the drug that would stop my heart and thus lead to death through cardiac arrest.

'The order of the drugs is to rapidly cause unconsciousness so that you won't suffer,' the warden said. 'You will feel no pain. I can assure you of that. And the whole process will take about seven minutes.'

When the warden was finished with me he introduced the prison chaplain, a tall guy with a stoop and a shiny bald head. I noticed he was wearing brown tasselled loafers.

'I can't begin to imagine what you're going through,' he said to me. 'But I want you to know that you are not alone here. God is with you.'

He recited a couple of prayers and then read out his own translation of Psalm 51 from The Book of Psalms, which began:

'Have mercy on me, O God, according to your loving kindness; in your great compassion blot out my offences. Wash me thoroughly from my wicked-ness and cleanse me from my sin. For I know my sin is ever before me. . . .'

He then told me he would be with me in the death chamber. His parting words were: 'You must now make your peace with God.'

I was left alone then to stew in a cauldron of fear and regret.

The guards gathered in the corridor outside the cell just before six. The warden was there too. Their faces were expressionless, their eyes blank. This was routine to them. They were going through the motions.

The warden said, 'It's time to go, Lee.'

My breath suddenly roared in my ears and I felt a cold terror in my chest.

The cell door was unlocked and I was told to stand up. At first I didn't respond because I couldn't. It was as though I had been unplugged from reality. Then I felt a hand grip my arm and I was pulled to me feet.

'Come quietly, son, and we won't have to use cuffs or chains.'

They led me along the corridor to the chamber. A short, silent walk.

Tremors started to move through my limbs and my legs felt weak and rubbery.

The heavy metal door was opened. No one spoke. For just a fleeting moment I thought about putting up a fight and making it hard for them. But what was the point? I'd just be making it harder for myself.

As I stepped inside the chamber I felt something cold and solid form in my stomach. The image that confronted me was one that had been drilled into my consciousness over the years by countless TV documentaries, news reports, movies and photographs. The place where hundreds of men and women had come to die.

The chamber was smaller than I imagined it would be. It was bright and sterile, with turquoise walls and a gurney in the centre with arm supports. On one side was a small mirrored window beyond which the drugs team were waiting to do their job. On the other side curtains were drawn across the windows through which the witnesses would observe the proceedings.

A ripple of fear convulsed inside me and a wash of acid scalded my oesophagus. I felt my lips move. No sound came out. But I heard my own tortured words in my head.

Please God let it be quick. And let me be strong.

'I need you to hop onto the gurney,' the warden said. 'Lay your head on the pillow and put your feet at the other end. Then stretch out your arms.'

There were five guards in the tie-down team. It took them about thirty seconds to strap me down in a crucifixion pose. The leather belts went across my chest, arms, abdomen and legs. And then a heart monitor was attached to me.

As this was happening my eyes drifted in and out of focus and I found it hard to breathe. I flinched as two IVs were then inserted, one in each arm. I'd been told that only one was necessary to carry out the execution. The other was a back-up in case the primary line failed. The tubes led through the wall into the drug room next door.

At this point the curtains across the viewing windows were pulled back. One room was empty because I'd told Emily and Zimmerman to stay away. In the other room stood a group of about half a dozen people. Reporters, I guessed, along with the friends and relatives of Kimberley Crane. One of them I recognized instantly.

Gideon Crane.

His hair was greyer now and he had lost weight. He was wearing a dark suit and a bright red tie. We locked eyes. His were wide and hostile. I tried to hold his stare and not to blink, but I found it impossible to focus on even that one small task.

'Would you like to make a final statement?' the warden said.

I turned away from Crane but I could still feel the heat from his eyes on me. A microphone was suspended from the ceiling above the gurney. The warden lowered it towards my face. I hesitated for a weighty second before I found my voice.

'I'm innocent,' I said. 'I did not kill Kimberley Crane.'

No one responded, but I didn't expect them to. Instead I heard the chaplain start to read out a prayer. At the same time the warden must have given the signal because the lethal drugs started to flow through the tube and into my veins.

In seconds my lungs felt like they were being squeezed shut. A cold sweat broke out on my forehead. I stared at the ceiling as my breathing became more and more laboured.

Then I felt myself letting go.

Just before the darkness took me I heard myself call out Marissa's name.

6

GIDEON CRANE FELT a cold numbness envelop him as he watched Lee Jordan die. The guy's body shook a little, his lips seemed to turn blue, and finally his chest stopped moving.

'Oh, my God,' Pauline said in a hushed tone, as she grabbed his arm and buried her face against his shoulder.

Crane continued to stare into the death chamber, his heart pounding, his mouth dry. It's over, he thought. At long fucking last.

Pauline squeezed his hand. He felt a shiver grab hold of his spine. Almost ten years to the day after Lee Jordan invaded his home with his accomplice, he was dead. Thank God.

The congressman watched as a suited physician entered the chamber. He checked the heart monitor, then Jordan's pulse and eyes. He then turned to the warden and pronounced that Jordan was no longer alive. Time of death was recorded as fifteen minutes past six.

As Crane walked out of the viewing room with the other witnesses he could feel a rush of adrenaline circulating through his system.

'Are you all right, Gideon?' Pauline asked him as they stepped outside the death house.

He came to a stop and filled his lungs with heavy draughts of sweet, cool air.

'I'm fine,' he said. 'What about you?'

'I'm relieved it's over,' she said. 'It wasn't an easy thing to watch.'

He gave her arm a squeeze. 'It was brave of you to come.'

A TV crew and a couple of reporters were waiting outside to get his reaction. He was careful what he said and made a point of not looking too pleased.

'I'm just glad that after ten years I can put this terrible ordeal behind me,' he told them. 'I can at last focus on the future, especially the Presidential nomination race. Lee Jordan can now answer to God for what he did to my darling wife.'

7

MARISSA IS WAITING *for me. She's standing in the front doorway of a small, timber-frame house that has been painted a brilliant white. When she sees me she beams a smile and waves.*

My heart leaps and I start to run towards her. She looks beautiful in a lilac-blue summer dress, her long blonde hair framing a face that has not aged in seven years.

But she doesn't wait for me to reach her. Instead she steps backwards into the house and closes the door behind her. I try to pick up speed, but realize that I'm not getting any closer. It's like I'm running on a treadmill.

Then I see a dark plume of smoke escaping from an open window on the ground floor. Half a second later the smoke turns into a bright orange flame that seizes the timber framework and spreads with lightning speed. I hear my wife scream. I feel the fierce heat of the fire on my face as the flames quickly engulf the entire building.

And then suddenly I wake up. Just as I always do when my recurring nightmare reaches this point.

'Welcome back from the dead, Lee.'

A man's voice. One I don't recognize. It's coming from somewhere in the darkness. I move towards it. But it's slow going. Like climbing up a greasy wall out of a deep hole in the ground.

'You're not dreaming, Lee. You really are alive.'

The voice again. Soft. Almost a whisper. Burred with a southern drawl. My eyes spring open. Everything's a blur. Like staring into a mist. I'm aware of an ache in my head and a soft rattle in my chest as I breathe.

The mist clears. I'm now staring up at a ceiling that's off-white and flat. A flicker of movement draws my eyes to the left. I see a man's face. He's *unfamiliar. A square jaw and thin mouth. Brown hair parted with surgical precision. Eyes bloodshot and glassy, with heavy pouches beneath them.*

'It's a hell of a thing to absorb, Lee,' the man says. 'So take it slowly. And try not to overreact.'

I'm drifting in and out of awareness. Not sure what this stranger is telling me. I feel sick. The pounding in my head is growing more intense.

And then an image flashes in my mind, swirling into a mental hologram. A room with turquoise walls and windows on either side. People staring at me through the glass. There's a gurney in the centre of the room and I see myself strapped on top of it, my arms outstretched as though I'm on a cross.

Holy crap.

It all comes back to me then in a great savage flood of memory that leaves me breathless.

The execution chamber, where they gave me a lethal injection. I can even remember floating into oblivion as the drugs shut down my mind and body.

So why am I still breathing?

'My name is Aaron Vance,' the man says, holding up an ID badge. 'I'm a Special Agent in Charge with the FBI. I'm here to tell you that you've been given a second chance at life.'

8

I STARED UP at Aaron Vance, my alarm clouded with confusion. Was this really happening? How could I possibly be alive? It made no frigging sense.

My head started spinning with questions. I felt disoriented and only half coherent.

'What's going on?' I blurted. 'I should be dead.'

I gazed up at the FBI man's face in disbelief. A slight smile played at the corners of his mouth and I could smell tobacco on his breath. He was well groomed and expensively dressed. 'To all intents and purposes the execution took place, Lee,' he said. 'As you can no doubt remember. But the audience were conned. And so were you. What happened in that chamber was an elaborate illusion.'

I shook my head. 'I don't understand.'

And I didn't. How could I? The memory of what had happened to me was now so clear. It couldn't possibly have been an illusion.

'It wasn't deadly poison that was pumped into your bloodstream,' Vance said. 'It was a cocktail of drugs that rendered you unconscious and in effect simulated death. The heart monitor was rigged to flat-line at the touch of a button and the drugs made it look like you'd stopped breathing.'

I hauled myself to a sitting position. But it was difficult. A wave of nausea washed over me. I sucked in a breath and closed my eyes for a couple of seconds. When I opened them again Vance was holding out a glass of water.

'Drink this,' he said. 'It'll make you feel better.'

I took the glass but my hand was trembling so he helped me raise it to my mouth. The water was cold and fresh and it tasted good.

I noticed for the first time that I was on a double bed in a large, bright room. I was still wearing the prison jumpsuit. Vance was standing next to the bed and there was someone else over by the door. A hulking guy with a boxer's nose and a black crew-cut. Dressed in a loose sweater and jeans. He was sitting on a chair with his arms folded across his chest.

I wiped spilled water from my chin with the back of my hand and said, 'There were witnesses. They all saw it happen.'

Vance put the glass down on the bedside table and shook his head. 'As far as they're concerned you died on the gurney. They saw you lose consciousness and assumed you were dead. It was up to the physician to examine you to provide confirmation. And the physician was installed by the FBI. So was the official who administered the drugs in the other room. The warden who oversaw the proceedings is also on our payroll. A lot of planning went into it, Lee, and in the end it was pretty easy to pull off. You see, people tend to believe what they see. And after the witnesses saw you fry they didn't hang around. Your body was moved out of the chamber and away from there in minutes. A van was waiting to bring you here.'

I sat there in reverent silence, my back against the headboard. It was difficult to separate emotion from logic. A second chance at life, the man had said. Was it really possible? Should I feel elated?

Or was there a catch?

I just couldn't get my mind around what was happening. My execution had been faked, for Christ's sake. After almost ten years on death row the authorities had only pretended to kill me. It was extraordinary. Mystifying. Beyond fucking belief.

'I can tell you're bewildered, Lee,' Vance said. 'That's only to be expected. I know I would be.'

He took something from his inside pocket. A sheet of paper. He held it in front of me. I could barely focus, but it looked like some kind of official document.

'In case you're in any doubt that the world at large believes you're dead you should take a look at this,' he said. 'It's a copy of your death certificate. Because it was a legal killing your death is recorded as homicide. That's normal in these circumstances.'

I took the certificate from him. Ran my eyes over it. Certain words and phrases stuck out.

Court ordered lethal injection.

Manner of death – homicide.
Lee Martin Jordan.

I felt goose bumps crawl up my arms and my pulse started to race. I tried to swallow but my throat clicked dry.

'There's more,' Vance said. He looked at his watch. 'It's now three in the morning. You officially died seven hours ago. In four hours from now an empty coffin supposedly containing your body will slide into the furnace at a crematorium a mile from the Walls. Your remains will be scattered in the grounds of the prison cemetery where more than a hundred other inmates are buried.'

It was all too much to take in. My thoughts were burning like a fuse, but they were muddled and abstract. I looked at Vance. He had intense brown eyes and a coating of stubble on his chin. His body beneath the suit looked stocky and toned.

'Where am I?' I said.

'You're in an FBI facility near San Antonio,' Vance said. 'We'll provide you with everything you need while you come to terms with what has happened. There's an en-suite bathroom through that door. You've got a refrigerator with some food and drink. In the closet you'll find some clothes. There's a TV, books and magazines. There's also a button next to the door. If you need something just press it.'

He gestured towards the other guy. 'That's Daniels. He's my right hand man and he'll be looking after you.'

I tried to rein in my thoughts so that I could formulate what I wanted to say. But the words got stuck in my throat.

'The door will stay locked and the window is barred,' Vance said. 'You won't be going anywhere, at least not right away. But I can assure you that you will find this place far more comfortable than the cell you've been in for the past ten years.'

Vance reached down and picked something up off the bedside table.

'We retrieved these from the death house,' he said, handing me my Bible and the photograph of Marissa.

At last I found my voice.

'Why did you save me?' I asked.

He smiled, revealing straight bone-white teeth.

'Obviously we had a good reason,' he said. 'There's something you're going to have to do for us. In return you'll be given a new identity on our witness protection programme and a new life. You're a very lucky guy.'

'What do I have to do?' I said.

'All in good time, Lee. For now just rest up and relax. You need to get your thoughts together. I'll be back to have another chat later.'

Vance and his side-kick left me alone then. As they closed the door behind them I passed a hand over my face and pressed my eyes shut.

Then I prayed that what was happening was real. And not a dream that would soon come to a sudden, gut-wrenching end.

9

I OPENED MY eyes, letting my senses soak up everything in the room. The beige carpet. The black leather sofa. The yellow curtains on the window. The TV on a stand. The dressing table with a coffee machine on it. The small refrigerator. The stand-alone mahogany closet.

I drank in the colours, the soft tones, the aesthetic contours. It was a world away from the dung heap of a cell I'd lived in on death row.

I got up off the bed and started to explore, enthralled by a sense of wonder. I hadn't watched TV in years. I could barely remember what it was like to open a fridge. So being here was nothing less than an emotionally charged adventure. Like suddenly being cured of blindness.

I opened the fridge door and gasped. There were several bottles of Bud. A carton of milk. A plate of white-bread sandwiches. Even a bottle of red wine with a screw top. One of the shelves contained candy bars and pastries. I blew out a whistle and felt my face crack a wide smile.

I grabbed a beer. There was an opener on top of the fridge. My hands shook as I levered off the top. The first slug was amazing. The ice-cold nectar exploded in the back of my throat and the sensation almost moved me to tears. I downed the whole bottle in about five seconds flat and helped myself to another. Jesus, it was good. I then picked up a sandwich. Ham and sweet pickle. Bit into it. It was quite the best thing I had ever tasted.

I walked over to the en suite bathroom, opened the door, turned on the light. The tub was white and pear-shaped and there as a separate shower cubicle with a frosted glass door. On a shelf next to the sink was a toothbrush, toothpaste, shaving kit and soap. I looked at myself in the mirror. My hair was long and dark and untidy. My eyes were deep set and bloodshot. The skin sat in folds beneath them. People used to say

I looked like my grandfather, a half Mexican who had moved across the border from Tijuana when he was a teenager. From the photos I had seen he had clearly been a handsome young man, but right now I looked like he did when he was in his late forties and dying from pancreatic cancer.

I couldn't resist the urge to take a bath. I'd forgotten what it was like. The thought of a long soak in hot scented water made my heart beat faster. Steam rose as I started to fill the tub. It was a beautiful sight, almost sensual. On death row the water never rose above lukewarm.

I went back into the bedroom to get another beer and sandwich. The TV beckoned. I turned it on with the remote and clicked through the channels. It was intensely thrilling. A simple, everyday task that had been denied me for so long.

I was mesmerized by the images and colours and sounds. There were half-dressed women, men with guns, wild animals, baseball games, commercials, talking heads, riots, speeding cars. . . .

And suddenly there was me. Staring out of the screen.

My photograph was being shown as part of a news report. I cranked up the volume and heard the newscaster tell his audience that Lee Jordan had been executed at the Walls prison in Huntsville, Texas.

'Jordan always claimed he was innocent, but all his appeals were rejected,' the newscaster said. *'After the execution we spoke to congressman Gideon Crane, whose wife Kimberley was Jordan's victim.'*

Crane gave his reaction outside the prison. As he spoke I could see veins throbbing across his forehead. He said he was relieved that it was over and he wanted to look to the future and concentrate on trying to become President. He ended by saying that I would now have to answer to God for murdering his wife.

And that's when it really hit me. I was alive. Drinking beer and watching TV. And Gideon Crane and the rest of the world thought I was dead. It was ridiculous. Insane. Beyond comprehension. No wonder I could feel a strong sense of unease building up inside me.

Just how high was the price I would have to pay for this second chance at life?

10

ON THE TUESDAY before Thanksgiving, Gideon Crane woke up at seven and could not get back to sleep. There was just too much racing around in his head.

He left Pauline in bed and got up to shave and shower. Then he made himself a coffee and carried it into his study. Outside, the sun had just broken through the patchy clouds. There was the promise of another fine day.

He planned to spend it with his wife because he'd told her that he would. She'd made a lunch reservation at a local restaurant. This afternoon she wanted to do some light shopping. He was OK with that. But then tonight her asshole brother Travis and his girlfriend were coming over for dinner and he most definitely wasn't looking forward to that.

Travis was a seedy, arrogant loser and Crane had never liked him. He tolerated him for his wife's sake and was grateful that they did not have to socialize on a regular basis.

Crane booted up his computer and checked his various email accounts. Lots of congratulatory messages following the New Orleans debate. A few alluded to the execution of Lee Jordan. One fellow congressman wrote that when he was next in Washington they should go out and celebrate.

The execution was prominent in most of the online news pages. Crane scanned through them. There were photographs of him and Kimberley and Jordan, plus shots of their old home when it was a crime scene. There were syndicated quotes from an Associated Press reporter who described in detail what had happened in the execution chamber.

Crane sat back and compressed his lips. The words and pictures had stirred up his emotions to the point where he felt his eyes dampen. He drew a sharp breath and pinched the bridge of his nose between fore-finger and thumb. He was about to go outside to clear his head when he had a thought.

He clicked on Google and typed two words in the search box: *Aaron Vance*. He'd been curious about the FBI agent since the governor mentioned him. He wanted to know why the Bureau had been so keen for the execution to go ahead.

There were a few hits of guys with the same name. But the one he was looking for came up on the news search. Aaron Vance, Special Agent in Charge of the FBI's San Antonio field office. He was featured in a couple of dozen news stories going back four years. Usually it was because he had given evidence in a trial.

Crane then went on to the San Antonio field office home page which had a picture of Vance. He looked to be in his forties. He had neat brown hair and high cheekbones. Clicking on his name brought up a short bio that had been produced by the FBI National Press Office. It said that Vance had been appointed to his job four years ago and had previously worked in the Criminal Investigation Division in New York.

His first assignment had been to the Miami Division, where he worked general criminal and organized crime matters. After that he was transferred to Los Angeles and was made team leader of a violent street gang task force.

His experience with gangs had helped him secure his promotion to his current position as SAC in San Antonio. The city was one of several in the state where criminal gangs – in particular the Texas Syndicate – were causing major problems for law enforcement agencies. Only eight weeks ago four men had been shot dead and dumped in an alley close to the iconic Alamo. The killings had prompted calls for more to be done to curb the power and influence of the gangs who thrived on drugs, extortion and prostitution. Vance would no doubt have been in the firing line along with the San Antonio police department.

But none of what Crane read gave a clue as to why Vance had told the governor not to grant Jordan a stay of execution. As far as Crane knew, Lee Jordan had nothing to do with the Texas Syndicate or any other gang. And he was pretty sure he had no connection with San Antonio.

Crane made a note of the field office phone number and jotted down a few details from Vance's bio. He would make a few inquiries and perhaps give the guy a call just to satisfy his curiosity.

Just then his cell pinged with a text message from Beth. He expected it to be about the execution, but instead she'd written: *Call me asap – we might have a problem.* He didn't like the sound of that because Beth wasn't one to get anxious over anything trivial. So he rang her straight back.

'Gideon?'

'I got your message,' he said. 'What's up?'

He heard her draw breath. 'Someone broke into my apartment while I was out jogging this morning.'

'What? Are you serious?'

'Deadly. I realized as soon as I got back. Stuff had been moved and I think I might have disturbed whoever it was because the balcony door was left open.'

'Did you see anyone?'

'I'm not sure.'

'What's that supposed to mean?'

'Well there was a car parked out front when I left the apartment. A guy sitting behind the wheel. He was watching me, I think. But when I looked at him he turned away. I didn't think anything of it. I couldn't even describe him – or the car.'

'Are you all right?'

'I'm a little shaken.'

Beth's apartment was on the ground floor of a block set back from the road and close to Bendwood Park. The balcony overlooked a small landscaped garden.

'I was only out for about an hour,' she said. 'I stopped at a juice bar on the way back.'

'Then that left plenty of time for someone to break in. Was the door forced?'

'No, and before you ask, it was definitely locked when I went out. It always is.'

'So have you informed the police?'

'Not yet. I wanted to talk to you first.'

'Well I think you should call them right away. What's been stolen?'

'That's what's so strange about it. The burglar left all my jewellery and even a wad of cash that was in a purse on the kitchen table.'

'So what the hell did he take?'

Beth left it a beat, said, 'My diary. I was writing in it in bed this morning and I left it on the pillow. But it's gone. I've searched everywhere and it's not in the apartment.'

'I didn't know you kept a diary.'

'I've always kept one. And that's the problem. I take it very seriously and fill the pages with details of what I get up to every day.'

An alarm sounded in his head. He felt a shiver of apprehension.

'Please tell me that's an exaggeration, Beth. Surely you've not been stupid enough to write about us.'

Another long pause, then, 'I'm sorry, Gideon, but that's what diaries are for.'

He felt an angry fire flare up inside him.

'Are you insane? Do you realize how serious this could be if that diary ends up in the wrong hands?'

'Of course I do,' she said. 'Why'd you think I called you and not the police?'

'If it's a dirty trick by one of the other candidates then they'll use it against me for sure.'

'I know that.'

He shook his head. 'Before we go into panic mode I want you to have another look for it. Turn that fucking apartment upside down. Then call me back in an hour. If you don't find it I'll make an excuse and come over.'

'OK, but what about the police? Should I call them now?'

'Not on your life,' he said. 'Don't do anything until you hear from me.'

11

I WAS LEFT alone for six hours. And it was wonderful. I spent the first hour in the tub, soaking away ten years of prison grime from my body. The water was scorching hot and scented. I could feel my flesh soften.

I drank another two beers and ate three more sandwiches. I slipped on a towelling robe I found in the closet and lolled around watching TV and reading the magazines and newspapers that had been left in the room.

It was surreal. But I wasn't complaining. Death row had made me appreciate the little things. Like not feeling too hot or too cold. Being able to take a dump without someone peering at me through the door. Having enough space to take more than four paces in any direction.

I tried to play down the sense of unease in my gut. I told myself that whatever was going to happen to me next would have to be better than being dead.

I dropped off to sleep for a couple of hours. The bed was so big and soft that it was hard not to. I had the dream again, the one where Marissa retreats into the house that starts burning down.

I woke up with a jolt, sweat on my face. But the stark images in my head instantly evaporated when I saw the sunlight splashing through the window.

I got up to have a look. The view was of a well-tended garden. The short grass was moist with dew. There was a fence at the bottom of the garden and beyond it a forest of high trees. Above the forest the sky was blue glass.

I gazed out at all the colours of the day. Browns, greens, yellows – and I couldn't help thinking how lucky I was.

*

Things started to happen just after ten o'clock. Daniels brought me a breakfast tray that had me salivating. Eggs, bacon, toast, pancakes, hot coffee and orange juice. I stuffed my face until I was so bloated I could barely move. But it felt good. An hour later Vance came back with Daniels in tow. They were both casually dressed in short-sleeved shirts and jeans. Daniels was carrying a small black leather holdall.

I was lying on the bed drinking coffee and watching a movie on TV.

'It's time to get this show on the road,' Vance said. 'I hope you're feeling refreshed.'

He pulled a chair up next to the bed and sat down. Daniels stood awkwardly with his back to the door and ran his tongue back and forth across his teeth.

'So how do you feel?' Vance asked.

'Confused,' I said. 'But I can live with that.'

'Have you made the most of the facilities here?'

'If you mean the beer and the bath and the TV – then you bet I have.'

He grinned. 'That's good. It'll take time to adjust. The shock to your system is immense. We understand that.'

He stroked his jaw and straightened in his chair, as much as the curvature of his spine would allow.

'Your head must be filled with questions,' he said. 'And they will all be answered in time. I promise.'

There was a beat of silence, save for the hum of the air-conditioner – a constant white noise.

'I want to make one thing clear at the outset,' he said. 'We don't care that you murdered Kimberley Crane.'

'I didn't murder her,' I said flatly.

Vance shrugged. 'For argument's sake let's accept that the jury got it right. But I want you to know that it doesn't matter. As far as we're concerned you've done your time. Killing you would serve no useful purpose now. Especially given the fact that you're in a unique position to help the FBI and therefore your country.'

'What's so special about me?' I asked.

'That will be explained to you later today. We're taking you to see a man who will spell it out and lay the deal on the table. He'll tell you everything you need to know. Such as which country you will move to and how much money will be put into a bank account in your name. He'll give you reassurance in respect of how we intend to keep our secret. For instance, the Bureau will wipe your prints and DNA from the database. So in future if you're arrested anywhere in the world a guy who should be dead won't show up on any computer.'

'What if I'm not happy with the deal you're offering?' I said. 'Or I don't want to move abroad?'

His grin widened. 'We're confident that that scenario won't arise. We're offering you a chance to live a full and comfortable life. Probably in South America. The only condition we'll impose is that you must never contact people from your past life – and that includes your sister.'

'And if I do?'

His face became serious. 'Then you'd create a situation that would have to be dealt with. We would take whatever action is necessary to stop that person or persons from passing on that information to someone else.'

He didn't have to spell it out. If the world suddenly discovered that I was still alive it would cause a media firestorm that would rage across the country. Heads would roll and there would be a series of high-profile arrests. The FBI would be seriously damaged and the fall-out would probably even engulf the President. Not to mention my own fate. I would almost certainly find myself back on death row.

All this told me one thing – whatever they wanted me to do for them had to be important enough to justify the incredible risks they were taking.

'We leave here at 6.30 this evening,' Vance said. 'You'll be meeting the guy I've mentioned at a restaurant in the city centre. He insisted on it being informal, which means that you've got most of the day to wind down. And it gives us time to prepare you.'

'What do you mean by that?'

'You need a makeover,' Vance said. 'We can't have you leaving here looking like Lee Jordan, the guy who just got executed in Huntsville.'

'So what have you got in mind?'

'Don't look so worried,' he said. 'It's nothing drastic. We're going to cut and dye your hair and provide you with some smart clothes. We want you to wear tinted glasses and fake tan so you don't look like a guy who's spent years without going out in the sun.'

He had a point. I'd studied myself in the mirror earlier. My face looked like the blood had been sucked out of it.

'We'll start right away,' he said. 'Daniels has got everything we need in his bag. After it's done you can chill out and you can have a taste of freedom in the garden.'

Vance was an impressive guy, I decided. He possessed a shrewd, calculating intelligence that showed in his eyes. But I didn't know him well enough to be able to read his face beyond that. So I had no idea if he was telling me the truth. For that reason a simmering unease continued to erode my optimism.

Daniels turned out to be pretty nifty with the comb and scissors. I'd let my hair grow long on death row so he cut quite a bit off. Then he applied the dye, which turned my dark brown hair to black. It made me look considerably younger. The fake tan I applied myself, which was fairly easy and made an instant difference. In the mirror I looked like a new man.

True to his word, Vance then let me go out into the garden. He and Daniels stayed close to me and we didn't encounter anyone else. From the garden I saw that I was being kept in a large detached house surrounded by Texas woodland. It was a beautiful red-brick building with a slanted grey roof.

But I barely paid attention to it because my senses were seized by our surroundings. The trees and the grass and the buzz of the insects. The smell of wild flowers and the gentle breeze on my face. I felt a shiver of excitement and my heart started thumping against my ribcage. As I stood there taking it in I thought to myself that it was surely all too good to be true.

12

BETH LOOKED PALE and anxious when Crane got to her apartment at lunchtime. She was still wearing her jogging suit and had not applied any make-up. He noticed immediately that she smelled of stale sweat.

'I didn't think you would come,' she said.

'Pauline wasn't happy,' he told her. 'She'd made arrangements for us to have lunch out and then go shopping.'

'I'm really sorry, Gideon.'

Pauline had been furious, in fact. She'd reminded him that he had promised to take a few days off. And she'd been more than a little sceptical when he'd said that an emergency had come up at the office. But he'd felt compelled to come to Beth's apartment. He needed to assess the situation for himself and decide what, if anything, could be done about it. He was worried because her diary had not turned up and she swore that she had searched every inch of the apartment.

'You're sure that nothing else was taken?' he asked as he perched himself on the arm of the sofa.

'I'm absolutely positive,' she said. 'Things had been moved around. A drawer was left open. But it seems that whoever broke in wasn't interested in anything but my diary.'

Crane sucked in his breath. 'I wish you'd mentioned it before. I would have told you that it was stupid to keep one.'

'I realize that now, but it never occurred to me that someone would steal it. I've never taken it out of the apartment.'

Crane chewed on a thumbnail, his stomach churning with dread. He couldn't believe this was happening. Not when things seemed to be going so well. His fears were compounded by the fact that there was very little he could do about it.

He didn't think it would be a good idea to contact the police. That way the news would spread like wildfire and speculation would be rife. Questions would be asked as to why anyone would want to steal Beth Abbot's diary. Did it contain explosive information about her job, her boss or her personal life? Crane liked to be in control of events that impacted on his life and right now he wasn't. He felt angry and impotent.

He gritted his teeth. 'Jesus fucking Christ, Beth.'

The fury in his voice made her flinch. As she looked up at him a muscle under her right eye started to twitch. It was the first time he had shouted at her but she needed to understand that she'd let him down big time. A diary for pity's sake. Who the fuck kept a diary in this day and age?

At that moment his cell pinged. He fished it from his pocket, thinking it was bound to be a message from his pissed-off wife. But it was from an anonymous source. It read: *What a night. Gideon told me he loved me. Then we fucked like rabbits on the floor of his apartment. Later I sucked his cock as he spoke to Pauline on the phone. Life just doesn't get any better!*

'What the hell is this crap?' Crane fumed.

He thrust the phone at Beth. She took it from him. The colour drained from her face as she read the text.

'Oh my God,' she exclaimed.

Crane glared at her. 'What?'

She swallowed hard. 'It's an extract from my diary. I wrote that months ago.'

Crane's mouth fell open and his heart froze in his chest.

'Oh shit,' he said.

13

I SPENT MOST of the afternoon pacing the room, feeling restless and edgy. My mind resolutely refused to switch off.

It was a great shame because I should have been spoiling myself. The fridge had been restocked with a few more beers and snacks. Daniels had also delivered some more newspapers and magazines. And there were dozens of TV channels to keep me entertained.

Eventually Daniels returned carrying a beige summer suit, a dark blue shirt and a pair of brown leather shoes. He told me to get showered and dressed.

'We'll be leaving in half an hour,' he said. 'And cheer up, Mr Jordan. This is where your new life begins.'

Mr Jordan! It sounded weird. It had been a long time since anyone had been so respectful towards me.

As I got ready I felt the excitement build. I thought about all the wonderful things I might now experience and all the paths that were going to open up to me. A new life. A new identity. A new country. Not bad for a man who only hours ago had been led into the execution chamber to be put to death.

But it wasn't easy to focus just on the positive. I couldn't totally ignore an underlying uneasiness – a vague sense of disquiet that refused to go away.

At six thirty I stood in front of the mirror and found it hard to believe that it was me staring back. I was a complete stranger. Smart and respectable. Tanned and well-groomed. I was pretty sure that even my sister wouldn't recognize me.

'The transformation is amazing,' Vance said when he came into the room. 'Nobody would guess you're a dead man walking.'

'Very funny,' I said.

Vance was wearing a black suit and carrying a black leather briefcase. He motioned for me to follow him outside.

There were two cars parked in front of the building. One was a grey Dodge Durango with darkened windows. The other was a silver Taurus. I counted four guys standing to one side smoking. One of them was Daniels. They were all wearing dark suits and they all snapped to attention when Vance and I stepped outside.

Daniels opened the rear door of the Dodge and Vance told me to get in. He climbed in beside me and Daniels got behind the wheel. The other guys got into the Taurus.

'So let's go,' Vance said.

The Dodge followed a long, gravel driveway to an automatic gate that opened as we approached it. The Taurus stayed close behind.

'What's with the muscle?' I asked. 'You afraid I might take off?'

Vance shook his head. 'You're not that stupid, Lee. You know there'd be no point. But you're a precious cargo and we have to make sure you're well protected.'

'Do they all know who I am?'

He shook his head. 'They think you're some nameless dude on our witness protection programme.'

This whole thing was becoming more puzzling. The questions were piling up inside my head. Why the hell was I so important to the FBI? Who was going to meet me in the restaurant? What did they want me to do for them? Why was I the only person who could do it?

So many thoughts were rattling around inside my brain that it was making me dizzy. As we passed through the gate onto the road I experienced a frisson of unease. Every muscle in my body felt taut and the blood was pounding in my ears.

There were plenty of distractions, though, and I tried to focus on them. I stared out of the window and drank in the sights, which became more interesting the further we travelled from the house. At first there wasn't much to see other than a few houses set back from the road. But after about five minutes the buildings started to bunch up and I realized that we were pretty close to the city.

It was already dark and the moon looked small, as though it were moving away from the earth. As we veered onto a freeway I saw a familiar landmark in the distance – the Tower of the Americas, which stretches 750ft above San Antonio.

Marissa and I had spent a weekend in the city early on in our relationship. We'd ventured up to the tower's observation deck from where the views are spectacular. We'd also visited all the other major tourist attractions, including the Alamo and the River Walk, with its various restaurants and bars.

It had been a wonderful couple of days during which we'd talked and walked and got to know each other. The memory brought tears to my eyes and I couldn't help wondering if Marissa could see me now. Would she be happy that I was still alive or sad that I wasn't with her?

'We'll soon be at the restaurant,' Vance said. 'It's in the downtown area. How are you holding up?'

I looked at him. 'Pretty well, I guess. I just want to know what's going on.'

'And you will soon enough. As I said before, all of your questions will be answered and your concerns addressed.'

'This guy I'm meeting – is he FBI?'

'He'll tell you himself who he is.'

'Why can't you tell me?'

'Because I've been ordered not to. That's the way it has to be. There's a lot at stake here and we all have to do exactly what we've been told to do. We can't afford any mistakes. I'm sure you can appreciate that.'

A few minutes later we were in the heart of the city and driving past the Alamo – that long-standing symbol of American freedom. Along with most other Texans, the old mission held a special place in my heart. It was where almost two hundred volunteers, including Davy Crockett, died at the hands of Santa Anna's Mexican army in the great battle for independence.

'It brings a lump to my throat every time I pass it,' Vance said, and I believed him.

Less than two minutes later, Daniels pulled the Dodge to a stop outside a brightly-lit restaurant called The Cactus Flower.

'This is the place,' Vance said.

I released a slow breath and gritted my teeth. It looked like a classy joint. There were large windows through which I could see inside and it was pretty busy.

'Just go in and ask for Mr Martinez. He's inside.'

'Are you not coming?' I asked, surprised.

'No. But we'll be waiting out here to take you back to the house.'

I glanced at the restaurant and then up and down the street.

'Just walk slowly and casually,' Vance said. 'You'll be fine. And I want you to take this.' He handed me his briefcase which had been pushed between the seats. 'You'll look like you just finished a hard day at the office.'

Something just didn't feel right, but I couldn't put my finger on what it was. My heart started to thunder against my chest.

'You'll be perfectly safe,' Vance said. 'See the guy standing in the doorway to the right? Well he's one of ours and he's there to make sure that nothing goes wrong.'

The guy was wearing a dark top with a hood so I couldn't see his face.

'Go on, Lee,' Vance said. 'Go and find out what we want you to do for us in return for bringing you back to life.'

I got out of the car and closed the door behind me. It was a cool, clear evening and the pavement was empty except for the guy in the hood. I could hear music coming from inside the restaurant and could see several people at window tables. One guy actually acknowledged me with a wave. He had jet black hair and was wearing a white jacket. He was Hispanic, probably Mexican. I reckoned he must be the mysterious Mr Martinez.

I threw a glance back at the Dodge but I couldn't see Vance through the darkened window. So I took a deep breath and started walking towards the entrance, briefcase gripped in my right hand, glasses resting on the bridge of my nose.

I told myself to stay calm. The Feds were not going to let anything happen to me. Not after going to all that trouble to stop me being executed.

I just had to go inside and hear what the guy had to say. Simple and straightforward.

But then something happened that I didn't see coming.

The Dodge suddenly pulled away from the curb with a loud screech of tyres. I spun round and saw it speeding along the road away from the restaurant.

At the same time I noticed that the hooded guy had stepped out of the doorway and was standing a few yards behind me. He was holding a revolver in his outstretched hand and it was aimed at my chest.

A chill of fear swept through me as he squeezed the trigger and the gun flashed and roared.

14

I WAS LUCKY. The would-be assassin must have thought that he was too close to miss his target because he was holding the gun in one hand instead of two. And as everyone knows – especially FBI agents – that leaves too much room for error. His arm was not as steady as it should have been and when the Dodge screeched away from the curb the noise appeared to distract him.

It caused his trigger finger to hesitate for a fraction of a second. Time enough for me to already be moving as he fired off the shot. The bullet sliced a path right where my body would have been if I'd stayed still. I felt the slug whizz above my head as I ducked down. I sprang forward, slamming into him with considerable force. The guy fired a second round, but he was off balance and the bullet went skywards.

He let out a sharp grunt of pain as his knees buckled and he fell onto the pavement. But I managed to stay on my feet, my ears ringing from the blasts. I dropped the briefcase and grabbed his wrist with one hand while seizing the gun with the other. Panic and rage cut through me like a hot knife. I took a step back, threw off the glasses and pointed the gun at him.

His face was visible beneath the hood and he stared up at me in slack-jawed disbelief. I saw that he was middle-aged and pale-skinned, but nothing else registered. I had no intention of shooting him, but I had no intention of hanging around so that someone else could try to shoot me.

I looked around, my heart drumming frantically. I saw diners in the restaurant looking out at me, some of them standing. I felt giddy and disoriented. Cold fear hardened in the centre of my stomach.

Then I heard a car door open. I turned and saw the Taurus across the road. Two of the suited men I'd seen earlier had got out. My gut told me that they were not coming to my rescue.

They're going to kill me, I screamed at myself.

So I did the first thing that came into my head – I raised the gun and fired off a shot in their direction, making sure the bullet went well above them.

As they both ducked behind the Taurus I broke into a run, moving like a panicked deer. My heart was pumping its way out of my ribcage as I hurtled along the street with no idea where I was going. I knew only that I had to put distance between myself and the FBI agents.

The muscles in my thighs burned as I hammered my feet on the pavement. At the same time the shoes they'd given me were hurting like hell.

The street was quiet. Too quiet. I was far too exposed. I came to a cross-street and chanced a look back over my shoulder. What I saw flooded my veins with ice. The Taurus was bearing down on me with its headlights blazing.

Without thinking, I turned left and went at full sprint along a street that was better lit and busier. As I ran, I shoved the gun into my jacket pocket, but not before the sight of it alarmed a bunch of people. One guy jumped out of my way and tripped over the curb, landing on his ass.

I saw a road bridge up ahead and a sign for the River Walk, with an arrow pointing down. I remembered how crowded the walk was when I came here with Marissa, so I followed the arrow and dashed down a long flight of steps. Behind me I heard the Taurus screech to a halt on the road.

At the bottom of the steps was the river that meanders through the downtown area of the city. On either side it was lined with restaurants, bars and boutique shops. A steady stream of people was moving in both directions, most of them tourists. The air was filled with the sound of flamenco music and the smell of exotic foods. But I did not stop to admire the colourful scene. Instead I ran straight onto the pavement and jostled my way into the crowd.

Someone swore at me. Someone else yelled for me to slow down. But I ignored them and pressed on, praying that I'd eventually shake the men who were pursuing me.

Brightly lit pleasure barges cruised along the river, and families and couples sat at outside tables soaking up the atmosphere, unaware of the drama that was unfolding around them.

I continued to attract attention as the throng dispersed to let me through. After about a hundred yards I came to a small footbridge over the river. I veered onto it and as I crossed it I slowed to a fast walk so that I could look down along the route I'd come.

I saw two dark suits cutting through the crowd of bright shirts and dresses. One of them looked up and pointed at me. That was my cue to break into another run.

The other side of the river was just as busy and the bars, cafes and shops were doing a roaring trade.

By now my breath was rasping in my throat and it felt like there were daggers in my lungs. I wasn't sure how long I could keep up the pace. A decade on death row meant that I had very little stamina. It was proving to be a real struggle. Could I outrun them? I didn't know. But I had to try. I had to push myself hard and fast.

But I quickly felt myself slowing, and as my breath became more laboured my head started to spin with the effort of staying on my feet. Trauma and exhaustion were taking their toll. Then I suddenly collided with the edge of an outside table and stumbled. There was nothing to hold onto so I went over and ended up splayed out on the path.

It caused a fair amount of commotion. People scattered, probably thinking I was drunk. A thought flashed in my mind. *Would I be recognised?* Surely that wasn't possible. Or was it?

'Are you all right, sir?'

I rolled on my side, looked up. The voice belonged to a black girl in a skimpy summer dress. She was holding a pile of menus under one arm and standing outside a Mexican restaurant. Just as she extended her free hand to help me up she was elbowed out of the way by one of the suits who'd been chasing me.

'OK folks,' he shouted, holding up his badge. 'No need to be alarmed. We've got this situation covered.'

His partner stepped into view, a cellphone pressed to his ear. No doubt he was telling Special Agent Vance that they'd caught me.

They hadn't taken out their guns. Was that because they didn't expect me to resist or they didn't want to cause panic? As far as I was concerned it was a mistake on their part.

I raised both arms, palms out, in a gesture of defeat. The two agents seized an arm each. They were both big guys with army-short haircuts. As they lifted me to my feet one of them leaned close and said, 'Don't make a scene, pal. If you do you'll get hurt.'

I let them think I was resigned to my fate. But when I was standing up I went for it, catching both of them off guard. We were all just a few feet from the edge of the walkway. One of them had his back to the river and I took a deep breath and then pushed at him with my shoulder. As he teetered backwards I jerked my arm free and gave him another shove to send him splashing into the river.

Then I twisted my body and drove my forehead straight into the other guy's face. He let go of my arm and staggered backwards, blood spurting from a broken nose. I leapt forward, grabbed his jacket, and whirled him round so hard and fast that he couldn't stop himself plunging into the river along with his partner. The river wasn't deep at this point and when I looked over the side they were both standing up, with the water reaching their chests.

A woman behind me screamed and there was shouting. Fear pulsed through me and my knees felt weak.

Fresh panic sent me plunging ahead along the river bank. When I'd covered maybe sixty yards I slowed down and looked to see who was on my tail. I saw no one.

The River Walk became less busy. I passed a couple of smart hotels and a few more restaurants. When I came to some steps I dashed up them. I found myself on a busy road. I heard a police siren in the distance, maybe a few streets away.

I had no idea where I was or how many people were looking for me. But I did know that if I didn't make myself invisible soon I'd be snared like a wounded animal.

I crossed the road and ducked into a doorway to catch my breath. I was completely winded and gasping for air. I ran the splayed fingers of both hands through my hair. I kept a sharp eye out for the Dodge and the Taurus. Where was Vance? Where were the other agents? Were the cops also looking for me?

I was certain of only one thing. Aaron Vance had set me up. He and Daniels had sped away from the restaurant because they had known what was going to happen. I'd been taken there not to have dinner with a mystery man but to be murdered in cold blood by a guy in a hood who was supposedly working for the FBI. I'd been an easy target. But the would-be assassin had messed up. He'd either been over confident or inexperienced.

None of it made any sense. Why go to extraordinary lengths to keep me alive only to have me gunned down just over twenty four hours later? And why do it outside a busy restaurant in the centre of town? And what did the guy I was supposed to meet have to do with it? Mr Martinez was the name I was given. Was he the guy who had waved at me through the window?

It meant I was on my own now. I couldn't expect help from anyone – not even the cops. I was supposed to be dead. My body cremated. And those who knew I was still alive – including the FBI – were going to be desperate to ensure the truth did not get out.

Their diabolical plan had backfired. I'd got away, and they now faced the threat of exposure. For them the consequences could be catastrophic. Faking an execution was not an acceptable practice – even for the FBI.

But what about me? I was a man who no longer officially existed. What was I going to do? I had no name, no money, no friends, no home, no prospects. I couldn't approach anyone I knew. The Feds would put everyone from my past under surveillance. They'd know everything about me – right down to my old haunts and the names of people who might be willing to help me. So how would I survive? Where would I go? What did the future hold for me, assuming I was still alive by this time tomorrow?

I stood there, feeling dread pour through me. A drum was beating in my head and my scalp felt tight. I could taste the fear in my mouth. I could feel the excess adrenaline burning me up. I had no plan of action other than to stay one step ahead of Vance and his crew.

Stay calm, I told myself. *Think. Think fast.* But my head began to ache as my brain grappled with what was a hopeless predicament. And suddenly I was struck by a strange truth – that there had actually been an upside to life on death row.

At least there I had never had to think for myself.

15

I CHOSE THE wrong moment to step out of the doorway. As I started walking along the pavement a grey Dodge with tinted windows came crawling out of a side street up ahead.

I breathed a sigh of relief when it turned left and started moving away from me. But then the brake lights suddenly came on and the vehicle did a frenetic U-turn in the road. I took to my toes again and ran at full pelt in the opposite direction. My heart surged into fifth gear.

A part of me wanted to stop and confront Aaron Vance. Find out why he now wanted me dead. But the other part of me, the rational part, told me it would be suicide.

So I took a determined breath to stiffen my resolve and picked up speed. But I couldn't outrun the Dodge. Its engine was soon roaring in my ears as it closed in.

As luck would have it I came to a low wall just in the nick of time. I scrambled over it, dashed across the forecourt of a clothes store, then charged head first into a narrow alley alongside it. The Dodge couldn't follow, but I didn't pause to find out if it had stopped. I tore through the alley, which was unlit and smelled of something rotten.

My chest heaved, thirsty for oxygen, and my legs hurt. I wondered if Vance or Daniels, or maybe both of them, had got out of the Dodge and were now coming after me on foot. If so I was in trouble. They'd be faster and fitter than me, and they would obviously know their way around the city. Whereas I was lost, with no idea where I was heading.

The alley discharged me onto another street. It was lined with trees and parked cars. I spotted the entrance to a hotel on my left. To my right was an intersection. I darted across the road, dodging a couple of cars. One driver blasted his horn because he had to swerve to avoid me.

I was looking back after every few strides, but I didn't see the Dodge or any Feds. Had I lost them? I doubted it. I feared it was only a matter of time before I was spotted again. The city centre was too bright, and away from the River Walk the streets were fairly quiet. There were too few pedestrians which meant I was pretty conspicuous.

Exhaustion forced me to slow down. I walked past an office block and then a fast-food restaurant. Beyond that I turned right onto another street that was part of a square. In the centre of the square there was a grassy area and a small water fountain with coloured lights. On the other side of the square I saw a large retail grocery store.

I stopped to look around. There was some traffic but no sign of the Dodge or the Taurus. I quick-stepped across the road and onto the grass, pausing next to a tree to catch my breath. From there I had a good view of the square and all the roads leading onto it. It looked like any normal weekday night away from the tourist area. There wasn't much action. Very little noise.

If the FBI had ordered a lockdown of the city centre to stop me escaping then there was no evidence of it. That probably meant the police had not been told about me. The cops were therefore oblivious to what was going on. That was why the streets were not swarming with uniforms and cruisers.

It made sense if my faked execution was part of a secret operation known only to a small team inside the FBI. A team headed up by Special Agent Aaron Vance. The last thing he'd want now would be for me to be arrested by the police who would quickly discover that I was Lee Jordan. The same Lee Jordan who was executed yesterday evening at 6 p.m. in Huntsville.

I suddenly caught sight of the Dodge. It was cruising along the road I had just crossed. I stepped back behind the tree, waited a couple of seconds, then peered out to see where it was.

To my dismay it had stopped at the curb. I had to assume they were looking out through the darkened windows, trying to decide which way to go. They were uncomfortably close. It made me wonder if they'd seen me and had radioed or phoned the other members of the team in the Taurus. If so I could soon be a sitting duck. I had to get out of the square.

Keeping the tree between myself and the Dodge, I started walking backwards, conscious of the fact that it was a risky manoeuvre. I got to within a few feet of the road, and was about to turn and hurry across it, when the Dodge suddenly lurched forward with a screech of rubber.

They'd spotted me.

My stomach did a backflip. I threw caution to the wind and hurtled full-throttle across the road towards the retail grocery store. It was a big, two-storey building and there was a large parking lot in front that was almost full.

I was wheezing with every breath as I jogged through the entrance. I then lowered my head and tried to lose myself amongst the vehicles. I moved as quickly as I could between cars and trucks and vans. I passed a couple of people loading groceries into their trunks and it gave me an idea.

But as I rushed forward I began to panic because I felt sure the Feds were about to entrap me. I was on the verge of bolting back out onto the road when I saw a woman who was by herself. She was piling bags into the back of a dark blue Ford Explorer.

I stopped in my tracks about twenty feet from her and watched as she unloaded her trolley. I couldn't see anyone else in the car. She was in her mid to late thirties and was wearing jeans and a tight black T-shirt. She had coppery brown hair that was tied back and beneath it I noticed her neck was pale and slender.

When her bags were packed she left the trolley where it was and moved towards the driver's side door. That's when I rushed forward, whipping the gun from my pocket. Just as she closed her door I wrenched open the door on the passenger side and slipped into the seat next to her.

She gasped and her hand flew to her mouth.

I pointed the gun at her face and said, 'If you scream you'll be very sorry.'

Fear contorted her features as she locked her frightened gaze on me. Her hand started to shake and a low moan issued from between her lips.

'I want you to switch on the ignition and drive out of the parking lot,' I said in a soft, controlled voice.

'Please don't,' she said. 'I have money and credit cards in my purse. Take them and go.'

'I don't want money,' I said. 'There are people after me and I need to get as far away from them as possible. If you cooperate you'll be OK.'

Her eyes shifted nervously to the left and I followed her stricken gaze.

Damn.

There was a young child strapped into a safety seat in the back. A girl, aged between eight months and a year I guessed. She was fast asleep with her mouth open.

'Oh my God please don't hurt us,' the woman said, her voice cracking.

I looked at her and gritted my teeth.

'Either you start driving or I kick you out and take the kid.'

That did it. She turned the key and the Explorer came to life.

'Don't rush it,' I said. 'Drive slowly and carefully. And for your sake don't try to signal to anyone.'

She shoved the stick into drive and we moved forward. Thankfully she stayed calm and gripped the wheel so tight her knuckles turned white. I saw the Dodge as we rolled towards the exit. We had to pass it and as we did I slunk down in the seat and hoped to God they didn't see me.

I focused my eyes on the wing mirror as we eased out of the parking lot onto the road, then let out a shaky breath when I realized the Feds weren't following us.

'I'll give you anything you want, mister,' the woman said, her voice so thin I could barely hear it. 'Just don't harm my baby.'

I put the gun back into my pocket, said, 'I won't harm either of you so long as you do as I tell you.'

She turned to look at me with a mixture of fear and confusion.

'Just keep your eyes on the road,' I said. 'And don't even think of crashing the car deliberately. It'd be a big mistake.'

She faced forward again and said, 'Where do you want to go?'

'Good question,' I replied. 'Just keep driving. I need to think this through.'

16

GIDEON CRANE KNEW he'd already drunk too much. He was slurring his words and feeling light-headed. He would have to ease up if he was going to avoid getting completely smashed.

It was only eight o'clock. The evening had barely begun. Pauline's brother, Travis, and his girlfriend Cindy, had come over as planned to celebrate Thanksgiving, as well as Lee Jordan's execution.

The four of them were now sitting around the dining table, working their way through their third bottle of wine. The dinner plates had been cleared and Crane was trying to look as if he was interested in the inane conversation. But he had too much on his mind to focus. That was why he was drinking heavily. He was desperate to quell the hysteria that was rising in his gut.

He'd been disturbed by a sense of monstrous tension since returning from Beth's apartment at about three. The theft of her diary and the text message sent to his phone had really got to him. Pauline had made things worse by refusing to cancel the dinner, telling him that she was determined to salvage something from what had been a miserable day.

As a result he'd had to put up with her brother's annoying drivel and grating arrogance for the past hour. Travis was in his late forties. He was a whippet-thin man with sunken cheeks and unruly fair hair. He ran a small and moderately successful private investigations agency in Houston. Crane reckoned he was well suited to the job because he was sleazy and without scruples. He was also addicted to gambling, and on three separate occasions over the past nine years Crane had had to bail him out when he couldn't pay his debts.

Only two months ago Travis had approached Crane for more money, this time the princely sum of twenty thousand dollars. But Crane had turned him down flat, a decision that had shocked and angered Travis and had upset Pauline. But Crane had stuck by it, insisting that Travis sort out his own problems.

This was the first time they had got together socially since then, and to Crane's immense relief the subject of the money had not been raised. He therefore assumed that Travis had managed to come up with it by some other means.

As far as Crane was concerned the guy was a sponge, soaking up the goodwill of those around him and giving nothing back in return. Crane had never tried to conceal his contempt for Travis. Pauline knew what he thought about her brother, but she defended him to the hilt on the grounds that he was her only blood relative.

Travis, for his part, didn't give a monkey's ass what anyone thought about him. He had elephant-thick skin and the morals of an alley cat.

'I'd like to propose another toast,' Travis said, after Pauline had refilled the glasses. 'This time to the next President of this great country of ours.'

Travis raised his glass towards Crane and the others followed suit.

Crane smiled grudgingly, said, 'There's a long way to go and it might not happen.'

Travis shook his head. 'Come off it, Gideon. You're way ahead in the polls. Once you've got the Republican ticket you can set your sights on that moron in the White House. And he'll be a walkover.'

'I don't think it's going to be as easy as that.'

Travis fixed him with a drunken stare. 'It will be so long as you keep your nose clean and don't fuck up.'

Crane was used to Travis's crass and insensitive remarks, but he feared that what he just said might prove prophetic. After all, he hadn't kept his nose clean had he? He'd been having an affair with his press secretary and whoever had stolen her diary was in a position to destroy his political ambitions.

'Don't look so glum,' Travis said. 'I'm a hundred per cent confident that you won't put a foot wrong. You'll be taking the oath of office next year.'

'It's good to know that you don't have any doubts,' Crane said, resisting the urge to adopt a sarcastic tone.

Travis grinned. 'In fact I'm so sure you'll make it that I'm going to place a hefty bet on it. The odds are currently three to one, so I can look forward to a big pay day.'

'You told me you'd given up gambling,' Cindy said in that loud Texas twang that Crane found so irritating.

She was a good ten years younger than Travis, with breasts the size of melons and a brain the size of a pea. She had ash-blonde hair and deer-like eyes, and Travis had been with her for six months.

'I *have* given up, sweetheart,' he said, and was clearly lying through his teeth. 'But this bet is a one-off. Call it a gesture of faith in my brother-in-law.'

Crane hated it when Travis referred to him as his brother-in-law. It made him cringe.

'Look, I need some fresh air,' Crane said. 'Does anyone mind if I pop outside to smoke a cigar?'

'I'll join you,' Travis said. 'There's something I want to talk to you about without boring the ladies.'

Crane's heart sank, but he tried not to show his disappointment.

'It's too chilly for me,' Pauline said. 'Cindy and I will clear the table. When you come back maybe we can play a game of cards.'

Crane took a couple of Dominican cigars from his humidor and he and Travis went outside. The temperature had dropped quite a bit. The night was clear and crisp and they stood under a glittering canopy of stars to light their cigars. Then they sat at the patio table from where they had a view of the moonlit lake. The cigar smoke hung above them like a pale cloud.

'So what is it you want to talk to me about?' Crane asked without preamble.

Travis picked off a piece of tobacco that had got stuck to his tongue. Then he smiled, which surprised Crane, who had expected him to adopt a pathetic expression and plead for money.

'I want to talk about your bid for the Presidency,' Travis said. 'And what you're going to have to do to stop me derailing it.'

Crane stared at him, confused.

'What the hell are you on about?'

Travis sucked wetly on his cigar and blew the smoke out slowly between pursed lips.

'I've never liked you, Gideon,' he said. 'There's something dark about you. And you're the most self-centred man I know. I don't understand why my sister was attracted to you in the first place, or why she still loves you. And it *is* love by the way. Your wealth has never had anything to do with it.'

Crane felt his blood boil. He said, 'What the fuck has got into you, Travis? How dare you talk to me like this?'

Travis flicked ash from the end of his cigar onto the patio.

'That's the trouble with you, Gideon. You think that because you're a wealthy politician you can be condescending and patronizing to people like me. People you regard as flawed and inferior. Well you can't – at least not anymore.'

It must be the alcohol talking, Crane thought. He'd never known Travis to be so truculent and offensive. Clearly the wine had unleashed a torrent of bad feelings that had been festering inside him for ages.

'Where's this coming from, Travis?' he said. 'Is it because you're still pissed off that I didn't give you that money in September?'

Travis made a thoughtful noise in his throat. 'I guess it's true to say that if you had given me the money I wouldn't have started my investigation. And I wouldn't therefore be in a position now to blow your campaign out of the water.'

Crane's nostrils flared like a bull about to charge.

'What investigation? Have you been prying into my affairs, for God's sake?'

Travis rolled the cigar between his fingers, clearly enjoying the moment.

'My job is to investigate people,' he said. 'So I decided out of anger to investigate you. And guess what? I found stuff out that will scupper your chances of ever becoming President.'

Crane's stomach knotted like a ball of twine. For several long beats he didn't know what to say or how to react. He felt his chest tighten up and his heart rate quicken.

Eventually he found his voice and said, 'This is bullshit. You're drunk. And you're talking crap.'

Travis bared his teeth. 'Unfortunately for you I'm not. You see, I'm the one who took your girlfriend's diary. I sent you the extract so that when we had this conversation you'd take me seriously.'

Crane felt a flood of panic wash over him. The bastard had not exaggerated when he said he could derail the campaign. He had taken possession of a grenade and all he had to do was pull the pin if he wanted to cause untold damage.

'As soon as I started following you I realized what was going on,' Travis said. 'You were careful, but not careful enough. I've got photos of the pair of you entering and leaving her apartment together. I've got one of you kissing her in her car. But I wanted more so I broke into her place this morning to plant some bugs. I actually didn't expect her to be around until this afternoon. Anyway, whilst in there I came across her diary. I couldn't believe my luck. It's all there, every sordid detail about what you've been up to.'

Crane gulped in a few deep breaths and swallowed a lump the size of a walnut.

'Have you told Pauline?' he asked in a hoarse voice.

Travis shook his head. 'I haven't told anybody. And I don't intend to so long as you and I can come to an arrangement. If we can't then I'll release everything to the media.'

'You'll break your sister's heart,' Crane said.

'Which is exactly what you're planning to do anyway. It's only a matter of time before you dump her. That's what you've been telling your bitch.'

Crane felt more helpless than he ever thought possible. He could see no way out of the situation he was in, other than to allow himself to be blackmailed by Travis.

'So what is it you want in return for keeping quiet?' he said.

Travis took another drag on his cigar. 'Money, of course. I want you to transfer a hundred thousand dollars into my account by noon tomorrow. I need the money to pay some very important people. And then we're quits. Oh, and I'll give you back the diary.'

Crane felt the fury build up inside him almost to the point of eruption.

'You son-of-a-bitch,' he seethed.

Travis chuckled. 'You can afford it, congressman. In fact, you should count yourself lucky that I'm not asking for more.'

Crane narrowed his gaze, said, 'So what if I tell you to stick it? That I'd rather take my chances than pay you a single cent? Sure, I'll suffer badly in the polls, but I could well ride out the storm. I wouldn't be the first politician who has gone on to achieve his ambition after being caught out having an affair.'

Travis sat back and ballooned his cheeks, letting the air out slowly between his lips.

'You're full of bluster, Gideon,' he said. 'You'll be finished and you know it. You'll be exposed as a serial philanderer. That won't play well with your middle-class supporters. So just shut up and pay up and maybe you'll get to be president.'

Crane felt his mind shut down. For several minutes he couldn't move or speak.

He knew he didn't have a choice. Travis had him over a barrel. He was well and truly fucked.

17

MY THOUGHTS WERE gnashing in my head as the woman drove me around the city in the Explorer. I had to force myself to remain calm as I tried to assess the situation. But it was hard to concentrate and harder still to decide what to do next.

The woman said nothing, but the fear she exuded was almost palpable. She was probably thinking that I was going to rape her and then kill her and maybe do something awful to her child.

I turned to look at her and in the glow from the dashboard I could see the tension along her jawline and in her neck. She was quite pretty, with eyes that were large and round and a nose that was sharp and delicate. She had tiny gold studs in her earlobes. Her face was made more interesting by a small, jagged scar just below her hairline. It was about an inch long and was a shade darker than her skin.

'Where do you live?' I asked when I glanced at the clock and realized that five minutes had passed since we left the grocery store parking lot.

'Why do you want to know?' she said guardedly.

'Because I'm going to have to stay there, at least for a while.'

She gave a sharp intake of breath.

'You can't. No. Please.'

'Don't freak out,' I said. 'I need someplace to stay while I get my thoughts together. It's either your place or on the street, and I'm not bedding down on the street.'

'My husband's home,' she said quickly. 'So it's impossible.'

'You're not married,' I said.

'What?'

'No wedding ring. Dead giveaway.'

Her lips started to tremble. 'I live with someone. My boyfriend.'

I shook my head. 'If that were the case then you'd have said boy-friend or partner in the first place and not husband. So you screwed up.'

Beads of sweat appeared on her forehead. She was close to losing it and I didn't want that. But at the same time I didn't want to start wandering the streets with nowhere to go.

'Look, I haven't got the time or the inclination to argue,' I said. 'So please don't make things difficult for me. Just do as I say.'

'Why don't you let us get out?' she said. 'You can take the car. Leave the city and go wherever you please.'

'Too risky,' I said. 'The moment I drive off you'll call 911 and I'll have every cop in the state on my tail.'

'I won't. I promise.'

She was doing well to control her terror. I had to give her that.

'Just tell me where the fuck you live,' I snapped and it made her jump.

'Out towards Eisenhower Park,' she said.

'How long will it take to get there?'

'About twenty minutes.'

I nodded. 'In that case put your foot down and get us there in fifteen.'

She started to cry and her shoulders heaved with every sob. I felt my stomach fall. I didn't want a hysterical woman on my hands.

'Stop crying,' I said. 'Just concentrate on the road.'

I watched her as the sobs gradually subsided. She tightened her grip on the wheel and I noticed her eyes kept flicking towards the rear-view mirror to check on her kid.

The child carried on sleeping, oblivious to her mother's ordeal. I prayed that she wouldn't wake up and raise the stress level still further.

'What's your name?' I asked.

She wiped tears from her eyes. 'Kate. Kate Pena.'

'And your daughter?'

'Anna.'

'How old is she?'

'Eight months.'

'So where's the father?'

'I told you. He's at home.'

I shrugged. 'I think you're lying, but if you're not then it's no problem. I'll just have to deal with him.'

Kate was scared for sure, but I wondered how much more scared she'd be if she knew the truth about me; that I had spent the last ten years of my life on death row having been convicted of killing a defenceless woman.

In all that time the only woman I'd seen had been my sister and the only sex I'd had had been with myself. I was pretty sure that her lightly scented perfume would have encouraged most death row inmates to pounce on her given the opportunity that I now had.

So what did that say about me? Well for one thing I hadn't turned into a sex-starved beast. And for another I still lived by a moral code. All the pain, loneliness and deprivation of the past decade had not robbed me of every last ounce of decency. All the horrible things I'd seen had not blunted my sensitivity, at least not to any significant degree.

So in a sense Kate Pena was lucky. If anyone other than me had jacked her car then she probably wouldn't be as safe as she was right now.

18

THE DRIVE TO Kate's place was uneventful. She drove quickly, but carefully, and seemed determined to meet the deadline I'd set.

The silence stretched between us, broken only by the sound of the traffic and the baby's occasional light snoring. But that suited me. I needed to think about what had happened and where to go from here. But it was like trying to make sense of life itself. The answers were beyond me.

I had no idea why the FBI had faked my execution only to set me up to be murdered. It seemed pointless. And it was a brutal fact that I might never know, not unless I turned myself in or was captured.

It wasn't as if the story, complete with a full explanation, would be carried on the news. The FBI – and whoever else was involved – were going to do everything they could to keep a lid on it. I was sure of that. And I figured they would put even more effort into trying to find me.

Despite that I had to keep reminding myself that I wasn't dead so I still had a good reason to be thankful. I was alive and free – for now at least. And there was a slim chance I might stay free for years to come. God willing.

'W-we're here,' Kate said suddenly, breaking into my thoughts. 'This is where I live.'

I glanced at the dashboard clock. She'd done it in just under fifteen minutes. Impressive.

'Pull onto the driveway,' I said.

It was a quiet residential street of small detached houses, most of them made of timber. The street was dimly lit, with no movement anywhere. The brakes squeaked as the Explorer slowed to a crawl and turned onto a short gravel drive.

It was a rundown single-storey house with a shingle roof and peeling brown paintwork. The front yard had been colonized by unsightly weeds and the low fences on either side had slats missing. To my relief there were no lights on inside or outside the house. And no sign of life.

Kate switched off the engine and gave me a fearful look.

'Please just go,' she said. 'I give you my word that I won't call the police.'

Her voice trembled as she struggled to speak and breathe at the same time.

'Is the house empty?' I asked.

Her chest heaved and she gave a reluctant nod.

'Are you expecting any visitors tonight?' I said. 'And bear in mind that it won't stop me coming in.'

She hesitated a second before shaking her head.

'That's good,' I said. 'Then I want you to get out of the car.'

I reached over and removed the key from the ignition, then threw open the door and got out. I dashed around to her side and as she stepped from the car I took out the gun and pressed it against her lower back.

'First we get your groceries from the rear,' I said. 'Then we come back for the baby.'

I looked around. The street was still quiet and gloomy. I didn't see any nosy neighbours. Kate peered through the window at her daughter who was still fast asleep in her chair. Then she walked slowly to the back of the Explorer. I could feel her body shaking against the gun.

'Don't do anything stupid,' I said. 'I really don't intend to harm either of you. I just need a place to stay for a while.'

She turned to look at me and I could sense the tension in her.

'Why should I trust you?' she said, her voice pitiful.

'Because you have no other option,' I told her. 'Now get the door open and let's get inside.'

She complied without another word. She took out two bags and carried them to the front door. I gave her back her keys and she opened up the house, stepped inside, and deposited the bags on the hall floor.

'Leave the light off for now,' I said. 'Let's get the baby.'

To my amazement the kid didn't wake up as her mother extracted her from her seat and carried her into the house. I guessed she'd had a tough day and it was way past her bedtime.

Once inside I shut the door behind us. The house did not have a homely feel to it. It smelled damp and stale, like something was rotting beneath the floorboards. I followed Kate along a short hallway into a small bedroom containing a crib and a night light. Kate gently lowered the baby into the crib and covered her with a blanket.

'Sleep tight, sweetheart,' she whispered. 'Everything will be OK.'

We stepped out of the bedroom and she left the door ajar. I stood and watched, gun in hand, as she retrieved her groceries and carried them into the kitchen. After placing the bags on the floor she flicked on the light.

I got a good look at her then. Her bright blue eyes puffy from crying were set against the deathly pallor of her skin. She was about five six and in good shape. She stood with her back to the countertop, her tight T-shirt and jeans accentuating her fine curves.

I let my eyes linger on her body for a second too long and she obviously sensed this because she inhaled deeply and said, 'I'll do whatever you want so long as you don't touch my baby.'

There was a hint of steel in her voice that hadn't been there before. The guilt came over me like a wave. This woman was terrified beyond reason. And who could blame her? I was a complete stranger and I was standing in her kitchen threatening her with a gun. There was nothing to stop me doing bad things to her and her child.

I stared at her for what seemed a long time, the only sound the hum of the refrigeration unit.

Then I said, 'Let's get one thing straight. I'm not interested in doing anything to you or your child. I'm not some sicko if that's what you think. So just stay calm and be patient. You're perfectly safe.'

Her eyes narrowed a little.

'Who are you?'

I ignored the question and waved the gun at the door.

'I need to check the rest of the house. Lead the way.'

The rooms were unimpressive and the furniture looked as though it had been collected from flea markets. There was a small living room with a threadbare carpet, a TV, sofa and coffee table. The main bedroom was clean but shabby and consisted of a double bed, a dresser, a stand-alone closet. I checked inside the closet. Only female clothes, and not many of them.

In the tiny bathroom-cum-toilet the light was a single bulb with a pull-string. When I turned it on I caught sight of myself in the medicine cabinet mirror. I looked a mess. My dyed hair was wet and matted and there were stains on the lapels of my jacket.

I made sure the curtains were closed in every room before we went back to the kitchen, which contained a table and two chairs and a bunch of cheap-looking white goods. The lino on the floor was faded and without colour.

'Is this your own house?' I asked.

She shook her head. 'I rent.'

'You on welfare?'

She nodded.

I grabbed her handbag from the back of a chair where she'd hung it. Emptied the contents onto the table. A cellphone, purse, lipstick, some tissues and a pen. I picked up the cell, switched it off and said, 'I'll keep hold of this for now.'

She didn't react, other than to breathe out slowly and touch a thin film of sweat on her forehead.

I shoved the gun into my jacket pocket and sat down at the table. My eyes ached with tiredness and my limbs felt stiff and brittle.

'Why don't you make some coffee?' I said. 'This is gonna be a long night.'

She didn't move, just continued to stare at me from where she stood by the sink. Her eyes were scared. I could practically see the wheels spinning in her head as she tried to assess the level of threat that faced her.

'Are you really not going to hurt us?' she asked after a beat.

'I've no reason to,' I said. 'I'm not some insane pervert.'

She swallowed hard. 'So are you running from the police?'

I felt the skin on my face stiffen. 'Not exactly.'

'What does that mean?'

'It means I'd rather not talk about it.'

I sat back in a daze, mentally rewinding everything that had happened. My blood began to race and every nerve in my body was bristling with electricity and urgency. I wanted to close my eyes and retreat within myself, but I knew that wasn't possible.

'Why have you got a gun?' Kate asked.

'It doesn't belong to me,' I said. 'I took it from a guy who tried to shoot me.'

Her eyes stretched wide. 'So why did he try to shoot you?'

'I don't know.'

I could see what she was doing. By engaging me in conversation she was thinking I'd be less inclined to turn on her. But I was OK with that if it made her feel more secure.

'So how about that coffee?' I said.

This time she responded. As she set about making it I kept a close eye on her in case she decided to grab a knife from a drawer or something.

I leaned on the table and pressed my fingers into my temples. My mind was in chaos, a mixture of anger, fear and bafflement. I wondered where Aaron Vance and his agents were and what they were doing. Were they still looking for me in downtown San Antonio? Had the cops been called to the scene of the shooting? Who else knew that Lee Jordan was still alive? Had my disappearance caused a major panic?

Questions, questions, questions.

'Do you take sugar?'

Kate's voice seized my attention and I smiled.

'No thanks. Just milk.'

I watched her pour hot water into two mugs. I couldn't help but appreciate the curve of her waist where it met her shapely butt. She was very attractive, I realized. But then after ten years in prison maybe every woman was going to seem attractive to me. She turned, holding the steaming mugs, and placed one on the table in front of me. Then she pulled out the other chair and sat down opposite me.

A bit of colour had crept into her cheeks and it seemed that her shoulders had relaxed a little. Maybe I'd finally convinced her that I wasn't some gun-toting psycho. Or maybe she was just trying to lull me into a false sense of security until she got an opportunity to raise the alarm or escape with her baby.

'Have you lived here long?' I asked, for want of something to say.

'Three months,' she said. 'It's a dump, I know, but beggars can't be choosy.'

I sipped at the coffee. It tasted good.

'How long have you been separated from your boyfriend?'

'Three months,' she said. 'I walked out, took the baby, came here.'

'That bad, eh?'

She nodded and pointed at her forehead. 'I have the scar to prove it.'

I raised my brow. I couldn't imagine anyone wanting to hurt her like that.

'What about you?' she asked. 'Do you have a wife or girlfriend?'

The question surprised me. I didn't really want to get drawn into an intimate chat. And yet having spent so long talking only to myself it was a temptation I couldn't resist. I felt I needed to offload on someone.

'My wife died seven years ago,' I said. 'There's been no one since.'

How could there be? I've been holed up in a tiny prison cell waiting to die.

'That's sad,' she said, and I thought I detected a note of genuine compassion in her voice.

I drank more coffee, tried to decide if I wanted the conversation to continue and if so where I wanted it to go. My mind was rambling as though on a loop and it was hard to control my thoughts. It meant I couldn't focus and that was what I needed to do. It was obviously too soon to come up with a mid to long term plan, but I had to decide on my next move. I'd managed to secure myself some breathing space. But that was all. There was no point getting too comfortable.

'Are you from around here?' Kate asked. 'Only you look kinda familiar.'

I felt a surge of warm blood into my face. Would she soon see through the feeble disguise and recognize me as the man whose face had been splattered all over the TV and newspapers? That was all I needed.

'No,' I said. 'I'm from a long way off.'

A frown tugged her eyebrows together. 'Do you have family here in San Antonio then?'

Family.

The word sent a thought cracking through my head like a lightning strike.

My sister Emily!

Why hadn't it occurred to me before now that she could be in danger? The Feds might assume that I'd make contact with her. And if so they might try to prevent it happening.

I took out Kate's phone and switched it back on. Emily's home and cellphone numbers were committed to my memory. But should I call her? Did I really want her to know that I was alive? Would that put her in even greater danger?

'What's wrong?' Kate said.

I didn't answer. I had to think this one through. There was a lot riding on whatever decision I made. It was a real dilemma. My breathing turned shallow and rapid.

But after thirty seconds I tapped in Emily's home number on Kate's phone. I felt I had to warn her. She needed to get away from her house and go somewhere safe.

My God. How was she going to react?

I didn't get to find out because the call did not go through. It didn't go to an answering service either. There was just a continuous beep, as though her phone had been disconnected. I tried Emily's cell and that also failed to connect.

'Shit.'

The sudden change in my demeanour alarmed Kate. She put her fist against her mouth and bit into her knuckle.

'I have to go,' I said, getting quickly to my feet. 'I think my sister might be in trouble.'

I switched off Kate's phone, then crossed over to the countertop and picked up her keys.

'I need your car,' I said.

I looked down at her, wondering whether I should take her with me. If I didn't she was bound to call the cops and chances were I'd be stopped during the hour long drive between San Antonio and Mountain City where my sister lived.

But before I could make up my mind I heard something that sent a cold rush of blood through my veins.

Someone was banging on the front door.

19

'It must be Frank,' Kate said.

'Who?'

'My ex-boyfriend. Frank Larson.'

'You said you weren't expecting anyone.'

'I'm not, but he's done this before. He won't leave me alone.'

'Then get rid of him.'

'It won't be as easy as that. He's probably drunk.'

She sprang to her feet, clearly mortified at the prospect of a confrontation with her ex-boyfriend. He continued to thump the door and was now shouting to be let in. I took out the gun, felt it necessary to show her that I still had it.

'Will he go away if you don't answer the door?' I said.

She shook her head. 'He'll keep on until I let him in.'

I gritted my teeth. This wasn't good. I could feel the panic starting to churn in my belly.

'You'll have to try to talk him into going away,' I said.

'And if I can't?'

'Then let him in before he wakes the whole neighbourhood. I'll just have to deal with him.'

I felt a trickle of sweat run down between my shoulder blades. My heart rate started to ramp up.

'I'm going into the baby's room,' I said, and saw the abject fear return to her eyes. 'You'd better not try anything stupid. If you do there'll be consequences.'

I grabbed her arm before she could protest and pushed her into the hallway.

'For everyone's sake just go and sort it out,' I said. 'And if you mention me all hell will break loose. You got that?'

She gulped in air and her jaw hardened. Then she nodded and turned away from me. As she shuffled along the hallway, I slipped into the baby's room, leaving the door slightly ajar. I peered through the crack, my pounding heart flooding my system with oxygenated blood. The angle was such that I could see into the kitchen and along the hallway. I watched Kate reach the front door and pause, her body stiff and straight.

'What do you want?' she shouted.

'To talk for Chrissake,' a male voice yelled back from outside. 'So open the fucking door.'

'It's late, Frank. And I've got nothing to say to you.'

'I want to see my daughter.'

'No you don't. You want to give me a hard time.'

'Cut the crap will you?' he said furiously. 'If you don't open the door I'll come in through a window.'

Kate threw a glance back over her shoulder. I eased the bedroom door open and showed her the gun. She swallowed hard and wiped her palms on her jeans. Then she reached for the lock, twisted it and pulled open the door.

The guy who came bounding over the threshold wore jeans and a black leather jacket. He had cropped hair and looked like he spent a lot of time pumping iron. His nose was splayed and crooked and it gave his appearance a vague warning of menace. He brushed past Kate and strode aggressively along the hall. I expected him to head for the baby's room and I braced myself. But instead he went straight into the kitchen.

Kate closed the door and followed him. She threw a glance my way and gave a desperate shrug as if to say *what am I supposed to do now?* I didn't respond, just peered through the inch-wide gap as she stepped cautiously into the kitchen.

'I need a drink,' Larson said. 'You got any?'

'Please, Frank,' Kate pleaded. 'Go home. I'm tired and I want to go to bed.'

'Then you should have answered my calls,' he told her. 'I phoned you dozens of times.'

I could hear him opening and shutting cupboards. Kate stood just inside the kitchen door watching him, her arms folded.

'It's over between us, Frank,' she said, her voice starting to crack with emotion. 'I don't want to talk to you, and I don't have to. Why can't you just leave me alone?'

He stepped into view, his shoulders hunched, his face flushed red with anger.

'You can't just walk away,' he said, jabbing a finger at her. 'Anna is mine too. I've got a right to see her.'

'I can't trust you, Frank. You know that. The last time you took her out you refused to bring her back.'

'I would have eventually.'

'That's not good enough.'

He moved towards her and I saw her body flinch.

'You're a callous bitch, Kate. Why can't you just give me another chance? We can make it work. I can change.'

She shook her head. 'No way, Frank. You've had all your chances. And you blew them by using me as a punch bag.'

He took another step towards her and I was surprised that she stood her ground.

'I've only given you what you deserved,' he yelled into her face. 'You're too fucking disrespectful. I won't stand for it.'

My pulse was spiking like crazy. I tightened my grip on the gun, curled my finger around the trigger. Things were going to turn ugly. The guy was working himself into a frenzy and it looked to me as though he was about to explode. There was no way he was suddenly going to calm down and leave. He was on a mission to upset his ex-girl-friend. And it was clear to me that his aggression was fuelled by booze.

And then things suddenly got a whole lot worse because the baby started wailing. She gave no warning and I all but jumped out of my skin. I could barely believe that something so small could be so loud. I looked across the room at the crib. In the soft glow from the lamp I could see her flailing about under the blanket.

'No you don't,' Kate shouted. 'Leave her be, Frank.'

I peered again through the crack, saw Kate trying to stop Larson from leaving the kitchen.

'Out of my fucking way,' he screamed at her. 'I want to see Anna.'

'You're drunk, Frank,' she said. 'She'll go back to sleep.'

I was sure that was wishful thinking on Kate's part. It sounded to me like the baby was becoming more distressed and needed to be comforted.

'Out of my way, you whore.'

Larson spat the words into Kate's face and then back-handed her across the cheek. Kate was thrown sideways by the blow and crashed into the doorframe. Larson then grabbed her by the neck and threw her into the kitchen. She let out an anguished cry as she hit one of the chairs and went sprawling on her back, limbs flung wide. The bastard then kicked her in the ribs, driving the breath from her lungs. A second swinging kick thudded into her shoulder as she tried to shield herself.

By this time I was out of the baby's room and hurtling towards the kitchen. Larson must have heard me because he whirled round just as he was about to deliver another blow.

His eyes bulged to the size of egg shells when he saw me bearing down, but I was on him before he could defend himself.

I cracked the butt of the revolver across his left cheekbone. It sent him staggering across the room, away from Kate. But he managed to stay on his feet and regain his balance. As he straightened up, gulping air and dripping blood, I hit him again and opened up another cut above his left eye.

This time he went down in an untidy heap and started writhing in agony. I stepped up to him and aimed a kick at his face with everything I had. But he shifted his weight and it connected with his shoulder.

The guy must have been as strong as an ox because he rolled away from me and pulled himself up onto his knees.

I pointed the gun at him, and was about to bark out a warning, when he threw himself at my legs, catching me unaware. I stumbled backwards against the table and dropped the gun onto the lino.

In the blink of an eye he was on his feet and coming at me, his face an ugly red mask. He managed to get a purchase on my jacket with one hand and lunged at my face with the other.

But in doing so he left himself exposed. I brought my knee up into his crotch with such force that his entire body sagged and he doubled over, letting go of my jacket.

I seized the advantage by ramming a fist into the back of his neck. He went down again and this time I made sure he stayed there. As he hit the floor I smashed my heel into his nose. There was a crack of bone and then blood started spouting from the wound like a garden sprinkler.

But he remained conscious, breathing heavily, and that meant he was still a threat. So I scooped up the gun, knelt beside him, and brought it down forcefully on the top of his head. He was out cold then, still breathing but not moving.

Bile rose at the back of my throat as I hauled myself up. My breathing was short and erratic, and every muscle in my body seemed to be trembling.

'Have you killed him?'

I turned. Kate was sitting up looking at me. There was blood on her mouth and fear in her eyes.

'He's still alive,' I said. 'He'll need stitches and pain killers when he wakes. And maybe he'll have a scar.'

I realized then that her baby was still crying in the other room, although it didn't seem quite so loud.

'Are you hurt badly?' I asked, crossing the room.

She shook her head. 'My ribs hurt and so does my mouth, but I'll live.'

I held out my hand and she took it. I pulled her to her feet, said, 'You'd better go to your baby. I think she needs you.'

Her eyes flicked across the kitchen to Larson.

'Thank you,' she said. Then she forced a low-voltage smile that revealed blood-smeared teeth. 'You know what's really crazy. If you hadn't been here he probably would have beaten me to a pulp and taken Anna.'

I smiled back. It felt strange.

'Glad to be of service,' I said.

She went into the other room and I was left standing there with my thoughts swimming in feverish circles. I found it hard to grasp anything. Nothing seemed real. Not this, or the extraordinary events of the last twenty-seven hours.

How would it end? I wondered. There was only so much drama I could take. I felt drained already. Tired. Exhausted. My head was throbbing and adrenaline was flushing through my veins like a drug.

And then I remembered what I'd been about to do before Frank Larson turned up. I was going to go to Emily's house in Mountain City because I feared she was in danger. A cold sense of dread was growing inside me like a build-up of toxic gas.

Then Kate came back into the kitchen carrying her baby. And the sight of the little girl had a profound effect on me. My breath caught in my throat and I experienced a strange explosion of warmth in my chest.

The child was wide awake and what little hair she had was wispy and fine. Her eyes were red rimmed and her bottom lip was trembling. When she saw me she looked confused for just a moment before her tiny face broke into a big, beaming smile. I was so touched by it that for a couple of seconds my mind shut out everything else.

What I saw in that smile were the things I'd been starved of during ten years on death row – love, beauty, innocence, trust, tenderness, purity. This child did not see me as a threat or as a monster. She didn't judge me or fear me. She was like a tiny light in all the darkness that had surrounded me for so long. So I smiled back. And I felt it come from deep inside me, the first smile in a decade to be honest and heartfelt.

'She likes you,' Kate said.

Anna raised her arm and pointed at me.

'She's beautiful,' I said.

'Frank didn't want children,' Kate said. 'Anna was an accident and he told me to have an abortion. The first time he hit me was when I refused.'

I could see that she was struggling to hold back the tears. Her features were tight, her lips pale and thin as she ran her tongue over them.

Mention of Frank reminded me that he was lying on the floor a couple of feet away and he would soon wake up despite the blows I'd inflicted. Kate seemed to read my mind.

'So what are you going to do?' she asked.

'I told you earlier,' I said. 'I think my sister is in trouble. I have to go to her.'

'You can't just leave us here. When he comes around he'll go berserk.'

'Well I can't take him with me.'

'Then take us,' she said, and I could see that she was serious. 'We can go to a hotel. At least we'll be safe there and I can decide where to go next.'

I gave her a look. 'Just a few minutes ago I was your worst nightmare.'

She shrugged. 'Let's put it this way. I'm still scared of you and I know I might be making a huge mistake.' She glanced at Larson. 'But right now I'm more scared of him.'

'But you'll have to come back sooner or later and face him,' I said.

'He'll have calmed down by then. And it'll give me time to think about where to go. I've had enough of this place anyway. I want out. My life is shit here. And Anna and me are not safe. It's time I moved on for her sake.'

I thought about it, but only briefly, because I knew it made sense from my point of view too. If she was with me then she wouldn't be able to call the cops before I got to Emily's.

'OK,' I said. 'But what about all your stuff?'

'I'll just take what we need,' she said.

'Have you got money and credit cards? I don't have a cent.'

She nodded. 'I've got enough to last me a few days.'

'Get to it then,' I said. 'I'll tie up lover boy so he won't be raising the alarm when he wakes.'

'That'll have to wait,' she said. 'I need you to hold the baby while I sort things out.'

Before I could resist she stepped up to me and thrust the baby into my arms.

I was taken aback and expected the infant to start wailing again. But she didn't. Instead, she sat happily in my arms, staring at me with bold curiosity. Then she began making slurping noises with her lips. I could not believe how light she was. It was like holding a bag of sugar, albeit one that smelled of stale urine. She looked up at me, her face about six inches from mine, her eyes as blue as a summer sky. And then she beamed that smile at me again, revealing tiny teeth and pink gums, and I was aware of the sting of supressed tears under my lids.

Jesus, I thought. What's going on? She's just a baby for pity's sake. Pull yourself together.

I started walking her around the kitchen, careful not to let her see her father lying unconscious on the floor. I bounced her up and down and she began to giggle, and I was reminded of something Marissa once said to me.

You'll make a great father, Lee. I can see it in you.

Well I never got the chance to find out if she was right. Life and bad luck had shattered the dreams I'd once had. Sure, I was still young enough to father a child, but the odds against it ever happening were about a million to one.

Kate appeared in the doorway after just five minutes, with a tired looking suitcase and fold-up stroller. She'd also slipped on a short, beige coat.

'I'm done,' she said. 'Is Anna OK?'

'She's fine. Smells a bit, though.'

'I'll change her diaper in the car. You ready?'

She took the baby from me and I said, 'I need some rope or something to restrain your ex.'

'I don't have any. But if you check his pockets you should find a set of handcuffs.'

I stared at her, open mouthed.

'Why would he have cuffs?'

'Because he's a cop,' she said.

20

On the small black and white monitor a man in a light coloured suit could be seen wending his way between cars in the grocery store parking lot.

'That's him,' Vance said.

The footage had been recorded on a security camera and it was of a pretty high quality. Not half as grainy as most he'd seen. He watched as Jordan came to a halt close to where a woman could be seen packing bags into the back of an Explorer.

Vance and Daniels were crowded around the monitor in the store's tiny security office. It had been the obvious place to come after they lost sight of Jordan when he ran into the parking area.

On screen Jordan pounced the moment the woman got behind the wheel of the Explorer. He wrenched open the passenger door and climbed in beside her. It was a classic car hijacking. Forty-five seconds later the Explorer started up and drove out of the parking lot – straight past the Dodge. In fact Vance could even remember watching it go by, which served only to rub salt into his wounds.

'We need to ID the vehicle,' he said, his voice clipped.

It meant switching to another monitor which carried the recorded feed from another camera. It took about a minute to rewind to the relevant time code.

'That's it,' Vance said.

The camera had picked up the Explorer as it exited the parking lot. And there was a clear image of the plate.

'Get the number into the computer right away,' Vance said. 'I want to know who owns that fucking vehicle.'

*

While the wheels were put in motion to identify the owner of the Explorer, Vance stood outside the store and lit a cigarette. He needed to steady his nerves and slow his heart rate. It felt like he was on the edge of an aneurysm.

Almost two hours had passed since Lee Jordan had run away and he still hadn't informed Washington. He couldn't leave it much longer. Unless he caught Jordan soon then he'd have to tell them about the mother of all fuck-ups. He still couldn't believe that the shooter had missed from a distance of only about twelve feet.

It wasn't as if the guy had never fired a gun before. He was a member of the Bureau's Clandestine Operations Unit. He supposedly had three kills to his credit and was an expert marksman. So how the hell had he botched it?

I had him, the shooter had said after they picked him up in the Dodge a few blocks from the restaurant. *But he suddenly turned because you sped away like a fucking Indy car. I didn't expect it and I hesitated.*

Vance couldn't believe the guy had the temerity to try to pass the buck. He'd wanted to smash a fist into his face. It took a lot of will-power not to. Instead, he'd called him a fucking prick and a total moron. And told him he was in deep shit. But Vance knew that nothing much would happen to him. It was the agent in charge who always shouldered the blame for operations that went wrong.

But in this case it wouldn't just be his own head on the block. The consequences would be felt all the way up the chain of command to the Director of the FBI. And maybe beyond!

His scalp prickled at the thought and he inhaled an anxious lungful of smoke. He could feel the pressure forming behind his eyes. The shooter did not realize how serious the situation was because he didn't know the identity of the target. And neither did the rest of the ops team – except for Daniels.

They'd been working from the start on a need-to-know basis. The fewer people who knew about the faked execution, the better. Now there was a chance that the whole fucking world would find out and that would be a disaster for everyone involved, as well as for the Bureau itself – and even the integrity of the entire American justice system.

The Bureau had been involved in past scandals, including allega-tions that agents had assassinated US citizens. And conspiracy theorists had long maintained that some lethal injection executions were faked so the military and CIA could carry out illegal experiments on 'dead' inmates. The truth had always been successfully covered up. But in this case there was irrefutable evidence in the form of a resurrected Lee Jordan.

It was supposed to have been a no-risk operation. When Vance had laid out his plan to the powers-that-be, he had assured them that it was fail-safe. He'd thought it through, worked it out, told them he was confident that nothing could go wrong. He had even put pressure on the state governor to make sure that Jordan did not get a last minute reprieve.

According to the plan, Jordan was going to be alive for just over twenty-four hours. Then he'd be shot. Only a few people would ever know what had happened and why. But now the murdering scumbag was on the run and therefore able to reveal to everyone he came into contact with that he was still alive.

That was why Vance had already got the Bureau to block the phones of Jordan's sister Emily and his lawyer Mark Zimmerman. In the last half-hour he had also arranged for special ops teams to be sent to their homes and wait in case Jordan turned up. Their orders were to arrest him or take him out. And if he managed to make contact with his sister or lawyer then they too had to be neutralized.

The orders carried the highest priority tag, meaning the individuals posed a serious and imminent threat to national security. Vance was praying that it wouldn't come to that. If they could find Jordan then they could limit the damage. But Vance knew it was not going to be easy. It wasn't even as if they could enlist the help of the cops because they weren't in the loop either. And if by chance they arrested Jordan, for whatever reason, then the game would be up.

Vance even imagined how it might go down if Jordan was stopped by a patrolman.

What's your name, fella?

Lee Jordan.

The same Lee Jordan convicted of killing Kimberley Crane?

You got it.

But aren't you supposed to be dead?

That's right.

Then how come you're not?

Good question. You should ask the FBI.

A bad situation was made worse by the fact that the audacious plan had got the go-ahead for a good reason. A successful outcome would have given them the ammunition to inflict the biggest blow so far against the Texas Syndicate. And that was something they had been desperately trying to do for years. But now it almost certainly wouldn't happen. Instead, if Jordan remained at large, a lot of good people were going to be in big trouble.

'We've got a name, boss.'

Daniels's voice snapped Vance out of his thoughts.

'The owner of the Explorer is a woman named Kate Pena,' Daniels said. 'She lives across town.'

Vance smiled without opening his mouth and a glimmer of hope blossomed in his chest.

'Then what are we waiting for?' he said.

21

DANIELS RECKONED IT would take about fifteen minutes to get to Kate Pena's house. The Dodge took the lead, followed by the Taurus.

Vance kept hoping that the woman had not recognized Jordan for who he was. And that Jordan had not revealed his identity to her. If she did know then she was as good as dead.

Nobody who learned the truth would be allowed to communicate it to anyone else. It was the only way to contain it. Otherwise it would spread like a destructive virus and the whole house of cards would collapse.

Vance was already cursing the night he received the call from the man he came to refer to as the Lawyer. That's when it all started, just minutes after he turned up at the crime scene in the alleyway eight weeks ago. The Lawyer had known about the four dead Hispanic men. He'd also known about a crooked cop named Dennis Cross. And he'd known so much more about the workings of the Texas Syndicate, the state's most notorious gang.

If you want me to expose the whole fucking operation then you have to give me what I've asked for. If you don't, then you can kiss goodbye to the best chance you'll ever get of smashing the Syndicate.

Those were the words the Lawyer had used at their first face-to-face meeting. And he'd been right. It was an opportunity of a lifetime and the Bureau decided not to pass it up. But now Vance wished they had. At least he wouldn't be in this predicament. If his career was flushed down the toilet then that would be the least of his worries. In the worst case scenario he would surely face criminal charges and serve a long time in prison. And all because of the one thing you could never rule out in even the best laid plans.

Human fucking error.

When they got to the house it was in darkness. The short driveway was empty. No sign of the Explorer. But Vance noted that there was a Lexus parked at the curb. It was closer to this house than any of the others.

'He probably got the woman to take him somewhere out of town,' Daniels said.

It made sense, but it was not what Vance wanted to hear.

'Let's check it out anyway,' he said.

They didn't have a warrant, but that wasn't going to stop them going inside if nobody answered the door. Two agents went around the back and Vance and Daniels took out their service revolvers and walked up to the front door.

They rang the bell. There was no answer. They tried opening the door, but it was locked.

Then they heard a sound from inside, like someone calling out. The voice was muffled and they couldn't tell if it was a man or woman. They checked the windows on either side of the door, but the curtains were pulled across them on the inside.

'Help me.'

This time they heard the words clearly. Definitely a male voice and very distressed.

'Let's go in,' Vance said.

The property was old and worn out so the door was a pushover. It took just two violent kicks to break the lock. They executed a textbook entry, arms outstretched, shoulders hunched, ready to open fire at the first sign of danger.

'FBI and we're coming in,' Vance shouted at the top of his voice. 'If you're armed then put down your weapons.'

Daniels switched on the light as they moved along the hallway, yelling as they went. After a tense few seconds they had the lay of the land. The house was small and shabby. There was only one occupant and he was in no position to put up any resistance because he was handcuffed to a radiator in the kitchen.

Vance felt the bottom drop out of his stomach when he saw it wasn't Lee Jordan. This guy he'd never seen before. He had cropped hair and was wearing a leather coat. He was sitting against the wall and there was blood on his face.

Vance knelt down beside him and asked him what the hell had

happened.

'I'm a cop,' the guy said, and Vance experienced a billowing sense of dread. 'Check my pocket.'

Vance shoved his hand into the guy's inside pocket and came out with a police ID. His name was Frank Larson and he was a detective with the San Antonio police.

Vance couldn't believe it. Things were going from bad to worse. A cop, for Christ's sake.

'Some guy took my kid,' Larson said.

Vance squinted at him. 'What guy? Who was he?'

Larson winced as he moved his head. 'Never seen him before. I just dropped by to see my baby. When I came through the door he hit me with a pistol.'

'So you don't live here?'

'No. My girlfriend rents the place.'

'Would her name be Kate Pena?'

Larson frowned. 'That's right.'

'Where is she?' Vance asked.

'Took off with the guy,' Larson said. 'And they have my kid.'

'Where have they gone?'

'How the fuck should I know?'

'We'll call an ambulance,' Vance said. 'Get you to a hospital. Where are the keys to the cuffs?'

'No idea. I was unconscious when he put them on me. Look, are you gonna tell me what's going on here? How did the FBI know what had happened?'

'We didn't,' Vance said. 'The guy who slugged you is on our wanted list. He jacked your girlfriend's car earlier. We traced it here.'

'Jesus.'

'How old is your kid?'

Larson had to think about it.

'Eight months,' he said. 'Her name's Anna.'

Vance took out his notebook and started scribbling.

'And your girlfriend – has she got a cellphone?'

'Sure.'

'Do you know the number?'

Larson summoned it up from his memory. Vance took his own phone out and rang the number. It was switched off.

Larson tried to say something else, but his words were snatched by a paroxysm of coughing.

Vance got to his feet and told the other agents to find the keys to the cuffs and check out the rest of the place for any clues as to where they might have gone. But he didn't expect to find anything. It was his guess that Jordan had got the woman to drive back here so he could rest up and get his mind around what had happened to him. Maybe he had even intended to stay the night just to get off the streets. But then Larson had turned up and he'd been forced to leave, taking Kate Pena and her baby as hostages.

It was a seriously bad development because now they had to decide whether to involve the police. A woman and her child had been kidnapped. Plus, a San Antonio detective had been attacked.

Vance pondered this and finally concluded that he was not going to be the one to make a decision on what should happen next. The whole thing had spiralled out of control and he just wasn't sure how to handle it.

It was time to call Washington.

22

IT TOOK ME just ten minutes to get used to driving the Explorer. I hadn't been behind a wheel in over ten years, but I discovered it's like riding a bike. Once you know how to do it you never forget.

It didn't mean I wasn't nervous, or rusty, though. During the first half mile or so I ran it up a curb and almost collided with a stationary truck.

Kate had screamed at me to be careful because she began the journey on the rear seat changing the baby's diaper. Now she was back riding shotgun and we were making good progress heading north-east along Interstate 35.

Our destination was Mountain City, about eighteen miles south of Austin. Luckily Emily's address was stored in my memory because I'd written countless letters to her from prison. I thought I'd have trouble finding it until Kate pointed out that the Explorer had a built-in satnav. She'd tapped in the details as we left San Antonio and we were now following directions given by a disembodied female voice.

I felt wired, and was aware of the blood rushing around inside my body. Or maybe it was adrenaline. I had so much to think about that it was hard to concentrate on the road.

I'd asked Kate about her ex and she'd told me he was a detective as well as a violent bully. For weeks she had been planning to flee the city and cut off all contact with him. Now she was determined to do it. He had beaten her up once too often. She would go someplace and start a new life. Change her name and her appearance. Perhaps even seek help from one of the organizations set up to assist battered women. She knew it wouldn't be easy given that he was a police officer.

I couldn't help but admire the way she was coping with the

situation. Her life had been blasted to hell by her psycho ex and a gun-wielding stranger. And yet she was holding it together and using all the drama as a catalyst for change. She reminded me of Marissa in that respect. My wife's unflinching resilience and strength of character had belied her angelic looks and timid charm.

I was uncomfortably aware that Kate and her baby were in mortal danger as long as they were with me. It was only a matter of time before Larson was able to raise the alarm and the Feds started looking for the Explorer. Hopefully that wouldn't be for some hours as I'd left the bastard cuffed to a radiator.

I had no idea how the rest of the evening was going to pan out. I was desperately worried about my sister and I wanted to get to her. But then what? Once she knew I wasn't dead would the Feds allow her to live? Probably not, in which case she would have to go on the run with me – like a hunted animal.

That wasn't fair on her, but there was no easy way out of this mess. Even turning myself in wouldn't bring about a happy ending for anyone. Likely as not there'd be a massive cover-up and I'd be disposed of quickly and quietly. Along with everyone I'd come into contact with.

'You know my story,' Kate said suddenly. 'Don't you think you should tell me yours? After what you've put me through you owe me that.'

'It's best you don't know,' I said.

'Have you robbed a bank or something? Is that it?'

I shook my head. 'No I haven't. Now, for your own sake let it be. I'll soon be just a bad memory. You can drop me off near my sister's place and be on your way. Find a motel and get a good night's sleep.'

'Is this thing with your sister really true?' she asked.

I looked at her. 'That's a stupid question.'

'Not really,' she said. 'I don't know anything about you, remember? Except that you kidnap defenceless women and carry a gun. For all I know you don't even have a sister. It could be bullshit about her being in trouble.'

'Her phones have been disconnected. That's why I'm concerned.'

'Maybe there's a simple explanation.'

'I doubt it. Too much of a coincidence.'

'So you think she's in danger – from the same people who are chasing you?'

'That's right.'

'But if they're cops they won't hurt her, so what's the problem?'

I hesitated. 'They're not cops. They're federal agents and they want me dead. I don't know why.'

She drew a breath and I saw the doubts clouding her features.

'I'm not sure I believe you,' she said.

I shrugged. 'If I was you I wouldn't believe me either, but it's the truth.'

She started to say something, but the baby began crying because she was hungry or thirsty or just plain miserable. So Kate had to climb in the back to sort her out.

After she was done I told her I didn't want to talk anymore. I said I had some more thinking to do.

So we sat in silence during the rest of the fifty minute journey to Mountain City.

23

It was too dark to see much of Mountain City. The night was heavy and oppressive by the time we got there. The moon was full, stars no more than pale pinpricks of light.

When the satnav indicated that we were almost at Emily's house, I rolled the Explorer to the curb and left the engine running.

'This is where we go our separate ways,' I said. 'It might not be safe for you to get any closer to the house. I don't know what to expect.'

I pinched the bridge of my nose and drew in a chest full of air to try to slow the pulse racing in my ears. Kate pressed her mouth into a thin line and the swelling on her bottom lip from Larson's backhander became more pronounced.

'So that's it?' she said. 'I can go now?'

I nodded. 'We've each got our own problems to deal with. I'm sorry I put the frighteners on you earlier. I was desperate and you happened to be in the wrong place at the wrong time.'

'It's the story of my life,' she said.

I grasped the handle, shoved the door open. Before getting out I looked back at Anna. She was still sleeping, her head lolling to one side, her eyes moving beneath the lids.

'You have a great daughter,' I said. 'She shouldn't have to see her mother getting hurt.'

'She won't anymore,' Kate said. 'I can promise you that.'

I swung out of the Explorer and Kate got out her side and came around to the pavement.

We stood under a street light that glowed like a white halo. The cool air felt good in my lungs, but there was no time to savour it.

I took out her cellphone and gave it back to her.

'I'd like to ask a favour,' I said.

She looked up at me and I could see that her eyes were filmed with fatigue.

'You're going to ask me not to call the police,' she said.

I nodded. 'At least don't do it right away. Give me a chance to get my sister away from here.'

She cocked her head on one side. 'OK,' she said.

I had no way of knowing if she meant it. There was a good chance she'd call 911 as soon as I was out of sight. And nothing I could do about it.

'Don't look so worried,' she said. 'I won't call them. I promise. You saved me from a beating back there. I know from experience what Frank would have done to me. So I owe you that.'

'Thanks,' I said. 'I'm grateful.'

There was an awkward moment. I felt I should say something else but I didn't know what.

'I hope your sister is OK,' Kate said.

She got behind the wheel and pulled the door shut behind her. Then the Explorer pulled away from the curb and took off.

Even before the tail lights disappeared I was heading towards Emily's house.

Emily told me once that she moved to Mountain City because she had friends here. But she'd rarely spoken about the place or about the house she'd moved into after selling her apartment in Houston.

So I didn't know what to expect, except that it wouldn't be a palace. She only had a moderate income from her job as a secretary in a waste management company.

Her street was silent and peaceful, without traffic. There were about a dozen parked cars. I heard a dog's plaintive bark in the distance.

I walked along the street cautiously, my eyes searching the gloom for signs of life. I didn't see any. I stayed in the shadows and moved along the pavement. Pools of darkness crowded around the few street lights. It was a short, residential street with about fifteen detached houses, two of them with 'for-sale' signs out front. Emily's property, number four, was fenced with redwood tongue-and-groove and there was a rickety gate that was open. Her car, a battered old Ford, was parked outside.

I stood across the road, feeling wildly conspicuous in the grubby beige suit. I studied the house carefully for a couple of minutes. It was another single-storey affair, constructed of grey brick and with a small concrete porch. There were lights on inside.

Through one of the windows I saw a movement. I couldn't be sure if it was Emily so I started walking across the road. At the same time I reached in my pocket and clasped the gun I'd taken off my would-be assassin; it was starting to feel familiar, like an extension of my hand.

I got another fleeting glimpse of a figure through the same window as I approached the gate. This time I saw that it was indeed Emily. She was wearing a dressing gown and had a glass in her hand. The sight of her came as a tremendous relief. I took it to mean that I was one step ahead of the Feds. Either they hadn't thought to come here or they just hadn't arrived yet.

Now for the tricky part, I thought. I was about to give my sister the shock of her life. As far as she was concerned I was dead. We had said our goodbyes and I'd been consigned to her memory bank. Now I was going to reappear like a ghost and fuck up her life all over again.

I snapped my eyes up and down the street, my mind running through a labyrinth of possibilities. Was the house already under surveillance? Was I about to walk into a trap? Was I being totally reckless in coming here? All these questions were suddenly answered when something caught my eye.

A tiny flash of orange light, like you get when someone sparks up a cigarette. And that someone was sitting in a car that was parked along the street about thirty yards away.

I felt the air lock in my chest and the blood stop pumping through my arteries. This wasn't the kind of street where people sat in cars in the dark. Not unless they were watching and waiting for something to happen. Or someone to show up.

Shit. I'd made a mistake. A big mistake. I should have been more circumspect, maybe approached the house from the back like any sensible person would have. Well there was no turning back now. And no time to consider my options. I had to go for it.

The pathway scree scrunched under my shoes as I hurried up to the front door and rang the bell, all the time watching the car to see if anyone got out.

Emily's screechy voice suddenly came from beyond the door.

'Who is it?'

I noticed there was no spyhole. She couldn't see me. So how the hell was I going to convince her to let me in? It was something I hadn't given any thought to.

'It's Lee, Emily,' I blurted out. 'Your brother. I'm not dead. I know it sounds crazy, but you have to believe me.'

A beat of shocked silence. Then Emily said, 'Go away, whoever you are.'

'The execution didn't happen,' I yelled back. 'It was faked. Listen to my voice.'

'Fuck off you creep, before I call the police.'

'Please, Emily. Open the door. It *is* me. Lee.'

Emily responded again, but this time her words didn't register because at that very moment whoever was in the car along the street decided to get out. The vehicle's interior light came on and I saw two figures emerge. The darkness didn't allow a clear view of them, but I was pretty sure they were guys in suits.

I felt my heart start to gallop. I thought about taking off, but even if I got away I couldn't leave my sister behind.

I had a sudden brainwave and said, 'Emily, listen. We talked about Monty when you last came to see me. Do you remember?'

There was no reaction this time. Just a heavy silence from inside the house. I thrust my hand into my pocket and gripped the gun. My gaze was fixed on the two dark figures who were walking towards me. They looked ominously big. One of them discarded a lighted cigarette, sparks exploding on the road.

They were maybe twenty yards away now. Two men dressed in dark suits. Tall and ready for action. If they weren't federal agents then I was willing to bet they were part of the clandestine army of private operators who were frequently hired to do the dirty work for government agencies like the FBI and CIA.

Fear clawed at my belly like a tiger and my lungs started dragging in air. I pulled out the gun to let them know I had it. Slid off the safety. It stopped them in their tracks. Now they had a decision to make. Take me on or wait for back-up.

I was still waiting for them to decide when my sister threw open the front door.

She took one look at me and said, 'Oh my Lord. It *is* you.'

24

I CHARGED INTO the house, shoving Emily out of the way. She yelped in alarm and staggered backwards.

'Don't panic,' I shouted as I booted the door shut behind me.

But she did. Her eyes bulged out of their sockets when she saw the pistol. And she started screaming.

I raised my empty hand, palm out, said, 'Stop it, sis. Please. You have to calm down.'

She froze mid-scream. For a single terrifying moment the world seemed to stop still. My brain seized on various impressions like an automatic camera taking a series of still photos. My sister's face sculpted tight with terror. The sudden silence roaring in my ears. The sepia-toned walls of the hallway. The haze of cigarette smoke.

Then just as abruptly the world started spinning again and I found myself grabbing my sister's hand and pulling her roughly down the hall.

'People are after me,' I said in a voice I could barely control. 'You're in danger too. It's why I came here.'

'But you're alive,' she stuttered. 'That's not possible.'

At the end of the hall an open door led into the living room. Small and drab with a hardwood floor and a leather sofa that took up more space than it should have. There was a coffee table and a TV that was not switched on.

I spotted the window through which I had seen Emily moving around. I rushed across the room to close the curtain, mindful of the fact that I was presenting myself as a target to the guys outside. Luckily I wasn't shot at.

'What's going on, for God's sake?' Emily wailed.

I felt breathless as I turned to face her. She looked tired and strung out. Her hair was stretched away from her face by a ponytail and she was shaking, the tremors travelling down her arms to her fingers.

'There are two men outside,' I told her. 'They've come to kill me and I think they intend to kill you too.'

She shook her head. 'This is insane. I must be dreaming.'

I crossed the room, grabbed her by the shoulders and stared intently into her face.

'Listen to me, sis. We're both in danger. They were waiting for me outside. I don't. . . .'

She tugged herself away from me, and her eyes flared with anger and confusion.

'No, this can't be happening,' she shrieked. 'You were executed. I saw it on the news. The prison called to tell me.'

I felt my chest tighten. 'No, sis. As you can see I'm very much alive. But I'm in the middle of some kind of weird conspiracy. They want me dead and I don't know why.'

She frowned and the animal fear in her eyes softened slightly.

'Who? Who wants you dead?'

Before I could answer I heard the doorbell ring. My heart stuttered in my chest and I felt the acidic surge or heartburn flare in my stomach.

'The light switch,' I said. 'Where is it?'

I didn't wait for an answer. I looked to the obvious place on the wall and hurried over to flick it to the off position. As the room was plunged into darkness Emily let out a frightened whimper.

'Is there a back door?' I yelled.

She didn't respond. How could she? Her mind was blown. She had lost her grip on reality.

The doorbell rang again.

I reached out, seized Emily's arm, dragged her back into the hallway. There was just enough light to keep me from slamming into walls and furniture.

I pulled to the right, away from the front door, and saw a wedge of moonlight in front of me on what looked like the kitchen floor. But in that very instant there came an explosion of breaking glass from the same direction. There was no escape now, not unless I seized control of the situation before I lost it altogether.

And there was only one way to do that.

I let go of Emily's arm, took two steps forward, and fired blindly into the kitchen. The gun bucked dramatically in my hand and there was a deafening blast of noise. A millisecond later came a burst of return fire. Three shots and one of them almost had me. I felt an arrow of air whizz past my neck and hit the wall behind me with a dull thud.

I threw myself back into the hallway and collided with Emily, who was squatting on the floor. I clasped the sleeve of her dressing gown and tugged her to her feet. Her body shuddered and she gave a loud moan.

'Stay close to me,' I said. 'I've got you.'

I wanted to get her into the living room. I figured there was some cover for her there. And maybe, just maybe, we could escape through the window. But everything was happening in fast-motion, so when the front door was suddenly kicked in we were still in the hall with our backs against the wall. The guy responsible was framed in the doorway, a black shape against the muted street illuminations. He was slow to react even though he was waving a revolver in our direction.

So I didn't hesitate. I lifted my gun and shot at him first. Three rounds and each of them hit the target. His body convulsed as though he'd been wired to the mains. He gave a sharp grunt, let go of his pistol, and fell backwards onto the porch.

By now Emily was hysterical, floundering like a grounded fish. I took hold of her hand and pushed her into the living room. But then I got a shock. The room was no longer in darkness. There was a fierce shaft of light coming from the left. Too late I turned and saw a door I didn't know was there. The second guy had already come through it from the kitchen. He was holding a flashlight in one hand and a gun in the other.

The gun exploded in his hand and I heard a cry of agony that filled me with dread. My own gun went off even though I was unaware I'd pulled the trigger. But the bullet missed its target as the guy dipped his body to the right and ducked down behind the sofa.

My gut told me that once he reappeared he'd have the drop on me. So I lunged forward and dived over the back of the sofa just as he was struggling back up.

He bellowed as I crashed into him. The momentum sent him sprawling back onto the floor with me on top of him. But he was no slouch. He managed to heave his way out from under me before I could follow through. He rolled away and at the same time reached for his gun which had hit the floor.

I was still holding onto my own pistol so I brought it down hard on the side of his face. He let out a loud grunt and tried to turn towards me. But it was the wrong move because it meant I could deliver the second blow right between his eyes.

His body went limp, but I whacked his head three more times to make sure that he wasn't going to get up again.

My ears were pulsating and my heart was beating its way out of my chest. I jumped up and staggered over to the wall switch, flooding the room with jaundiced light. I knew what I was going to see but that did not diminish the shock of seeing it.

Emily was lying on her back and blood was oozing out of a gaping wound between her breasts.

25

My sister had taken a bullet that was meant for me. I didn't want to believe she was dead. It wasn't possible. Surely life couldn't be that cruel.

I rushed over to where she lay and knelt beside her. I placed two fingers against her carotid artery, praying for a pulse. Nothing. I lowered my ear to her chest, listening for the sound of her heart. There was no sound.

I stared at her lifeless body, mesmerized, transfixed, in shock. Her dead, empty eyes stared up at me and I felt myself go cold despite the warmth in the room.

Oh God, no. Not this. Not Emily.

I went numb. Everything receded around me, until I was left with a pain that was so intense it felt like my insides were awash with scalding water.

What had I done? Why had I come here? Why the fuck did this have to happen? I closed my eyes and abandoned myself to the sudden onslaught of grief. I felt my throat constrict until I couldn't swallow. A choking sadness surrounded my heart.

After the pandemonium, an eerie silence descended on the room, but in the distance I could hear the unmistakable sound of police sirens. The neighbours, alarmed by the shooting, must have called 911. But I didn't budge. I continued to kneel beside my sister, my hand on her cold forehead. An image of her as a child flashed in my mind; her infectious smile and bright blue eyes. She was a great kid who grew into a warm and considerate woman who should have gone on to have a bountiful life with a loving family.

But I had ruined things for her. Ten years ago I'd plunged headlong into an abyss and taken those I loved with me. First my wife and now my sister. Because of me, Emily's marriage was wrecked and she'd been forced to move away from the city where she grew up. And because of me she was now dead at the age of thirty-five.

The tears welled up and I buried my face in my hands and wept. I wept for my sister and for my wife and for all the years I'd lost. But I didn't weep for long because I knew that if the cops caught me here I would either be killed or put back in jail. Then I would never be able to find out why this had happened. And it was something I suddenly knew I had to do.

It was too late to atone for my own sins. But not too late to ensure that others paid the price for theirs.

I stopped sobbing and leaned over to kiss Emily on the forehead.

'Bye, bye, sis,' I whispered.

And the cruel irony of the moment was not lost on me. Just the day before yesterday she had come to the prison to say goodbye to me. I was the one who should be dead. Not her.

I filled my lungs with air that tasted of death and stepped over to the guy I'd battered. I was hoping he was still alive because I wanted to hurt him even more for what he'd done to my sister. Sure, he must have been acting on someone else's orders, but he'd pulled the trigger. He was the one who'd killed her and it was only right that he should suffer.

But he was dead already, his face a bloody mess, his legs crumpled beneath him at an unnatural angle. I thought it would please me but it didn't. It just made my stomach churn.

I turned and hurried out of the room. On the porch I had to step over the body of the other man. He was younger than his pal and wearing a similar dark suit that was soaked in blood. I didn't need a medical degree to know that he too was dead. From the state of him there wasn't any doubt. His eyes were open but glazed over. His mouth was agape and his tongue lolled out.

As I stepped onto the path, I realized that the police sirens were a lot louder and closer. And they were converging. I didn't have long. Still holding the gun, I ran to the road. I was aware of faces at windows in neighbouring homes, but sensibly none of the residents had ventured out to see what was happening.

I turned right and broke into a sprint. I was frantic. Desperate. And I feared I wouldn't get far before I was spotted by the cops. I didn't want to get into a shoot-out with someone who had nothing to do with my plight. But as I ran hell for leather along the street, I suddenly heard the roar of an engine behind me.

I spun around and was blinded by the glare of fast-approaching headlights. I twisted my body so that I was facing the vehicle, half expecting it to mow me down.

I raised the gun in a defiant gesture and got ready to fire. But instead of mounting the curb the vehicle screeched to a standstill in the road and my breath caught in my throat when I saw the familiar contours of the Explorer.

The driver's window was lowered and Kate's face appeared.

'Get in,' she said.

After I got into the passenger seat, Kate floored the gas pedal and we accelerated away from there. Fifty yards on she took a left, just in time to avoid two screaming squad cars heading for Emily's house.

I looked at Kate as I tried to regain my breath and my mental footing. She was gripping the wheel so tight her knuckles were bleached white.

I peered in the back and saw her baby asleep in her seat, without a care in the world. It was surreal.

'I don't get it,' I said. 'Where the hell did you come from?'

She took a deep breath, expelled it.

'I had to turn around,' she said. 'The road was taking me away from the interstate. Coming back this way I passed your sister's house and heard shots. Then I saw a man kicking the door down. I stopped to see what was going on. There were more shots and the man fell onto the porch. Then you came out and started running. It looked like you needed help.'

I gazed at her profile and felt a sharp pang of guilt. She'd taken an almighty risk for someone she didn't know. Someone who had put her through hell earlier in the evening. And even now she and her baby were very much in the danger zone.

My admiration for her soared into the stratosphere.

'I appreciate it,' I said. 'You saved my ass.'

She shrugged as though it was no big deal. 'We're not safe yet.'

'Then put your foot down,' I said. 'Let's get as far away as we can.'

'Do you want to drive?'

'No way,' I said. 'I'm still a bundle of nerves and my hands won't stop shaking.'

She threw me a glance. 'So what happened back there?'

A fresh wave of sadness washed over me. I stared ahead through the windshield, my jaw clenched.

'My sister was shot,' I said. 'Emily's dead.'

Tears exploded in the corners of my eyes and once again I was overwhelmed by emotion. An empty space opened up in my stomach and I began to cry.

My sister was dead. And it was my fault. How the fuck was I going to live with myself?

The film spooled in my mind, showing Emily on the floor with the bullet hole in her chest, her dressing gown a crimson mess. The image cut into me like a saw blade.

Kate said nothing as the tears flowed. She just continued to drive away from the scene of carnage and pretty soon I could no longer hear the sirens.

26

GIDEON CRANE WAS at last able to escape to his panelled study. His desk was bathed in the sapphire glow of an art deco lamp. It was ten o'clock and his head was pulsing.

Travis and his girlfriend Cindy had only just left after what had been an excruciating evening. Somehow Crane had managed to get through it without losing his temper. And that was no mean achievement following the conversation he'd had with Travis out by the pool.

His own brother-in-law had announced that he was going to blackmail him. Travis had used his skills as a private investigator to uncover the relationship with Beth. Now he wanted $100,000 transferred to his account.

Crane was livid. The rage burned inside him, hot as a blast furnace. His entire presidential campaign was in jeopardy. And he was at the mercy of an unprincipled sleazebag. Travis was bound to come back for more. A hundred grand would not be enough. He'd pay off what he owed and then quickly run up more debts. It was as certain as the sun rising.

Crane went to his drinks cabinet and poured himself a triple whisky. It went down his throat like liquid fire and he poured another. He sat behind his large mahogany desk and massaged his eyes with his thumb and forefinger.

What a fucking nightmare, he thought. He should have been on a high. The New Orleans debate had gone so well and then he'd had the privilege of witnessing Lee Jordan's execution. But instead it felt like his world was suddenly falling apart.

He reached for his humidor and took out a cigar, his second of the evening. His study was the only room in the house he smoked in. It was where he usually came to relax and let the day dissolve – or to worry about a problem he couldn't solve.

He lit the cigar and drew the heavy smoke into his lungs. Then closed his eyes and exhaled twin plumes from his nostrils.

Anger and frustration continued to blaze away inside him. And the anger wasn't just directed at Travis. He was furious with himself for the parlous situation he was now in. He'd been careless and complacent. He had made it easy for Travis to dig up the dirt. His brother-in-law was a skunk, a heel, a rat and a low-life piece of shit. But he was also very good at his job. He would have had no trouble gathering evidence of an illicit affair between Crane and his press secretary.

Crane was jolted out of his thoughts when the study door suddenly opened and Pauline walked in. She had already changed into her pink towelling robe and removed her make-up. Her features were white and brittle and he saw stress vibrating beneath her composure.

'I'm going to bed, Gideon,' she said. 'Why don't you come with me?'

If it had been Beth standing there he would have followed her straight up. She would have helped him to forget his troubles by fucking him hard and telling him that she loved him. But Pauline would just turn her back on him and go to sleep and he'd be lying there in the dark unable to drop off.

He needed a few more whiskies and maybe a couple of sleeping pills before he turned in.

'I'll be up in a bit,' he said. 'I'm feeling a little restless.'

She stepped further into the room and stopped when the cigar smoke caused her nostrils to flare.

'Was the evening really that bad?' she asked.

His face slid into a half smile. 'Not at all. Just been a tough day. I need to wind down.'

She narrowed her eyes at him. 'I'm no fool, Gideon. Your mood changed after you went outside with Travis. I'm guessing he said something to upset you. Like he usually does.'

A part of him wanted to tell her the truth. Make a full confession and get it over with. But the sensible part of him held sway and he said, 'He wants to borrow some more money and I said I'd think about it.'

Her face rippled with anxiety. 'I thought he'd got his finances sorted. He said he'd stopped gambling.'

'Well he hasn't.'

'I'm sorry, Gideon. I'll talk to him. He's my brother.'

'I'd rather you didn't. He doesn't want you to know. So leave it to me. It's not a problem.'

She took a breath, let it out in a long sigh.

'If you're sure.'

He nodded. 'I am. Now go and get a good night's sleep. You look tired.'

He got up, walked around the desk, and delivered a weightless kiss to her cheek. There was a time he would have ripped off her robe and ravaged her there and then.

A memory flashed through his head of him taking her over the desk. It was two years into their marriage when she was trying to get pregnant. And three months before cancerous cells in her womb led to the hysterectomy.

'Don't stay up too late,' she said.

When she was gone he poured another whisky and re-lit his cigar. Then he sat back down and tried to think. But his brain felt slow and full of mush. He couldn't focus. After a few minutes he gave up trying and switched on the wall-mounted TV using the remote. He flicked through to a news channel and wished he hadn't because he caught the tail-end of a background report on Lee Jordan.

There was an exterior shot of the prison in Huntsville and then some library footage of the execution chamber.

'And this is where the man who murdered Kimberley Crane was executed last evening by lethal injection,' the reporter said in voice-over. 'And where he finally paid the price for his callous crime.'

The events of that night ten years ago flashed unbidden into Crane's mind. The clarity of the images shocked him and he felt his blood chill. He saw himself shoot Sean Bates. Then crying out as Jordan lunged at him. In the struggle he pulled off Jordan's ski-mask and stared briefly into those cold, desperate eyes before he was knocked unconscious.

And then he saw himself waking up to find his wife lying in the hall with blood on her face and her clothes.

The memory shook him out of his stupor and a moan of despair issued from his mouth. It was all too much. He turned away from the screen and cupped his face in his hands.

Soon he felt the tears as they began to ooze through his fingers.

He was too distraught to hear the TV anchor refer to a breaking news story. There had been an incident at a house in Mountain City near Austin. Shots had been fired and there were believed to be multiple casualties.

27

A PHALANX OF local blue and whites had blocked off the street by the time Vance got there. He flashed his credentials and passed through the cordon, parking outside Emily Jordan's house.

Lieutenant Chris Mendoza, the detective in charge of the crime scene, had been expecting him. They knew each other so there was no strained introduction. Just a handshake.

'It's a bad one, Aaron,' Mendoza said. 'Two of the victims are carrying Bureau ID.'

Vance bunched his lips and nodded. 'What about the perp?'

Mendoza shook his head. 'Clean away. Neighbours saw a guy in a tan suit run from the house after the shootings. He took off down the street and at least one of them saw him hop into a car that stopped at the curb. Must have been an accomplice.'

Vance knotted his brow. 'Is the witness sure about that?'

'He seemed confident when I spoke to him. Said the car appeared out of nowhere.'

'Did he give you a description?'

'He was pretty sure it was an Explorer.'

'What about the driver?'

'He said it looked to him like there was a woman behind the wheel.'

Vance was confused. It could only have been Kate Pena. But it made no sense. She was Jordan's hostage. Not his fucking driver.

Vance's face took on a fiery intensity. He locked his jaw and spoke through clenched teeth.

'Look, I don't want anything released to the media until I've OK'd it. What's happened here relates to a highly classified operation. We're gonna have to restrict the information we put out.'

Mendoza bristled. 'Fuck you, Aaron. We've got a bloodbath here and it's my case. I won't. . . .'

'You'll do as I tell you,' Vance cut in. 'If you've got a problem with that then get your boss on the phone and I'll tell him to get you in line or take you off the case. Understand?'

Mendoza was about to react but thought better of it when he saw the look in Vance's eyes.

'I'm going inside,' Vance said. 'More agents will be here soon. I suggest you put your guys in the picture.'

The first body he came across was on the porch. Agent Craig Flynn. Vance had known him for two years. He had a wife and daughter. And he'd been in line for promotion.

Vance felt his heart plummet to his feet. A rush of heat burned his chest and when he swallowed he tasted bile. It was clear that the situation had gone from bad to catastrophic. The Washington chiefs were already in a panic so they would freak out over this. When he spoke earlier to his section chief he'd received a volley of abuse.

How the fuck did you let this happen?

You told us it was a fool-proof plan.

Why didn't you have more agents in the area?

Why didn't you use a shooter who could fucking shoot?

Do whatever it takes to keep a lid on this mess.

They were sending someone to San Antonio to help sort it. He didn't doubt they would also be working out a way to save their own skins.

Among the few people who'd known about the operation were the director and his deputy. They were the ones who had sanctioned it. But they would now try to distance themselves. Deny all knowledge and claim it had been carried out without authorization by a group of maverick agents in San Antonio. There'd be no physical evidence to suggest otherwise. Plausible deniability would be the name of the game.

And he'd probably be hung out to dry along with the prison warden, the physician who pronounced Jordan dead, and the other agents who had been directly involved. Anything that had been put in writing would be destroyed, and that would include confidential files on previous faked executions where the inmates were later subjected to medical experiments before being put down.

It was turning into a total fucking nightmare and he was right in the middle of it. As he ventured into the house the sense of impending doom intensified.

There were two more bodies in the living room. He recognized both. Agent Douglas Simms – a single guy who had recently been transferred from Baltimore – and Emily Jordan, sister of the man whose very existence now threatened to rock the country. They were in a terrible state. There was blood everywhere. It was a shocking scene of carnage.

It was obvious to Vance what had happened. The agents had forced their way into the house and Jordan had let loose with the gun he'd picked up from outside the restaurant. He'd killed both of them, but not before Simms shot the sister. However you looked at it, this was a tragedy.

The two agents hadn't known the true identity of the guy they were looking out for. They'd been given a description and told that he was armed and should be approached with caution if he showed up. But they had also been ordered to move in quickly so he wouldn't have a chance to get away. And to bring him down if he resisted. So there was always going to be a big element of risk.

An empty ache touched the pit of his stomach and he was suddenly desperate for some fresh air and a smoke. Back outside he fumbled in his pocket for his cigarettes. He was lighting one when his cellphone rang. He took it out and flipped it open.

'That you, Vance?' asked a familiar voice.

'Yeah, it's me.'

'I just heard that your boys fucked up and Jordan is still alive,' the Lawyer said. 'Please tell me it's not true.'

Vance's throat tightened. 'The shooter missed and Jordan ran off. We're tracking him down.'

'And in the meantime what am I supposed to do? I'm already getting calls.'

'Just sit tight. Act normal. We'll catch him. And then we'll work something out. Trust me, all is not lost.'

'You don't sound very confident.'

'Well I am. We're on his tail and closing in. He's only been missing for a couple of hours. So keep calm.'

'And what happens if the cops get him or he turns himself in?'

'He won't. He knows that if he does he'll go straight back to death row.'

'So has he any idea why he was sprung from the execution chamber and why you tried to kill him?'

'He hasn't a clue,' Vance said. 'So there's still a chance he'll assume we had nothing to do with the attempt on his life and get in touch.'

'That's not going to happen,' the Lawyer said. 'If he's got any sense he won't trust anyone. He'll just count himself lucky he's still alive and high tail it to Mexico.'

'We'll get him before that can happen. I guarantee it.'

There was a long span of silence on the line. Vance paced up and down the pavement in front of the house, only half aware of all the activity around him.

'Keep me posted then,' the Lawyer said. 'And remember this, Vance. If you guys can't deliver on your end of the deal then I won't deliver on mine.'

The Lawyer hung up and Vance pocketed his phone.

28

After leaving Mountain City we headed north along the 35 towards Austin. I figured it would be more difficult for the cops to spot the Explorer if we lost ourselves in the state capital.

We stopped at a gas station in the suburbs and Kate went in to buy some food and drink for us and the baby. It was an odd feeling watching her doing it and not worrying that she might rat me out. Somehow I'd earned her trust and she had earned mine. Who would have guessed it the way things started out?

Five minutes later she emerged with two bloated plastic bags. She told me to take the wheel because the baby had woken up and was becoming increasingly distressed.

'She's hungry,' Kate said. 'And she needs to lie down.'

I started the engine. 'We'll find a motel. There should be plenty around here. We can get out of sight and get some rest.'

'Hold on a goddamn minute,' she said. 'Are you suggesting we share a motel room?'

'We can't drive around all night,' I said. 'And right now we need to stick together. I don't know if you'll be safe on your own.'

'You're kidding, right? No one knows I'm with you except Frank.'

I pulled the Explorer out onto the road. 'Don't be so sure. Someone might have spotted you picking me up back there and got the plate number. And when Larson does raise the alarm it won't take the Feds long to realize it was me at your house.'

'But I'll say you abducted me.'

'And if they think you're lying you'll be in trouble. You need to stay close to me for now.'

She stared at me with her mouth sagging open in disbelief.

'Are you saying they might kill me to keep me quiet?' I could hear the panic in her voice.

'It's possible,' I said. 'You saw how ruthless they were back at the house.'

'This is not fair,' she said.

She was right and I felt another wave of guilt hit me head on.

'Look, we need to get off the road sharpish,' I said. 'The cops will be on high alert and the car could be spotted.'

'So why don't you drop us at a hotel and go steal another car? You could be halfway across the country by morning.'

'Because I intend to go back to San Antonio,' I said. 'So I don't want to go far.'

'Why would you do a crazy thing like that?'

'I need to find out why my sister was killed,' I said. 'And why the Feds want me dead too. San Antonio is the obvious place to start.'

'So what happens if and when you find out?'

My grip tightened on the wheel. 'Then someone is going to pay for what happened to Emily.'

Another question formed on her lips but she was distracted by a shrill scream from her daughter.

She drew a sharp breath and closed her eyes. After a heart-stopping minute, she said, 'OK, let's find somewhere to stay. But on one condition.'

'What's that?'

'You tell me what the fuck you've got me into.'

I thought about it and decided to lie.

'It's a deal,' I said.

Kate clambered into the back seat and I concentrated on where we were going.

Ten minutes later I spotted a small double-decker motel called the Tulip Garden. I pulled over and stopped outside the office. The parking lot was half full. I could see there was more parking at the rear of the building.

'This will do,' I said. 'It's not fancy, but it looks clean. You'll need to pay in cash.'

Kate snorted. 'So how come you don't have any money or credit cards? And yet you have a gun?'

'It's a long story,' I said.

'And one I'm looking forward to hearing.'

We went in together, Kate holding little Anna who had finally stopped crying and was now in a playful mood.

The manager was a friendly old guy with a shock of white hair and pale eyes that were rheumy under drooping lids. He didn't seem in the least bit surprised. In fact he welcomed us with a smile and made faces at the baby who giggled in response.

Checking in was trouble-free. We used Kate's second name and asked for a large room with two beds and Kate paid up front in cash and showed her ID. The guy only gave it a cursory glance.

We were able to park the car in front of the ground floor room and out of sight of the road. The room was small and basic with two double beds, an armchair, a dressing table with a TV mounted on top, and a separate bathroom with shower. There was also some coffee-making stuff. Compared to what I'd been used to it was a sultan's palace.

The first thing I did was slip into the bathroom to empty my bladder, which had been fit to explode for the last half hour. When I came back out Kate had taken off her coat and was sitting on one of the beds giving the baby some milk.

I went outside and unloaded Kate's case from the car. I left the stroller in the trunk.

'There's food and drink in the bags,' Kate said. 'And some toiletry things for you.'

'Thanks.'

I emptied the contents of the first bag onto the other bed. There were cans of coke, pre-packed sandwiches, some potato chips, a few candy bars, some fruit and yogurts.

In the second bag there was a toothbrush, toothpaste, razor and shaving gel. There was also a folded grey baseball jersey with a Texas Longhorns motif on the front, and a matching cap with a large T.

'That stuff didn't come cheap,' Kate said. 'But I figured you needed a change of clothes. You stand out like a sore thumb in that suit.'

Before removing the jacket I took out the gun. My fingers touched something else in the inside pocket which turned out to be a leather business card wallet. It was very light and thin, which was probably why I hadn't realized it was there.

I felt a tingle of excitement. I wondered if Vance had known about it. Could it have belonged to whoever wore the suit before me?

The wallet contained seven identical letterpress cards. They were a simple non-flashy design of black words on a white background. On one side was a small scales-of-justice logo above the name *Raymond Garcia, Attorney-at-Law*. On the other side was an office phone number and email address.

I went straight over to the room phone and called the number. A recorded voice informed me that the office of the Garcia and Cruz Law Firm was closed until after Thanksgiving.

'What have you got there?' Kate asked.

'I'm not sure,' I said. 'Could be some kind of clue. I'll check it out tomorrow.'

I dropped the wallet on the bed and opened a can of coke. I was parched.

'Do you want a drink?' I asked.

The baby had dropped off to sleep while drinking her milk and Kate was placing her gently on the pillows.

'Yes, please,' she said.

I went into the bathroom and brought out two glasses. I filled them both to the brim and handed one to Kate, who was sitting on the edge of the bed. She looked exhausted, her eyes red-rimmed and bleary.

I downed some coke, letting the bubbles blitz away in my mouth. That's when another blast of grief hit me and an image of my sister lying on the floor with a bullet hole in her chest reared up out of nowhere.

Tears sparked behind my eyelids and I had to sit down in the armchair to steady myself. It felt like my heart had just been kicked. I bit down hard on my lip and forced the image away by looking across at the baby. I couldn't help feeling responsible for both that sweet little bundle and her mother. I'd got them into this mess and I didn't want them to end up like Emily. But at the same time I wasn't sure I knew how to protect them – or myself for that matter.

'Are you all right?' Kate asked.

'Not really,' I said. 'What I saw tonight was too much. My sister didn't deserve that. And I blame myself. I should have stayed away from her.'

'Did she have a family – apart from you?'

I shook my head. 'Our parents are both dead. She was divorced. Never had children.'

'How old was she?'

'Thirty-five.'

'A year younger than me,' Kate said. Then she paused, before adding,

'I'm really sorry for your loss.'

My eyes misted. 'I appreciate that.'

'I can't imagine what it must have been like for you in that house,' she said. 'What happened exactly?'

So I told her, leaving out the bit where Emily was shocked to see her brother return from the dead.

When I was through, she said, 'Isn't it time you told me your name?'

I spoke without thinking.

'It's Lee,' I said, and immediately regretted it.

She nodded. 'So come on then, Lee. You agreed to tell me what's going on. I've a right to know why I'm here.'

So what was I supposed to tell her?

Well it so happens that I'm a convicted murderer who is meant to be dead. Now I'm on the run and the Feds are trying to kill me.

She was bound to freak out and become dangerously unpredictable. And I didn't want that. I decided therefore to buy some time in order to come up with a plausible story.

So I held up my hands and showed her the spots of blood that had dried on my palms. 'Can it wait until after I've taken a shower?'

She rolled her eyes and shook her head at the same time.

'I guess it can wait a short while. But in all fairness I think you should shower after I've had a bath. My muscles are hurting like hell from the kicking Frank gave me. And I smell like the inside of a sock.'

She didn't wait for a response. She got up, grabbed some things from her case and disappeared into the bathroom. I was left alone with her baby and for some reason that made me feel a little better. Kate trusted me. It was a mystery to me why she did, but she did, and it was like a small reminder that not everything in this crazy world was bad.

The first thing I did when I was by myself was to hide the gun under the mattress. I wasn't quite as trusting as Kate. Then I switched on the radio and sat in the armchair to try to clear my mind. But the soft music that filled the room served only to stir the emptiness inside me.

I sat there for maybe twenty minutes, re-living in my head all the stuff that I'd been through. The fake execution, the attempt on my life outside the restaurant, the confrontation with Frank Larson, the shoot-out which had left three people dead, including my sister. I told myself that tomorrow I'd start seeking answers to all the questions that were tormenting me. And this infused me with a sense of purpose.

When Kate appeared again her skin was flushed from the heat of the bath. She was wearing black tracksuit bottoms and a white T-shirt. Her hair was pinned back.

'It's all yours,' she said. 'How's my little girl?'

'Out for the count by the look of it.'

A wave of emotion barrelled through me. This time it had nothing to do with my plight or my sister's death. It was engendered entirely by this single, startling moment of normality. The circumstances were irrelevant. What struck me was that I was here in this room with a woman and a child. There was background music and the scent of bath oils.

The contrast with my previous life was beyond belief. For almost a decade I'd been alone in a grubby, smelly cell. I'd yearned for just a fleeting respite from ugliness and drudgery. A brief glimpse at something better. Something wonderfully ordinary. And here it was and I was blown away by it. But it was going to be short-lived. Just like every phase of my life that had not been pure shit.

'You'd better get in the shower,' Kate said. 'Then I want you to tell me what kind of trouble you've got me into and how I can get out of it.'

I took the toiletries she'd bought me into the bathroom. Brushed my teeth and stared at myself in the mirror. My eyes were lost inside the dark circles surrounding them. The rest of my face was the colour of dirty wax despite the self-tan.

I stripped off and stepped into the shower. I let the water pummel my face and body for a long time. It felt good. Eventually I turned off the water, stepped out and towelled dry. I put my trousers back on and draped the towel over my shoulder, too shy to let Kate see me naked from the waist up.

But I needn't have worried. She was fast asleep on the bed next to her daughter. It was a relief. It meant I had more time to make up a story about myself.

I switched off the radio and the main light and covered mother and daughter with the top sheet from my bed. I noticed a bruise on the side of Kate's face, not far from the scar that had also been inflicted by her brutal ex. She struck me as a good woman and mother. She didn't deserve to be treated like that. It made me wish I'd done more damage to the arrogant bastard back at the house.

I slipped off my trousers, leaving my underpants on, and got between the scratchy sheets. The mattress was hard but I was used to that. I braced myself for a long, restless night filled with tears and painful memories.

But once the bedside light was extinguished I went straight to sleep – fearful of what the new day would bring.

29

I WOKE UP early, my head pounding as if I had a migraine. I lay in the dark listening to Kate's heavy breathing in the other bed.

A maelstrom of thoughts stopped me from going back to sleep. My last conversation with Emily at the prison kept playing over in my head. Along with the image of her lying dead on the living room floor.

The grief would not ebb, but at least the pain had for now lulled to a dull, persistent throb. There would hopefully be time later to mourn properly for my sister. Right now I had other priorities – like where to start my search for answers and how to extricate Kate from the predicament I'd placed her in.

Eventually the morning light crept into the room through a gap in the curtains and started dancing on the walls. My bed was next to the window so I hauled myself up and looked outside. The new day had brought with it an angry mass of clouds. I watched them change shape as they drifted overhead towards the city centre. It looked like a storm was brewing.

'Since you're up can you make some coffee?'

I turned, startled. Kate was peering out from beneath the sheets. I could barely see her head in the half-dark room. My first reaction was to reach for my trousers at the foot of the bed and pull them on. But I made a clumsy job of it and cursed out loud as I fell between the bed and the wall.

Kate gave a soft chuckle. 'Please try not to make a noise. I want Anna to sleep as long as possible.'

I struggled to my feet, zipped up my trousers, and whispered that I was sorry. I still felt self-conscious because I was bare-chested, so I put on my new Texas Longhorns T-shirt.

While I was making coffee Kate slipped into the bathroom. When she came out the coffee was poured and I handed her a mug. Just then, the baby woke and at once introduced an element of chaos to the morning. She crawled across the bed with a speed that astonished me. I had to lunge across the room to catch her before she fell off the edge.

'That was close,' Kate said, with a smile.

The baby giggled and tried to poke her fingers into my eyes. She was a tiny ball of energy, and it was as though she had known me since she was born eight months ago. I was flattered and confused at the same time. I'd never had anything to do with babies and I felt awkward.

'Let her have a crawl,' Kate said. 'She'll be fine.'

I lowered her delicately to the floor, fearing she might break. She looked up at me, smiled, then moved on her hands and knees across the carpet, as though daring me to follow.

'I'm going to shower so you're in charge,' Kate said. 'There are toys in that case over there.'

She grabbed some clothes and dashed back into the bathroom.

I spent the next fifteen minutes sitting on the floor trying to get little Anna to play with the toys but all she wanted to do was crawl around the room grabbing things. Keeping her out of harm's way was enough to stop me thinking about the grim reality of my situation. Or rather *our* situation, because this child and her mother were in a bind too thanks to me.

Playing with Anna made me think of Marissa and what we could have had if I'd stayed on the right side of the law. My wife had always wanted a daughter – a little girl like Anna who she could dress in pretty clothes and show off to her friends. She would have been a brilliant mom and our child would have been given all the love and attention in the world. Unlike this poor kid, whose father had wanted her killed in the womb and whose formative years were likely to be blighted by trauma and uncertainty.

'I can see that you're not used to kids,' Kate said when she stepped out of the bathroom. 'You're all flustered.'

She was wearing faded blue jeans with horizontal slashes at the knees and a white silk blouse that clung to her curves.

'She won't keep still,' I said. 'I'm afraid she's going to hurt herself.'

Kate laughed as she rubbed her wet hair with a towel.

'She's stronger than you think. And she's making the most of it. She's not had much male company. I don't think Frank ever sat down to play with her.'

'That's a shame.'

'Damn right it is. But he was either too busy with his job or out drinking with his pals. And when he did come over I had to put her to bed so she didn't see him laying into me.'

'Why did you put up with it?' I asked.

'I guess I kept hoping he'd change, but he didn't. He got worse.'

'So what's his problem?'

She stopped rubbing her hair and pushed out her bottom lip.

'Apart from not being able to control his anger he's very resentful. And jealous. He wanted me, but not Anna. He already has two children by a previous marriage and didn't want any more.'

'But you did.'

'Hell, yeah. That's why I never told him I came off the pill.'

She gave me a look that challenged me to be critical of what she'd done. But I said nothing.

'Bathroom's free,' she said. 'You go ahead and shower. When you're done we need to talk.'

The moment I stood up Anna reached her arms towards me and started crying. I felt my heart lift and my throat catch.

'For some reason you've made a big impression on her,' Kate said.

It was a curious and not unpleasant feeling. Despite all that had happened I had somehow managed to find a new friend in this tiny bundle of mischief. Who the hell would have thought it?

'OK, I've got her,' Kate said, scooping her daughter up in her arms.

But Anna tried to struggle free and Kate had to whisk her away from me and distract her by taking her over to the window and pointing outside. I stared after them, bemused and disoriented by the disparate emotions that were converging inside my head.

'Hurry up,' Kate said, over her shoulder. 'If she can't see you she'll calm down.'

Once I'd closed the bathroom door behind me Anna went quiet, like she had been silenced by the flick of a switch. I examined myself in the mirror. My complexion was pallid and sickly. My eyes were crusty with sleep and there were dark bags under them. The stubble on my chin rasped as I rubbed it, but it went some way towards altering my appearance so I decided not to shave.

The shower revived me, but this time I didn't dwell under the steaming jets. I got out, dried, and dressed. I was brushing my teeth when

Kate started banging on the door and telling me to come out.

I swallowed a mouthful of foam and rushed into the bedroom. She had switched on the TV and was watching a news report on the shooting in Mountain City. There was night footage of the outside of Emily's house and lots of flashing blue lights.

'It just came on,' Kate said. She was holding the baby in her arms and staring intently at the screen.

I froze, feeling my gut twist and realized that the cat was about to leap out of the bag.

'The house belonged to Emily Jordan,' the newscaster said. *'According to police sources she was one of the three people found shot dead. The other two are unidentified males. Miss Jordan was the sister of Lee Jordan, the man who was executed on Monday evening at Huntsville in Texas for the murder ten years ago of Kimberley Crane, former wife of congressman Gideon Crane. The FBI, who are in charge of the investigation, say they have no idea at this stage who is responsible for the killings and whether it is in any way linked to Lee Jordan's execution.'*

The picture they put up was the one they had always used and despite what the Feds had done to my hair, there was no mistaking it was me staring out of the screen.

Kate's head whipped around. As she stared at me I heard the air rush out of her lungs.

'Let me explain,' I said.

She shook her head and her jaw twitched. I could see she was trying to swallow her panic.

'My God,' she exclaimed. 'I saw it on the news. They said you died. There were witnesses.'

'Please,' I said. 'Just hear me out.'

I shifted under the intensity of her gaze. Every cell in my body was shaking. I didn't know what I would do if she made a run for it or started screaming for help. There was no way I was going to hurt her.

After a few moments her nostrils flared, her mouth tightened, and she spoke in a taut voice. 'So how come you're alive?'

I slumped in the armchair, feeling desperate and defeated.

'That's the million dollar question,' I said.

30

To HER CREDIT, Kate listened without saying a word whilst pacing the room clinging to Anna. But it was clear she was struggling with what she'd learned. She had the look of someone trying to hold onto reality while their brain was screaming in disbelief.

I tried to keep my voice low and even, but it came out shaky and disjointed. It was a hard thing to explain. How I was led into the execution chamber and laid out on the gurney. How I saw the faces of the witnesses and listened to the chaplain's prayer. How I felt the 'lethal' cocktail of drugs enter my veins and then waking up in a strange room to be told by a man named Aaron Vance that the execution had been faked by the FBI. Followed by a trip to a restaurant in San Antonio where a guy named Martinez was going to tell me what I had to do for them.

'But it never happened,' I said. 'After I got out of the car it sped away. Then a guy who'd been standing on the pavement produced a gun and shot at me. By some miracle he missed and I managed to run away. They came after me, but I got another lucky break when I saw you in the parking lot.'

Kate just stared at me as her mind processed what I'd told her. A loose hair drifted into her eye and she tucked it up. The baby tried to wriggle free and kept pointing at the floor. Outside I could hear the low beat of the city.

Eventually, she said, 'As I recall you've always claimed to be innocent.'

'That's because I am.'

'So you're saying you didn't kill that woman?'

I shook my head. 'I did a lot of bad things back then, including invading that house with my partner. But I never killed anyone until last night.'

'So if you didn't kill her then who did?'

I shrugged. 'I had my suspicion, but I could never prove it.'

'So how come they convicted you?'

I shrugged. 'The evidence against me was strong. And I had a lousy lawyer.'

She put Anna on the floor and sat on the edge of the bed. Her eyes continued to drill into me, unblinking.

Did she believe me? I couldn't tell.

After a few seconds, she said, 'How did they fake the execution?'

I told her what Vance had said about the knockout drugs and the rigged heart monitor and the people like the warden who had been involved.

'And you have no idea why they did it?' she said.

'None at all. When I walked into the execution chamber I didn't expect to come out of it alive.'

'But faking an execution is a big deal. Why would they go to all that trouble only to have you gunned down the next day?'

'It's what I've been trying to figure out. But none of it makes a shred of sense.'

Anna had crawled across the floor to where I was sitting. She started climbing up my leg and wanting me to pick her up. But I didn't move, afraid that Kate wouldn't want me to touch her baby now that she knew the truth about me.

'It's a far-fetched story,' Kate said. 'And if you weren't sitting right there in front of me I wouldn't believe it.'

'I'm not sure I believe it myself,' I said.

Anna started bawling and tears spilled from her eyes.

'You'd better pick her up before her crying shatters the windows,' Kate said.

I leaned forward and lifted Anna up. But she didn't stop crying until I got to my feet and started walking her around the room.

'So what the hell happens now?' Kate said, her voice strained. 'Shouldn't you go to the police?'

'That's not an option. If I'm locked up or dead I'll never know who was ultimately responsible for Emily's death.'

She grunted out a bitter laugh. 'So what about me? What am I supposed to do?'

'You have to stay with me, at least until you know it's safe to go home.'

'But how will I know that?'

'I won't lie to you,' I said. 'Right now I don't have the answer. But if I can get to the bottom of what's going on I'm sure we'll see a way out.'

'But where will you start?'

'With Aaron Vance,' I said. 'The FBI guy.'

'You know nothing about him.'

'That's why our first port of call after leaving here will be an internet café. We'll look him up. See where it takes us. And we'll also find out what we can about Raymond Garcia.'

'Who?'

I took out the business card wallet from my pocket and held it up.

'The guy whose cards were left in my suit. Maybe he's somehow involved. I need to find out.'

'That's clutching at straws,' she said.

'Sure, but it's all I've got.'

She let a few moments pass in silence. Her face was red, her eyes moist. While I waited for her to speak my stomach grew heavy and I felt the bile rising. I needed her to stay on side. If she jumped ship now she'd put her own life at risk and make it impossible for me to seek out answers.

Eventually she said, 'You know there's only one thing stopping me walking out that door with my daughter and telling you to go to hell.'

'What's that?'

She took a quick breath. 'I happen to believe what you said about not being a murderer. Which probably means I'm really stupid.'

'You're not stupid,' I said.

'I guess that depends on whether you've told me the truth about Kimberley Crane.'

31

It was eight in the morning on the eve of Thanksgiving. Aaron Vance was back in his office, feeling like shit. He hadn't slept a wink all night and his eyes were sore and heavy.

He sat behind his desk in the building on University Heights Boulevard that housed the Bureau's San Antonio field office. On the wall behind him hung the FBI's seal and a ten-most-wanted poster. The poster was out of date, of course. The most wanted person in America was not an Al Qaeda terrorist or the lunatic who had murdered three women in Tampa.

No, it was Lee Jordan, the man who posed a diabolical threat to the Bureau and everything it stood for.

Vance still found it hard to believe what had happened overnight. First the bungled attempt on Jordan's life. And then the carnage up in Mountain City in which two FBI agents had been killed.

He dreaded to think what today would bring. Jordan could be anywhere by now. Maybe he was even thinking about turning himself in to the cops. That'd be tricky, but manageable. It'd be an altogether more difficult problem if he went directly to the media.

But Vance's instincts told him Jordan wouldn't do that because even in the best case scenario he'd end up back in prison.

He swivelled his chair and looked through the window. It was pouring outside, great sheets of rain lashing onto the street. The sky was an angry morass of clouds that just about matched his mood.

He felt really down. It was at times like this he wished he was still with Jennifer. At least he would then have someone in his corner. Someone he could trust to be there for him when his world collapsed. But she was now shacked up with a firefighter back in LA. So he was on his own and standing on the edge of an abyss.

His secretary, a matronly type in her fifties, knocked on his door and peeked in.

'What is it, Liz?'

'Sam Boyd is downstairs, Mr Vance. Do you want him to come right up?'

He nodded.

Liz was in the dark about Jordan, like almost everyone else in the building. She knew only that all hell had broken loose because of what had happened in Mountain City. But it was going to get more and more difficult to stop the truth from getting out.

Vance was still behind his desk, chewing his fingernails, when Boyd was brought in.

'I'll get some coffees,' Liz said and closed the door behind them.

Boyd had a reputation as a charmless manipulator who had back-stabbed his way to the top. He had a bland, symmetrical face and dark brown hair complete with a wave at the front. He was in his early forties and his head looked too small for his robust frame. For three years he'd been the FBI's deputy director of Special Operations. He'd been responsible for advising the FBI director to approve the faked execution plan that Vance had come up with. So he was up to his neck in this shit and that's why he was the one sent by Washington to get a handle on things.

'You look a mess, Aaron,' Boyd said, as he sat down on the other side of the desk. His voice was a deep baritone and it suited him.

His blue jacket was tight and ill-fitting and beneath it he wore a black open-neck shirt.

'I haven't been to bed,' Vance said. 'It's been a fucking nightmare.'

'So what's the latest on Jordan?'

'Nothing new. He's disappeared again.'

'And the woman and child – are they still with him?'

'As far as I know, they are. She may even be helping him.'

'Oh?'

Vance told him about the neighbour who claimed he saw Jordan get into an Explorer that was being driven by a woman.

'This gets worse by the minute,' Boyd said, his face tight with supressed anger. 'I can't believe you let it happen?'

'The shooter fucked up,' Vance said. 'He missed from almost point-blank range.'

'That's no excuse, goddamn it. You were in charge. You should have made sure there was no room for error.'

Boyd's words were as sharp as razor wire. Vance felt them stick into him. A bitter taste filled his mouth and an intense heat radiated from his brow.

'Fill me in on what happened at the sister's house,' Boyd said.

Vance sucked in a breath. 'We sent two agents to cover it. To be honest I didn't expect Jordan to show up there. But he did and when our guys tried to get him he started shooting at them.'

'So what story are we putting out?'

'We're saying Emily Jordan called the Bureau and asked to speak to an agent. We sent two along and when they got there they were fired on by an unidentified gunman, who then killed her.'

'Sounds plausible, I suppose. What about the cops? They can't be happy.'

'They're not, but they've been leaned on from on high.'

'I had to do the same with our field office in Austin. They were up in arms about it.'

'I'm not surprised.'

'What about our lawyer friend?' Boyd said.

Vance shrugged. 'He's pissed off. I spoke to him last night. Told him to hold fire and we'd get the deal back on track. I'll arrange to meet up with him later. Try to put his mind at ease.'

'That won't be easy.'

At that moment Liz brought in a tray with coffees and biscuits. She didn't hang around and quickly retreated from the office.

'The director says we have to do whatever it takes to stop this from getting out,' Boyd said. 'I don't need to tell you what the implications will be if it does.'

'I've thought about nothing else,' Vance said.

'If there's even a whisper of it outside the family then the media will start digging around. And we don't want that. They'll resurrect all those rumours from a few years ago. The ones about executions being faked so government agencies and the military could carry out medical experiments with impunity on guys who were supposed to be dead.'

'They were more than rumours, Sam.'

'I know it and you know it, Aaron. But the fucking public at large has no idea what we do in the interests of national security. And they don't want to know. That way they get to sleep at nights.'

A long, awkward silence stretched between them. Vance drank

some coffee and tried to ignore the buzz swirling inside his head.

Then Boyd said, 'We need to delete Jordan's prints and DNA from the database.'

'I've already asked for that to be done,' Vance said.

Then he sat back and felt his blood pressure rise a notch. The muscles in his jaw ached and he realized he'd been grinding his teeth.

There was a light tap at the door and Liz came back in.

'I'm sorry, Mr Vance, but there's someone on line two who insists on talking to you.'

'Tell them to call back,' Vance said. 'I'm busy.'

A puzzled look wrinkled her features. 'But he's a police officer and he says it's about Lee Jordan.'

Vance felt a chill spread through his belly.

'What's his name?'

'Frank Larson. Detective Frank Larson.'

'OK, put him through.'

'Is he the cop you came across in Mountain City?' Boyd asked.

Vance shook his head. 'Larson is the boyfriend of Kate Pena, the woman whose car Jordan hijacked.'

'Shit. Put him on speaker.'

The phone rang. Vance picked it up and pressed the speaker button. He tried to keep the tremor out of his voice.

'Hello, Detective Larson. How do you feel?'

'I've just left the hospital with a broken nose and ten stiches in my head. Plus, my daughter's been kidnapped. So how the fuck do you think I feel?'

'We're doing all we can to find your daughter and girlfriend,' Vance said. 'As soon as we—'

'Cut the bullshit, Vance. I want to know why the guy who took them isn't in a fucking coffin.'

Vance and Boyd exchanged anxious looks.

'What do you mean?' Vance said.

'I mean the whole world was led to believe that a murdering bastard named Lee Jordan was executed in Huntsville on Monday. Only he wasn't because last night he attacked me. I thought he looked familiar, but I couldn't be certain until I got the lab to check the coffee mugs for prints.'

'Coffee mugs?'

'I'm a cop, agent Vance. Did you really think I wouldn't try to find out who the guy was? The mugs were on the table. I took them with me. His prints were on one of them. There's only one way they could have got there.'

'Have you spoken to anyone about this?' Vance said.

'The lab guy thought it was odd, but assumed Jordan had used the mug in prison. I thought it best not to put him right on that score.'

'So who else have you told?'

'Not a fucking soul. But so help me everyone will know about it unless you clue me in.'

'OK, Frank,' Vance said. 'Stay calm. I guess you have a right to know what's going on. But we can't talk over the phone. Are you at home?'

'I'm at Kate's. Dropped by to pick up my car. I walked right in. Your guys did a piss-awful job of fixing the lock.'

'Are you alone?'

'Of course.'

'Then stay put and I'll come right over. And for your sake as well as ours please don't talk to anyone about this. It's all part of a highly classified operation.'

'I guess it would have to be,' Larson said. 'You can't make a noise about something this crazy.'

Vance hung up the phone and blew out his cheeks.

'This is all we need,' he said.

'Well you know what you've got to do,' Boyd said. 'He's not one of us. He's a fucking cop and he's bound to talk. So let's nip this one in the bud right away.'

Vance exhaled a long burst of air.

'Shouldn't we refer it up? Maybe the director himself should make the decision.'

Boyd shook his head. 'I've been given full authority to do whatever it takes to limit the damage. This guy Larson is a liability. He has to be taken care of.'

'I'll do it myself then,' Vance said. 'That way I know it'll get done properly.'

'You sure about that?'

Vance nodded. 'We can't afford to get any more of our people involved in this. It's getting completely out of hand.'

'Good point,' Boyd said. 'Just make sure you do a clean job. I'm guessing that like me you're a bit rusty when it comes to killing.'

32

WHILE KATE FED and changed the baby, I made some more coffee. We thought about going across the street to a diner for breakfast, but decided it wasn't worth the risk. Instead we ate the sandwiches from the gas station.

I watched more of the news, but heard nothing I didn't already know. When they showed an old photo of Emily the grief hit me again. Like a knife twisting in my gut.

Kate saw my reaction. 'You're not to blame you know. You went there because you thought she was in danger. She was.'

It didn't help. The guilt had already embedded itself in my soul and it was growing by the minute. Along with my determination to avenge her death.

'When was the last time you saw her?' Kate asked.

I swallowed hard. 'The day of the execution. She came to see me. We said our goodbyes and that's when I decided to tell my lawyer not to lodge another appeal. I'd had enough and so had she. All the time I was alive she couldn't get on with her life.'

'It must have been sad.'

I felt a lump rise in my throat. 'It was.'

'Did she believe you were innocent?'

I nodded. 'Always, but she was one of only three people who did.'

'And the others?'

'My wife Marissa and the lawyer I took on a few years ago. A guy named Mark Zimmerman.'

She left it a beat, said, 'What was it like on death row?'

The memory of that place dragged me back there. I had a vision of the tiny cell. I felt the cold and the loneliness and it sent a shiver through my body.

'It was like living in a bubble full of slime,' I said. 'When I walked out of the cell for the last time it was a relief.'

'And what was it like walking into the death chamber?'

I felt tears push against my eyes. 'It was weird, but I tried to empty my mind and tell myself that at least all the suffering was coming to an end.'

'And when you woke up in that room – what the hell did that feel like?'

I looked at her. She was sitting on the bed putting a clean diaper on Anna.

'I thought I was dreaming at first,' I said. 'But I quickly came to believe I'd been given a second chance. Vance said I would have to do something for the Bureau. Then afterwards they'd give me a new identity and move me to another country. I thought it was too good to be true. It was.'

'But at least you're alive,' Kate said.

'Yeah, but three other people are dead.'

As we checked out of the hotel I asked the guy on reception to point us in the direction of the nearest internet café.

'No need for that,' he said. 'There's a computer room down the hall. Guests can go online free of charge.'

It was a tiny windowless room with one computer on a desk. Alongside it stood a printer and fax machine. There were two plastic chairs so I positioned them in front of the desk.

Kate put Anna on the floor and gave her some toys to play with.

'So where do we start?' Kate said.

'Aaron Vance,' I told her. 'And you'll have to do it. I'm a bit stale when it comes to computers.'

We sat close together. Close enough for our arms to touch. The fact that Kate did not move away made me tense, but in a good way. I took it to mean that she wasn't afraid of me, in spite of what she now knew. That was a huge relief.

'Here we go,' she said, as the Google search page opened up on the screen.

She started tapping at the keys and the name Aaron Vance appeared in the search box.

'Is that your man?' Kate said.

Google had come up with lots of hits for Aaron Vance, but a number of people shared the same name. So we narrowed it down by adding the letters FBI. And that's when it got interesting. The first page we opened up happened to be the official site for the Bureau's San Antonio field office. And there was his picture. He was younger by about five years. But the jaw was just as square and the dark hair just as neat.

Kate clicked on his name and up came his profile. Before being appointed Special Agent in Charge in San Antonio he'd spent time in New York, Miami and Los Angeles. During much of his career he'd been attached to task forces set up to combat organized crime and street gangs. It was an impressive track record.

Vance's name also came up in quite a few stories involving high profile court cases and gang busting initiatives. Most of the stories, I noticed, mentioned the Texas Syndicate, one of the most notorious criminal gangs in America. At least seven of its members were on death row at the Polunsky Unit awaiting execution for murder. Hundreds more were in other prisons across Texas and there were thousands of them running illicit operations on the outside.

The stories went back years. In some of them Vance gave a quote to a newspaper or TV station after a successful bust or prosecution. In others he was named as the officer in charge of the latest push against the Texas Syndicate. Kate tapped into the stories and I scanned them.

August 3 2010: Five members of the Texas Syndicate were charged with drug offences today following an FBI operation that lasted eleven months. The agent in charge, Aaron Vance, said that the Syndicate had become 'one of the most violent and prolific drug trafficking organizations the state has ever seen.'

December 10 2011: Acting on a new federal indictment an FBI task force led by special agent Aaron Vance arrested three more gang suspects as part of an effort to disrupt the activities of the Texas Syndicate in San Antonio. But despite these latest arrests there's growing concern that the authorities are losing the fight against this powerful organization.

October 7 2012: Texas Syndicate boss Julio Martinez walked free from a court today after racketeering charges against him were dropped. It followed the sudden disappearance of two key federal witnesses. Martinez has been described by the FBI as one of the Syndicate's leading figures, with links to drug trafficking, prostitution, extortion and murder. FBI agent Aaron Vance said, 'This is a major disappointment for the Bureau. But I can assure the public that we will keep up the fight against the street gangs that are terrorizing our cities.'

I touched the computer screen with my finger. 'See if you can pull up other versions of that particular story. I want to see if there are any photos of Julio Martinez.'

Kate tapped the keys and several stories were listed. The second was a page from the San Antonio Express. And there was a photo of Martinez. He was coming out of a building, wearing a bright orange shirt, jeans and tinted glasses.

'That's him,' I said. 'That's the guy I was supposed to meet in the restaurant. He waved at me through the window just before I was shot at.'

Then something else caught my eye. The door behind him was open. On the wall to the right of it there was a small square plaque. I could just about see the words on it but I asked Kate to zoom in so that I could be sure. She did it by cutting and pasting the photo into the computer's documents file and them magnifying it.

And I was right. The sign read: *Garcia and Cruz – Attorneys at Law.* I took out the business card I had found in the jacket. Showed it to Kate.

'It's the same firm.'

'Could be a coincidence,' Kate said.

I shook my head. 'No way. This shows there's a link between Julio Martinez and Raymond Garcia. A lawyer and a gangster.'

'So what have those two got to do with you?'

'I haven't a fucking clue,' I said. 'But I'm gonna find out.'

The next step was to look up the Garcia and Cruz law firm in San Antonio. But the search proved less than fruitful. The company did not appear to have its own website, although its address was given in various business directories, along with the names of the partners – Raymond Garcia and Michael Cruz.

This surprised me as all the other law firms in the city were doing what they could to raise their online profile with photos of the lawyers and all kinds of information.

We couldn't find any photos of Garcia and Cruz and we didn't come across anything linking them to the Texas Syndicate or the FBI. There was a spiral notepad and pen on the desk so I jotted down the firm's address. Then I copied out the phone number and address of the FBI field office in San Antonio.

'Is this stuff helpful?' Kate asked.

I looked at her. 'Only in the sense that it gives me somewhere to look for answers. But for the life of me I can't figure out why I was drawn into something involving these guys.'

'Had you heard of either of them before?'

'No, but then I've been out of circulation. I rarely got to read a newspaper and I had no TV in my cell.'

'You want me to see what else there is on Martinez?'

'Sure.'

'In that case you'll have to pick Anna up.'

I looked down. I hadn't realized the baby was trying to climb up a leg of the chair.

'She's got that look on her face that comes when she's about to scream like a banshee,' Kate said.

I picked Anna up and gave her a smile. She stared into my eyes as if fascinated by them, and then started gurgling with a sloppy grin. It felt good to be holding this tiny living person on my lap. I rubbed her back and she snuggled against me. I could even feel her heartbeat.

'It says here that Julio Martinez has been running the San Antonio branch of the Texas Syndicate for about four years,' Kate said. 'He took over after his release from a short prison term for drug trafficking.'

She was reading more news stories thrown up by Google. Martinez was obviously a well-known gangster and the Feds had been trying desperately to put him away, but without success.

'According to this story, Martinez has been linked to no fewer than seventeen murders,' Kate said. 'Including the killings two months ago of four men whose bodies were dumped in an alleyway near the Alamo.'

I'd heard about that. It'd been a hot topic on death row. One of the guards had told me that the dead men were all police informants. The web was teeming with information about the Texas Syndicate, as well as all the other street gangs that had become the new face of organized crime in the US. The Syndicate was more prominent than most. It was formed in one of the state's prisons during the seventies when a group of Mexicans began extorting and raping weaker inmates. The Syndicate grew at an alarming rate and during the eighties gained full control of the prison system's drug trade across Texas.

The gang was now a highly organized outfit with a proper chain of command from foot soldier to chairman. There was even a board of directors who monitored the gang's funds, approved of new members and authorized killings. Joining the gang was a life commitment and all members had to bring in money.

The more I read the more puzzled I became. Questions were piling up inside my head. Did Julio Martinez have anything to do with my faked execution? Why was he waiting for me in the restaurant and what would he have told me if I'd gone inside? Did he have a relationship with Aaron Vance, the FBI agent who was trying to put him behind bars?

It was hard to believe that Martinez would have had anything to do with the attempt on my life. After all, he'd waved at me through the window, expecting me to join him at his table. He was probably just as shocked as I was when the gunman struck. I would have given a king's ransom to talk to him, but there was no way that was going to happen. I had no idea where he hung out and he'd almost certainly be heavily protected.

It meant I'd have to concentrate my efforts on Vance and the two lawyers, Garcia and Cruz. I was beginning to think that maybe they were part of some clandestine conspiracy involving gangsters, lawyers and government agents.

The rational side of my brain was telling me to walk away and get as far from Texas as possible – that no good would come of trying to seek answers to all my questions.

But the other part of my brain, the emotional part, was telling me that I had to find out why Emily had been killed and who was ultimately responsible. I owed her that much.

'I've seen enough,' I said to Kate. 'It's time we headed for San Antonio.'

33

THANKS TO A couple of sleeping pills and almost half a bottle of whisky, Gideon Crane had managed to get a good night's sleep. But when he woke up at nine his head ached and his mouth was bone dry.

He rolled over and saw that the other side of the bed was empty. It surprised him because he usually heard Pauline when she got up first, which wasn't often.

He still felt tired but his mind had shifted into gear and he knew he would not be able to get back to sleep. He sat up, mashed the heels of his hands into his eye sockets, and sat still for a few seconds to assess whether or not he had a hangover. He did, but only a mild one.

Still, as he got out of bed his neck was stiff and his limbs sluggish. It felt like he had sludge running through his veins. He shuffled into the bathroom, took a leak, and decided to shower before going downstairs. He turned on the water and while it was heating up he went back into the bedroom to open the curtains. It was overcast outside and raining. All the colours in the garden were muted.

He was reminded of his conversation outside last night with Travis and how calmly the bastard had revealed that he was going to black-mail him. Crane knew he had no choice but to pay the $100,000. Travis was an evil low-life who would not think twice about carrying out his threat to expose the affair with Beth. In fact the money was already in Travis's account. Crane had transferred it from one of his own accounts before going to bed.

It was a price he had to pay to keep his political ambitions alive. But it grated like rough sandpaper on his nerve endings.

The shower battered the tiredness out of him. He stood under the power jets for a full five minutes, then dried himself and got dressed in a pair of shorts and loose-fitting shirt.

Pauline was in the kitchen drinking coffee at the breakfast bar when he got downstairs. She was dressed in her designer tracksuit, her hair pulled back from her face.

'I'm going to the gym,' she said. 'I'll be a couple of hours.'

There was something in her voice that told him she wasn't in the best of moods.

'Since when did you start going to the gym first thing in the morning?' he asked.

She smiled at him, but the smile didn't quite reach her eyes.

'Since I decided to go on a serious diet,' she said. 'I told you about it but you probably didn't take it in.'

He detected the thinly veiled sarcasm in her words but chose not to remark on it. She poured him a cup of coffee and handed it to him. At the same time she offered her cheek and he gave her a gentle kiss. Then she collected her bag and left the house. He was used to her moods and had decided long ago that it was best to ignore them.

He carried his coffee into his study, glad that he had some time to himself this morning. He needed to focus his mind on how to resolve the issue of Pauline's brother. There were very few options open to him and those that were – like confessing all or having Travis killed – were simply unpalatable. But he had a feeling that if he didn't do something the whole blackmail thing would blow up in his face.

He sat down behind his desk and heaved a sigh. Just then a message came through on his cell. He dug it from his pocket and saw that it was from Beth.

Call me asap

He felt a frisson of guilt because he hadn't thought about Beth all morning. And he hadn't yet told her that it was Travis who took her diary.

He rang her and she answered on the third ring.

'Hi there, sweetheart. I was actually about to call you when your message came through.'

'Have you seen the news?' she asked with a sense of urgency that unsettled him.

'No. Why?'

'Check it out. There was a shooting last night near Austin. Lee Jordan's sister was killed.'

It came as a shock to Crane and he was lost for words. He had seen

Emily Jordan many times when she attended her brother's trial. She'd been distraught the whole time and he had actually felt sorry for her. He'd been surprised that she hadn't attended the execution.

'What happened?' he asked.

'It's all a bit of a mystery apparently. Two FBI agents were also killed. All three were shot.'

'My God!'

'The FBI have taken over the case. A special agent named Vance was interviewed at the scene in the early hours.'

Crane experienced a jolt of recognition.

'Would that be special agent Aaron Vance?'

'I think that was the name on the screen caption,' Beth said.

'But he's based in San Antonio.'

'You know him then?'

'Not at all, but for some reason he showed an interest in Lee Jordan on the morning of the execution.'

'What do you mean?'

Crane realised he'd said too muc'.. What the governor had told him about Vance applying pressure to ensure the execution did not get stayed was in confidence. And he wasn't about to betray his old friend.

'Oh, forget it,' he said. 'Look, I'd better get across this before some reporter rings me for a quote.'

'Will you call me later?'

'Sure will, and listen, there's something you should know. It's about your diary.'

'What about it?'

He told her about Travis. She reacted badly, appalled that his brother-in-law had violated her home. She wanted to call the police, but he managed to calm her down and talk her out of it.

'I'll get your diary back,' he promised. 'And I've already transferred the money to him so the immediate crisis is over.'

'But this is wrong, Gideon. How dare that man break into my apartment?'

'Call Butler and get him to sweep your apartment for bugs,' he said, referring to the campaign's head of security. 'And don't worry. I'll keep Travis sweet until we no longer have to care about what he says.'

He sensed that Beth was keen to carry on the conversation. She was obviously upset and wanted him to comfort her. But he was anxious to get off the line so he could check out the news. He promised he would call later and told her he loved her.

As soon as he was off the phone he booted up his computer and surfed the online news sites. Beth had been right about the shootings being a mystery. The Feds were saying that the two agents had gone to the house in response to a call from Emily Jordan. As yet they didn't know who had carried out the killings, but a man was seen by neighbours running away from the house.

Aaron Vance was quoted on some of the sites, but there was no explanation as to why he was in charge of the investigation. Crane sat back in his chair and his face folded into a frown. He decided it was time to find out why Vance had called the governor before Lee Jordan's execution. Why were the Feds anxious to ensure that it went ahead without a delay? Did that have anything to do with last night's shootings at the sister's house?

Crane knew people in Washington who would try to find out if there was something going on that he ought to know about. But he didn't see why he couldn't get that information direct from the horse's mouth. Now was probably not a good time to call Vance, though. He'd have been working through the night. So Crane decided to ring him later. In the meantime, he'd have to ponder the prospect of seeing Lee Jordan's face on the TV and in the papers for weeks to come. And just when the bastard was about to become old news.

It was ironic – and so damned unfair.

34

KILLING A COP was not a job that Aaron Vance could delegate. Sure, the Bureau had access to men and women who carried out assassinations, but this was different. And besides, those so-called shooters couldn't always be relied on to get it right – as was demonstrated outside the restaurant when one of them was meant to kill Jordan.

Vance went alone to Kate Pena's house. He didn't anticipate that it would take long. A bullet to the head from a silenced pistol would be swift and efficient. He'd leave the body and when it was found the cops would assume he was killed by an old enemy or perhaps the man who had abducted his kid.

Vance had killed before so he knew what to expect. He had claimed two lives in the line of duty and he kept telling himself that this was also in the line of duty. Frank Larson could never be trusted not to blab about what he'd discovered. And that made him a serious threat to the Bureau, as well as to a government that would have to deal with the fallout if what happened to Lee Jordan got out.

Knowledge was power and they couldn't take the chance that Larson would use it at some point to advance his own personal agenda. It helped Vance that Larson was apparently a douche bag bastard and a bad cop.

Vance had accessed his file before leaving the office and discovered that he had form for using unwarranted force against suspects. He'd also been suspended on one occasion for attacking a colleague.

But what really got Vance fired up was that Larson had lied about Kate Pena being his girlfriend. They'd split up months ago because he'd beaten her up and she'd filed a complaint against him, claiming it wasn't the first time he'd hit her.

But it *was* going to be the last time, Vance told himself. Larson wouldn't be attacking any more defenceless women. He'd thrown his last punch and inflicted his last wound. Now it was his turn to suffer.

Vance wanted to hate Larson and he wanted to believe that the world would be a better place without him. It was always easier to kill someone when you thought they deserved to die.

Vance parked his car two blocks away from Kate Pena's house. He put on dark fold-around shades and a plain baseball cap. He'd already removed his suit jacket and put on a navy blue windbreaker.

Before alighting the car he screwed the silencer onto the muzzle of the nine millimetre Glock that he'd kept in his office safe. He'd confiscated it a year ago from a Texas Syndicate foot soldier. It had never been fired and the serial number was filed down. Vance had always known it would come in useful one day.

It was a five minute walk to the house and Vance kept his head low and his hands in his pockets, where the right one maintained a firm grip on the Glock.

As he walked he tried to concentrate on his breathing. His body was fizzing with adrenaline. He found it hard to believe that this was really happening. Murders, whether justified or not, had never been a part of his job description as Special Agent in Charge. He was way out of his comfort zone and his stomach twisted with grim apprehension.

But this was the right thing to do. Of that he was convinced. No way was he prepared to risk any more fuck-ups. Not with so much at stake.

The street was empty. Most people were at work and the drizzle was keeping others inside. He kept his head down as he approached the house. Larson's car was parked outside in the same position it was in when Vance had last seen it. He scurried up the pathway and was about to ring the bell when the door opened and Larson was standing there.

'What's with the disguise?' the detective said, a note of concern in his voice. 'You trying not to be noticed?'

Vance simply pushed past him into the hall.

'Shut the door,' Vance said. 'We need to talk.'

Larson closed the door and followed Vance along the hall into the living room. Vance took off his shades and put them in his pocket.

'We've got to be careful,' he said. 'What I'm about to tell you is heavy shit. Are you sure you haven't told anyone what you already know?'

'Of course I'm sure. I could barely believe it myself. Now I just want to know what's going down. How come I was attacked by a guy who was supposedly executed by the state? I know you Bureau people like pulling crazy stunts that are not always legal, but this beats the shit out of anything I've ever heard.'

'Is anyone else in the house?' Vance asked.

Larson gave an impatient shake of his head. 'I told you. I just dropped by to pick up my car.'

Vance could feel his heart stuttering against his ribs. He knew that if he didn't act quickly Larson would get suspicious.

So he reached into his pocket, pulled out the Glock, and took aim with both hands.

Larson cocked his head to one side. 'What the hell—'

But Vance didn't wait for him to finish the sentence. He squeezed the trigger and put a bullet in the centre of the detective's forehead.

35

WE TOOK THE freeway south from Austin to San Antonio, the quickest and most direct route. There was a chance the Explorer would be spotted if the cops were on the lookout for it, but there was a lot of holiday traffic so I figured it was a risk worth taking.

I was behind the wheel, and made sure I stayed just below the speed limit. Kate hadn't said a word since leaving the motel. She knew I had to pull my thoughts together and try to make sense of what I'd learned. At the same time I was under pressure to come up with a plan of action – where to go and what to do next.

I wanted to avenge my sister's death if I could, and to somehow ensure that Kate and her child had a future. I felt a heavy burden of responsibility for them, having dragged them into something sinister and perilous – a situation that I now knew involved the FBI, a notorious street gang, and a city law firm that for some reason liked to keep a low profile. I was desperate to know what was going on. I'd been the subject of what must rank as one of the most elaborate cons ever – a faked execution under the watchful eyes of a bunch of witnesses.

And now I was being pursued by government agents who were prepared to commit murder in order to protect themselves and their ghastly secrets. On the face of it my situation seemed completely hopeless, as did my chances of taking care of Kate and her daughter. But I did have one thing going for me. That was the threat I posed to the Bureau and in turn the whole fucking establishment. It gave me a certain amount of leverage, an edge.

I just had to think of a way to use it.

The decision on what to do when we reached San Antonio was taken out of my hands by Kate when we were five miles from the city.

'I want you to take me home,' she said.

There was a lot of noise inside the Explorer. The windshield wipers were thudding back and forth and the baby was demanding attention in the back. Not crying exactly. More like a constant high-pitched whine that grated on the ears. So I got Kate to repeat what she'd said because I thought I'd misheard.

'I said I want to go home.'

I shot her a glance. 'Are you serious? How can you?'

She stared straight ahead, her eyes wide, jaw set hard.

'I don't mean to stay,' she said. 'I just need to collect some stuff for myself and the baby.'

'I don't think that's a good idea.'

'Well I do. It won't take long.'

'We don't even know if your place is empty,' I said. 'Frank Larson might still be there cuffed to the radiator.'

'But he's had all night to wake up and call for help. Unless you took his cell from him.'

'I didn't.'

'There you go then.'

'Do you have a phone in the house?' I asked. 'A landline?'

'Of course.'

'Then call it and see if anyone picks up.'

She rummaged in her bag for her cell and switched it on. It pinged with several messages.

'Two are from Frank,' she said, as she read through them. 'Both were sent late last night. In the first he's asking me where I am and if the baby and me are OK. In the second he says he's at the hospital. That means he probably won't be at the house.'

'I'm still not convinced it's the right thing to do,' I said.

'Well I am,' Kate said in a steely voice. 'I never want to stay in that house again so I want to get my stuff. As much as I can carry at least. And that includes some jewellery that I can sell. I'm fast running out of cash and we'll need it if we're going to stay in hotels.'

I shook my head. 'It's far too risky.'

She fixed me with a solid stare. 'Look, if we get there and it doesn't look safe we'll drive on by. OK?'

I sighed heavily, like a ball deflating. 'Fair enough. Just tell me how to get there.'

36

VANCE WAS BACK in his office thirty-five minutes after committing murder. He was still telling himself that he'd done it in the line of duty and in the public interest. And he repeated over and over in his head the mantra that had been drummed into him during his training.

Sometimes an agent will have to do things he or she doesn't want to do to serve the greater good.

Vance was a Bureau man through and through. He had devoted his life to it and it had cost him his marriage. He believed passionately in what it stood for and could never imagine working for any other organization.

But there were a lot of things he didn't question that were at odds with the FBI's core values – values that included uncompromising institutional integrity and rigorous obedience to the American Constitution. Dubious practices were too often tolerated within the Bureau and there were wrongs he did not try to put right, even though they sometimes caused him to have sleepless nights. But if it had been any other way he would not so easily have carried out the cold-blooded assassination of a serving police officer. That, surely, was a demonstration of his complete and utter loyalty to the cause.

'It had to be done,' Sam Boyd said, after Vance had briefed him on what had happened.

'I know,' Vance said.

'And we had no choice but to act quickly.'

'I know that too.'

Vance had put his suit jacket back on having dumped the windbreaker and baseball cap along with the gun. He was still shaking a little and there was an acidic taste in his mouth.

Boyd was pacing the office, wearing a worried expression, his apprehension growing. He told Vance there was still no sign of Lee Jordan or the woman and child. And he said that in Washington there was growing concern about what was happening.

'The director has been on the phone twice already since I've been here,' Boyd said. 'He sounds like he's fit to explode.'

That did not come as a surprise to Vance. The longer Jordan was free then the more likely it was that it would all come out. If Jordan spread the word about himself then they were in trouble. They couldn't very well assassinate everyone who knew the truth. Their best hope was still to catch him and kill him quickly, before he was able to wreak total havoc. Easier said than done, of course, unless he made a mistake or they got lucky. But so far the luck had been with Jordan and the only mistake he'd made had been to go to his sister's house.

The two men spent the next twenty minutes taking stock of the situation and liaising with some of the agents in the field. They'd issued a general description of Jordan – or rather the man seen running away from the house in Mountain City – and warned that he was armed and extremely dangerous. All police officers had been told that if they arrested him they were to inform the FBI without delay and he should be isolated immediately so he couldn't talk to anyone. Both Vance and Boyd knew that such an instruction would probably prove ineffective, but they had to say something in the hope that they could limit any potential damage.

At 10 a.m. Liz poked her head in to tell Vance he had a call from Congressman Crane.

Vance frowned. 'Shit. What's that about?'

'There's only one way to find out,' Boyd said.

Vance put his phone on speaker and waited for the call to be put through. He had never met Crane, but of course he knew a lot about the guy who was running for the Republican ticket in the Presidential nomination race.

'Is that Special Agent Vance?' Crane said when he came on.

'Yes it is, sir. What can I do for you?'

Crane cleared his throat. 'I assume you know that my wife Kimberley was murdered by Lee Jordan.'

Vance felt his heart lurch. 'Of course, sir. I'm well aware of that.'

'Well there's something I need to ask you, Agent Vance. I appreciate that you must be very busy right now with those shootings up near

Austin, but it is important, at least to me.'

'Go ahead, Mr Crane. What is it you want to know?'

'I want to know why you called the governor on the day of the execution to urge him not to grant Jordan a stay,' Crane said. 'And I want to know if what happened last night with Jordan's sister had anything to do with it.'

Vance thought quickly and said, 'There's no connection whatsoever, sir. We're beginning to believe that the shootings were carried out by someone known to Miss Jordan. It possibly involved drugs.'

'I see. Then what about your conversation with the governor? It seems odd to me that the FBI should apply pressure that way, although I have to say I'm glad you did. The last thing I wanted was for the bastard to be granted a stay of execution.'

Vance was a long time answering. Eventually, he said, 'There's a simple explanation, Mr Crane. I'll tell you but I must ask you to treat it in confidence.'

'Of course. That goes without saying.'

'Well I was instructed by someone in Washington to help ensure the execution was not put off. A lot of people up there were concerned that if there was a delay it would be a major distraction for you during your election campaign.'

Boyd gave Vance the thumbs up and Vance shrugged – it was the best he could come up with. But it obviously convinced the congressman.

'I'm grateful to you for telling me, Agent Vance,' Crane said. 'I'm only sorry you can't give me the name or names of whoever issued the instruction so that I can thank them personally.'

'There's no need, Mr Crane. Everyone is just glad it's all over and Lee Jordan is history. Now you can focus on your campaign.'

'And you can concentrate on finding out who shot your agents,' Crane said. 'Thank you again for your time.'

After hanging up, Vance felt his heart pounding in his throat.

'You did well,' Boyd said. 'I don't think I'd have been able to come up with such a good lie so quickly.'

Vance mustered a smile. 'Let's hope he doesn't pursue it. Could get awkward.'

At that moment Vance's phone rang again. He picked it up. It was Daniels.

'There's been a development, boss,' he said. 'Kate Pena's cellphone is back on. The guys are in the process of triangulating the signal. If it stays on we should have the location in a few minutes.'

'Bingo,' Vance said.

37

IT HAD STOPPED raining by the time we got to Kate's house. The clouds were breaking up and the sun was starting to force its way through.

In the daylight her street looked pretty rundown. It was wet and empty and grey. Most of the houses were in need of a fresh coat of paint. The front yards were cluttered and untidy and there were small pot holes in the road.

'That's Frank's car,' Kate said.

It was a Lexus. I'd seen it when we hurried away from the house last evening. It was parked in exactly the same place at the curb, just to one side of the short driveway.

'He probably hasn't come back for it yet,' I said. 'But to be on the safe side call the landline again.'

I slowed to a stop maybe thirty yards back from the house while Kate made the call.

'Still no answer,' she said.

When I pulled the Explorer onto the driveway, I switched off the engine and waited anxiously for someone to come out of the house. But nobody did so I assumed it was empty. I looked in the back seat. Anna was sleeping, her chin resting on her chest.

'Are you going to wake her?' I asked.

'No. She'll be OK. I won't be long.'

I took the key from the ignition. Kate's house key was on the same ring. I lifted the gun out of the door pocket, flicked off the safety.

I still wasn't comfortable with what we were doing. I would rather have taken Kate straight to a hotel. But she was insistent and I realized she had a point. I had no idea how long we'd be on the run. She obviously couldn't go on spending money on new things as well as hotel accommodation.

But as I walked up to the house my palms felt sweaty and the air around me seemed to be choked with a sense of foreboding. The street was still empty. The only sound the distant drone of traffic.

I handed Kate her keys but she didn't need them because the door was ajar and I noticed the lock was broken. I made sure I went in first. In the daylight the place was even less impressive. The hallway was narrow and gloomy. The yellow wallpaper was old and peeling at the joins.

'Anyone home?' I called out.

It seemed a stupid thing to say seeing as it was Kate who lived here, but I felt I had to say something. There was no reply. The house was dead quiet. No ticking clocks. No creaking timbers. No rush of water through the pipes.

The bedroom door to my right was open. The baby's room. I peered inside. Empty. On the left, the kitchen. Also empty. It was just as I remembered it from the previous evening. It looked as though nothing had been moved, except that Frank Larson was no longer cuffed to a radiator.

The next door on the right was slightly open. It was the main bedroom. Kate's room. Clothes were strewn across the duvet from where she had hurriedly packed.

The living room door at the end of the hallway was closed. I gripped the handle and turned it. The first thing that struck me when the door opened was the thick smell of cordite in the air.

The second thing was the body on the floor. Frank Larson was lying on his back and the front of his head was missing.

Kate was right behind me and saw the body a fraction of a second after I did. She let out a deafening shriek as I rushed into the room.

I stood over the body and felt my heart shudder at the sight of all the blood and shattered bone. It was pointless checking for signs of life because I knew there wouldn't be any.

Detective Frank Larson was very dead. The wall behind him was sprayed with blood. Whoever had murdered him had fired from close range and the bullet had pounded into his forehead, blowing his skull apart.

'Oh my God,' Kate gasped.

She backed out of the room into the hallway on shaky legs. Her face was scrunched up as though in pain, her mouth gaping in a soundless scream.

I strode out of the room, grabbed her arm, pulled her along the hallway to the front door. She became hysterical the moment we stepped outside. She dropped to her knees on the small patch of wet grass, shaking her head and sobbing uncontrollably.

I stood beside her and bent over, fighting a sudden urge to spew up my guts. My mind started racing along with my heart, telling me that Larson must have been murdered by the Feds. By Aaron Vance and his crew. Somehow they had followed my trail to this house last night and had found Larson cuffed to the radiator. Maybe he told them he'd recognized me. Or maybe they just killed him because they weren't prepared to take any chances.

Whatever the circumstances, his summary execution did not bode well for Kate. These bastards were ruthless beyond measure. It seemed inconceivable now that they would let her live, even if she made them believe she didn't know who I was.

'Come on,' I said. 'We should go.'

I was about to help her to her feet when I heard the roar of an engine. Looking up, I saw two familiar vehicles tearing towards us along the road.

The Taurus and the Dodge.

My chest exploded in a spasm of panic. I reacted by grabbing Kate's arm and jerking her up. The intention was to make it look like she was my hostage. I was still holding the gun so I raised it and fired a shot into the air. The two vehicles slewed to a halt about twenty yards from the house. The doors were thrown open and men armed with pistols jumped out onto the road.

For just a moment it looked as though a stand-off situation was going to develop. But then the sound of a baby crying came from inside the Explorer and Kate's maternal instinct kicked in. She shook her arm free of my grip and made a dash for the vehicle.

'Anna!' she yelled. 'I've got to get my baby.'

I was left standing on the front yard, fully exposed and unsure what to do. I aimed the gun at the Feds. There were five of them spread out in the road and one of them was Aaron Vance. Their arms were out-stretched and their pistols were pointing at me.

I was maybe three steps from the front door of the house and ten steps away from the Explorer. Everything froze for a couple of tense seconds when Kate reached the vehicle. I thought she was going to open the rear door to get at her daughter. But instead she stood with her back to it protectively and spread out her arms.

'There's a baby in the car,' she screamed at the Feds. 'Don't shoot.'

Then she turned to me and said, 'Run. There's nothing you can do for me.'

There was no way I could leave her alone so I took a side-step towards her. But it prompted Vance to shout a warning.

'Don't move. Just stay where you are and drop the gun.'

I ignored him and took another step. In response one of Vance's men opened up with a warning shot. I immediately returned fire. The Feds ran for cover and I instinctively moved back towards the house and away from Kate.

Two bullets slammed into the timber either side of the front door as I threw myself inside. More shots were fired and one of the bullets thumped into the hallway wall.

I caught a glimpse of Kate cowering against the side of the Explorer. There was no way I could get to her without taking a bullet. She was on her own now. There was nothing I could do for her but hope that Vance would not deem it necessary to kill her.

I scrambled on all fours along the hall and into the kitchen. In the hope of slowing them down, I let off a shot at the window, shattering the glass. Then I homed in on the door to the back garden. My only escape route. The key was in the lock. A quick turn and the door was open. I rushed headlong into the rear garden and then across a small soggy lawn to a low wooden fence.

I heaved myself over the fence into another garden that was slightly smaller and better looked after. I heard shouting behind me but I didn't look back. I just kept running, along the path at the side of the house, and then into another residential street. I veered to the right and sprinted along the pavement.

After about thirty yards I got lucky. A guy in a black SUV was just backing out of his driveway. He didn't see me until it was too late. I pulled the driver's door open and aimed my gun at his face. He braked instinctively and the SUV jolted to a halt.

'Get out,' I shouted. 'If you resist I'll kill you.'

The guy was no hero. He got quickly out of the car. I jumped straight in behind the wheel and pulled the door shut. Then I stamped hard on the gas and the SUV shot out onto the road.

There was no sign of the Feds in the rear-view mirror as I roared off. I knew they'd soon be on my tail so I had very little time to put distance between them and me. But as I drove I was oblivious to the speed I was travelling at and the direction I was going in.

All I could think about was Kate and her baby. And how I'd been forced to abandon them.

38

GIDEON CRANE FROWNED when he saw his wife's car pull up on the driveway. He looked at his watch. She'd only been gone an hour, which was hardly enough time for a proper workout at the gym. Normally she took twice that long. So he wondered why she was back so soon.

He turned away from the window and switched his attention back to the TV. He was still behind his desk and still following with interest the story that was unfolding on the screen.

The murders in Mountain City continued to dominate the news. The two FBI agents who'd been shot dead hadn't yet been named. And the killer was still at large. Neighbours who were interviewed claimed they'd heard the shots. One had seen a guy run out of the house and get into a waiting car, which suggested that there was more than one perpetrator.

Reporters were inevitably speculating that the killings were somehow connected to Lee Jordan's execution, but the FBI were saying this was highly unlikely. Crane was curious, but at the same time incensed that Jordan was still haunting him. The bastard's photo was popping up with alarming frequency, and each time Crane saw it he felt a chill in his bones.

It was like he was living through that terrible night ten years ago all over again in his head. The two men in ski masks bursting into his home. The explosion of gunfire. Jordan's desperate expression as he came charging forward. And then Kimberley lying on the floor. The images were crowding his mind and causing his eyes to become moist.

He was so caught up in this new blast of raw emotion that he wasn't aware that Pauline had entered his study and was standing in front of his desk.

Her sudden appearance made him jump and he was just about to smile at her when he realized she was staring at him with a look of cold contempt on her face.

'What's wrong?' he said.

She produced from behind her back a large padded envelope and without so much as an explanation emptied the contents on the desk. It took a second for him to realize what he was staring at and when he did he felt his heart shift in his chest. Four colour photographs and a book with a pink cover. The photos were of him and Beth together. In one of them they were kissing. The book had the word *Diary* emblazoned in gold lettering on the front.

'You low life piece of scum,' Pauline yelled at him.

Her words hit him like a series of blows to the solar plexus. He was too shocked to respond straight away. He just sat there feeling the heat of her anger, and wondering why he had been so stupid as to give her brother $100,000.

'I suspected for months that something was going on,' she said. 'I just didn't want to believe it. Not after all we'd been through. Maybe it wouldn't be so bad if you were just fucking the bitch. But it's clear from what she's written in her diary that it's a lot more than that. You bastard.'

She was struggling to hold back the tears and the hurt in her eyes made him ashamed of himself. Christ, it wasn't meant to be like this. And it wasn't meant to happen yet. This was a fuck-up on a grand scale. Horrible, ugly and potentially hugely damaging. He could see the headlines in his mind's eye.

Congressman quits Presidential race in disgrace.

Crane cheats on wife number two.

It would all come out. The details of his affair with Beth. His adulterous relationship with Pauline at the time of Kimberley's murder. He tried to swallow against the dryness in his throat. He opened his mouth to speak but nothing came out.

'God forbid that someone like you should ever become President,' Pauline said. 'You're a disgusting, deceitful excuse for a man. And you're stupid. Did you not think that I would find out? You were becoming more distant. And you stopped asking me how I was. I needed to know if something was going on so I asked Travis to find out. And he did. And he said you made it really easy for him.'

Crane managed to swallow down the growing lump in his throat.

He said, 'Do you know about the money I transferred into his account last night?'

'He just told me about it,' she said with a smirk. 'And do you know what? I'm glad he ripped you off. The fact that you were prepared to let him blackmail you makes you even more contemptible.'

She continued to glare at him, her lips pulled back, her muscles like rope under the pale skin of her neck. He knew he would not be able to placate her, or reason with her. She was too far gone for that.

'I know what's going through your warped mind,' she said. 'You're wondering if I'm going to bring an end to your naked ambition. Well for your information I don't know yet. I need to think it through and decide what's best for me. But I will tell you this. If you don't fire that whore right away then you can kiss goodbye to ever seeing the inside of the Oval Office.'

And with that she spun round and stormed out of the study, slamming the door behind her.

39

AFTER DRIVING AROUND for ten minutes I found myself in the centre of San Antonio, close to the River Walk. I pulled over to the side of the road and killed the engine.

A flood of thoughts, incoherent and corrosive, were rushing though my tired brain. I felt angry, guilty, frustrated. The inside of my chest was burning and blood was pounding in the top of my head.

I couldn't keep Kate's face out of my mind. I wanted to believe that she would be all right, that Vance wouldn't harm her, but I wasn't able to convince myself of it. His people had already killed Emily and Larson. So why would they spare Kate?

A sudden burst of music made my jump. I thought the radio had switched itself on, but I quickly realized it was coming from a man's jacket that was hanging on a hook behind the front passenger seat. I leaned over and pulled it down. In the inside pocket I found a cell-phone. I stared at it for a good ten seconds before I felt compelled to answer it.

'Is that you, Lee?' It was a familiar voice.

I didn't respond, but neither did I hang up. I waited for him to speak again.

'This is Aaron Vance here,' he said. 'The guy who owns the SUV told us he left his phone inside. I was hoping you'd pick up because we need to talk.'

'What have you done with the woman and her baby?' I said.

'They're safe, Lee. We're going to look after them.'

'She doesn't know who I am so there's no reason to hurt her.'

'We don't intend to. I promise.'

'I don't believe you,' I said.

'Look, I give you my word that no harm will come to them. Or you, Lee. Just let us come and get you and we can talk about what's happened. There's no reason to be scared. You've got it all wrong.'

'You bastards killed my sister. And you tried to kill me.'

'The man who tried to kill you outside the restaurant wasn't one of us.'

'You told me he was.'

'We thought he was, but someone paid him to take you out. We were as shocked as you were, but you didn't give us a chance to explain that.'

'What about my sister?'

Vance cleared his throat. 'My men went there in case you turned up. They were meant to bring you to me and not harm you or your sister. But as you know that went wrong. I'm really sorry. It was tragic.'

'This is all bullshit,' I said. 'You're intent on eliminating everyone who knows I'm alive. Like Frank Larson.'

'We had nothing to do with that.'

'You're a liar.'

'It's true. I didn't know he was dead until I just went into the house.'

Fury burned in the pit of my stomach. I wanted to get my hands on the bastard and wring his neck.

'So why did you fake the execution?' I said. 'What was the point?'

'It's a complicated story, Lee. I'll tell you everything but not on the phone. Let's get together. You have to trust me.'

'Why should I?'

'Because I'm here for you, Lee. You've got nowhere to go. You can't keep running. If you want a new life then you need a new identity. We'll give you that. Just like I told you.'

A warning light flashed in my mind. With all their technology the Feds would probably be trying to get a fix on the phone signal as we spoke. Maybe that was how they'd managed to track us down so soon after we arrived at Kate's house. We'd used her cell to call her landline.

Fuck!

I ended the call abruptly and threw the phone out of the window. It smashed on the pavement. Then I turned on the engine, pressed the gas to the carpet, and got the hell away from there.

Twenty minutes later I pulled up opposite the offices of Garcia and Cruz, attorneys at law, having put the address into the SUV's satnav. It was a sedate street with rows of trees and very little traffic.

I recognized the building as the one Martinez had been standing outside in the online news photograph. It was a two-storey affair that was part of a smart red-brick terrace. The building was narrow, with a single front door and a window on the ground floor. There were two other windows on the upper floor and no obvious access to the back of the building.

Raymond Garcia was my only real lead. I was convinced he figured in whatever was happening. Why else would his business card have been left in the jacket I'd been given? So maybe there was something in his office that would either lead me to him or help me unravel what was going on. But it was clearly not going to be easy to get inside – if at all possible. The building was probably alarmed and I had no tools to help me force open a window or door.

But as I was agonizing over what to do, I got lucky. A dark blue BMW pulled up outside the building. A guy in a light grey suit got out. He had dark hair and was in his late forties or early fifties.

He mounted the steps to the front door, which he opened with a key. Then he disappeared inside. I thought there was a good chance the guy was either Raymond Garcia or Michael Cruz.

I tucked the gun into my waistband and covered it with the now grubby Longhorns T-shirt. I was still wearing the baseball cap, but I wanted something to cover my face. I found it in the glove compartment, a long soiled rag that was probably used for cleaning the inside of the windshield.

I got out of the SUV and glanced up and down the street. Not much was going on. I saw a guy putting out the trash and a woman walking away from me along the pavement. I hurried across the road and up to the front door. There was a security buzzer on the wall next to it and underneath a small metal plaque with Garcia and Cruz engraved on it. I pressed the buzzer and had to wait twenty seconds for a response.

'The office is closed until after Thanksgiving,' a man's voice said. 'Please come back on Monday.'

'I have an urgent delivery for a Mr Raymond Garcia,' I said.

'Well he's not in right now. What is it?'

'A package. It needs a signature.'

A pause, then: 'OK, I'd better take it. I'm his partner. I'll be right there.'

I lowered my head and wrapped the rag around my face, covering my nose and mouth. I tied a knot at the back and braced myself. I figured I was now everyone's idea of a nightmare – a guy holding a gun and wearing a hat, shades and a face mask. Cruz was going to get the shock of his life.

In the event I didn't give him a chance to react. As the door started to open I pushed at it with such force that the guy was knocked onto the floor. I rushed in, kicked the door shut behind me, and pointed the gun at him.

'Do as I tell you and you'll survive this,' I yelled.

He paled instantly. His expression was somewhere between terror and confusion.

We were in a carpeted reception area with a desk and a water cooler on a stand. There were three doors leading off it and one was open.

'Why are you here if the office is closed?' I asked him.

He gazed at me fearfully. 'I just got back from a business trip. I stopped by on my way from the airport to pick up some papers.'

'So you're the only person in the building?'

'That's right. But if it's money you want there's cash in the safe. Lots of it. So there's no need to get violent. Just take it and go.'

'Are you Michael Cruz?'

He frowned. 'Yeah, that's me. I'm a lawyer.'

I waved the gun. 'Get to your feet.'

He struggled up and I got him to turn away from me while I patted him down like a cop. His suit was expensive, probably Italian, and the body inside it was lean and toned. He wasn't armed, but then I hadn't really expected him to be.

'Where's Raymond Garcia?' I said.

He turned to look at me, his eyebrows climbing up his forehead. 'Ray? Why do you want him?'

'I need to talk to him. So don't pretend you don't know where I can find him.'

'I haven't spoken to him in three days.'

'But you're partners. You must know where he is.'

His eyes widened suddenly and he raised his hands, palms out. 'Jesus, are you with the Syndicate?'

I didn't answer so he assumed I was.

'Look, man you gotta know that whatever Ray has been up to I'm not involved. That's the God's honest truth. I'm straight with you guys. Martinez knows that. He knows I'm loyal.'

'So what's Garcia been up to?' I said.

He shook his head. 'I don't know. Not for sure. I'm just saying.'

I raised the gun and aimed it at his face. He let out a creaking gasp.

'Let me be clear about one thing,' I said. 'When I ask a question, I want an answer. If I don't get one, or if I think you're lying to me, I'm going to smash the butt of this gun against your face. You got that?'

He swallowed a huge lump and nodded. 'Please don't hurt me. I've done nothing wrong. You have to believe that.'

'You'll need to convince me,' I said. 'So start with your partner. What's he been up to?'

He chewed on his bottom lip, said, 'You need to ask him that. He's probably at home for Thanksgiving. I can give you his address if you don't have it.'

I swiped the gun across his face. He was thrown sideways into the desk before collapsing on the floor. He moaned and put a hand against his left cheek. Blood trickled through his fingers from a rough cut.

'I told you I want answers,' I said. 'Not a bunch of crap. So let's try again. Tell me what Garcia has been up to.'

It took him a few seconds to recover. He sat up with his back against the side of the desk and wiped blood away from his face with his sleeve.

'There's no need to hit me,' he said. 'Just stay calm. I've got to get my head round this. You've taken me by surprise.'

'Just tell me what you know.'

'That's just the point. I don't know anything for sure.'

'So what do you suspect?'

He blinked a couple of times and said, 'I think maybe he's been misappropriating funds. I've noticed things in the accounts. I was going to talk to him about it because I knew you guys would find out eventually. If he has been doing it then he's a stupid motherfucker.'

'Are you talking about Texas Syndicate funds?'

He knitted his brow. 'What the hell else would I mean?'

When I didn't say anything it dawned on him.

'Shit, you're not with the Syndicate are you?'

I shrugged. 'Never said I was.'

A shadow crossed his face. 'So who the hell are you? What do you want?'

'I'm the one asking the questions,' I said. 'Tell me what your relationship is with the Texas Syndicate.'

He made steady, unflinching eye contact with me.

'Look, Mister. I don't want to. . . .'

I moved towards him, raised the gun above his head as though I was going to hit him again.

'OK, OK,' he said. 'It's no fucking secret anyway. We're the legal representatives for the Syndicate. They're our only client. We deal mainly with Martinez, who runs the show in this part of Texas.'

'What do you do for them?'

'We mainly look after the money. We help to launder and invest it. And we advise them on all kinds of stuff.'

'You're talking about money from their illicit operations?'

He nodded. 'For sure – drugs, prostitution, gambling. It runs into tens of millions every year.'

'So why do they use your firm?'

'We're very small, very discreet and very good. They get our undivided attention. Plus, Ray and I are half-Mexican, which helps.'

It made sense. There were hundreds of law firms across the country involved in organized crime, the highest profile ones being those aligned to the Italian Mafia. The firms fell into two categories. There were those who represented the gangsters in court and did what they could to keep them out of prison. They didn't care if their clients were guilty of the most heinous crimes, so long as they got their retainers and bonuses. Then there were the law firms like Garcia and Cruz who took care of the business side of the operations. They tended to keep a low profile and handled things like salaries, offshore accounts and property portfolios. They helped set up legitimate businesses with dirty money and ensured the cash was always on the move.

'Where does Aaron Vance come into it?' I said.

Cruz gave me a surprised look. 'You mean the FBI guy here in San Antonio?'

I nodded. 'What's his relationship with you guys and Julio Martinez?'

'I don't know what you mean by relationship. Vance has been gunning for Martinez and the Syndicate for a long time. It's a fucking war out there on the streets and Vance is the enemy.'

'Is he on the take?'

'Not as far as I know. If he was it would have shown up in the books.'

'Could there be a link between him and your partner that you're not aware of?'

He started to speak, but stopped himself and gave it some thought.

'If there was I'm sure I would know about it,' he said.

I felt he was telling the truth, which suggested to me that he didn't know of any arrangement involving Raymond Garcia, Julio Martinez and Aaron Vance.

'Why mention Vance?' Cruz asked. 'Have you heard something? Is that what this shit is about? You think Ray is involved with the Feds?'

I was certain of it. It would explain why Garcia's business cards were in the suit. Maybe the suit had belonged to Garcia?

I just couldn't get my head around any of it and it was driving me crazy. There were still too many unanswered questions. Like what was the nature of the relationship between Vance and Garcia? Why did Vance take me into the city for a dinner date with a gangster who happened to be Garcia's main client? Why was I sprung from the execution chamber? And was Vance telling the truth when he said he had not expected his own agent to try to kill me?

Cruz suddenly broke into my thoughts, his voice tinny and strained.

'Look, I don't know who you are but this is clearly heavy shit and I don't want you thinking that I'm part of whatever is going on here. I just look after the accounts. I hardly ever see the Syndicate people. Ray handles all that. It's him you should be talking to.'

'Then give me his address,' I said.

'It's in my office.'

'Get up.'

His office was through the open door. It was surprisingly small but tastefully furnished. There was a large teak desk and bookshelves on two of the walls. He copied out Garcia's address for me from a leather-bound book.

'He lives alone,' he said. 'A house just outside the city.'

I slipped the piece of paper with the address on into my pocket.

'Where's the safe you mentioned?' I said.

He bit on his lip and didn't answer. So I asked him again more forcefully.

'It's in Ray's office,' he said.

'Then let's go get that money you offered.'

He hesitated. 'But I'm not sure I can remember the combination.'

I grabbed his arm and pushed him towards the door.

'You've got a choice, Cruz,' I said. 'Open the safe and live or clam up and die.'

It was a wall safe and it was hidden behind a large framed photo of San Antonio that had been taken from the air. It took Cruz four turns of the dial to get it open.

My eyes lit up when I saw that it contained bundles of hundred dollar bills along with various documents.

'How much is there?' I said.

'About eighty grand.'

My heart bounced in my chest.

'Why so much?'

'It belongs to Martinez. It's for paying off officials, including the cops.'

Even back in the day when Sean and I were on the rampage I had never laid eyes on so much cash.

'I'll need a bag,' I said.

'There's a holdall in my office.'

We went back into his office and he took a leather holdall from a cabinet. Then I told him to lie on the floor while I snatched two power cables from the back of his computer and used them to hogtie him. He didn't try to resist. He was just relieved that I wasn't going to end his life.

'You gonna tell me who you are?' he said as I prepared to gag him.

'No point,' I said. 'You wouldn't believe me if I did.'

I packed the money into the holdall and then searched Garcia's office. But I found nothing of interest and I wasn't savvy enough with the computer to see what was stored on it.

Finally I ripped the rag from my face and let myself out of the front door. The sun had broken through the clouds and steam was rising from the street. I checked my watch. It was just after eleven. With luck Garcia would be in when I got to his house. And I'd hopefully move a step nearer to finding out what the hell I was caught up in.

40

Raymond Garcia lived in a development of large and small detached houses. It was a cosy upscale enclave – the perfect habitat for bankers, lawyers and media types.

By the time I got there the sun was a blazing ball in the sky. Only shreds of cloud remained. I drove past Garcia's house at school-zone speed to get a look at it. When I reached the end of his road I doubled back.

The house was a two-storey grey-brick property with bay windows and a double garage. All the houses had short driveways. But quite a few cars were parked along both sides of the road and I guessed they belonged to people who were staying with friends and relatives for Thanksgiving.

There was no car on his driveway and no sign of life. The only way I was going to find out if he was in was to take the most direct approach. I got out of the vehicle and removed the coat and hat so I'd look less conspicuous. Then I strolled casually up to the front door and rang the bell. No answer. I tried again, but there was still no answer.

I stood on his porch and wondered what to do next. I heard a child laughing along the street. Two cars drove slowly by. After about a minute I went back to the SUV and settled down to wait in the hope that he would show up. I knew I couldn't wait for long. Michael Cruz would eventually be discovered and would alert his partner and the Syndicate. But I reckoned I had a couple of hours.

It gave me time to think. And there was a lot to think about. The money for one thing. Eighty thousand dollars. It really hadn't sunk in yet, but it was going to make a big difference to my situation. It meant I could pay my way to a new life, maybe over the border in Mexico. With that kind of cash I could buy a fresh identity, even a passport. I could lie low in some godforsaken town until the heat was off and then try to carve out a future for myself.

Every instinct I had screamed at me to hit the road right now and head south, to seize the opportunity and flee the danger zone. But it'd mean never knowing what it had all been about and never finding peace because I'd be leaving Kate and her daughter to an uncertain fate. So I knew I couldn't do it.

Raymond Garcia would be able to help. I was sure of it. Not that I expected him to volunteer any information. It would have to be dragged out of him. I knew Garcia's type even though I'd never met him. He'd be a self-serving rat with no morals. Like all those other briefs who feed off the proceeds of organized crime.

I sat for a while mulling over all the questions I was going to ask him. But as the clock ticked the doubts began to form in my head. Who was I kidding? I was up against the titanic forces of the federal government and a powerful and ruthless criminal organization. I didn't stand a chance.

I was so inwardly focused that I didn't notice the silver Mercedes until it slowed to a crawl in front of me. As I watched it turn onto Garcia's driveway I felt a bolt of adrenaline. The car stopped in front of the garage and a man I assumed was Raymond Garcia got out of the driver's door. He was wearing chinos and a sleeveless red shirt. He went to the trunk and took out a set of golf clubs. That was when I got a good look at him. And realized that his face was familiar.

In fact it was a face I would have known anywhere.

41

Seeing Raymond Garcia came as a massive shock. I stared across the road in disbelief as he lugged his golf clubs into the house.

My breath slowed to nothing and every muscle in my body seemed to freeze over. I just didn't know what to make of it and for several minutes I couldn't move.

I sat there with my heart beating ferociously in my chest. For the first time since waking up in the FBI facility I was bleeding for a drink. I felt I needed a shot or two of something potent before confronting the lawyer.

There was no doubt in my mind that he was going to be as surprised as I was. Maybe even more so.

I started to think about how I'd approach him. He was bound to be a cautious guy. So if he checked first to see who was at the door there was no way he would answer it.

But then something happened that I didn't expect. The front door opened and Garcia came back out. He walked to the garage, unlocked it, and lifted up the slide-over door. Then he got into the Mercedes and started to nudge it into the garage. I saw my chance. He'd left the front door open.

I was out of the SUV in a flash and dashed across the road. The angle was such that he couldn't see me in the rear-view mirror. I hurtled through the door into a white-walled hallway. It was wide and bright, with a high ceiling and carpeted stairs. Ahead of me the hall opened out into a sunlit living room. I saw large windows and a sofa. There was a closed door to my right. Perfect, I thought. I could hide beyond it until Garcia came back into the house. Then I'd pounce.

I grabbed the door handle and pushed it open. Then I slid into a shiny, modern kitchen. It had marble countertops and stainless steel appliances. There was a breakfast bar and a dining area. I eased the door shut behind me and stuck my ear to it, listening for Garcia.

But I heard something else. Something that lifted the hairs on my arms.

A low, menacing growl.

I turned around and felt my system flood with fear.

A dog.

It was standing not seven feet away, having stepped out from behind the breakfast bar. It was a big, black Rottweiler, and it was looking at me like I'd invaded its territory. Its dark lips were pulled back in a ferocious snarl, revealing teeth like razor-sharp fangs.

I didn't move, not even to blink. I sucked in my breath and held it there. Why the hell hadn't it barked or howled when I rang the bell? Wasn't that what dogs were supposed to do? Maybe it had been sleeping. Or maybe it was deaf.

The animal stared at me. Its eyes were large and bloodshot, and thick muscles strained beneath its silky coat. I knew the breed to be one of the strongest and most dangerous, with powerful jaws and a vicious temperament.

I should have known that a guy like Garcia would have some kind of protection. And this killing machine was the ultimate fucking bodyguard.

I heard the garage door slam shut and realized I was done for. If I moved the dog would go for me. If I didn't move it would go for me anyway eventually. But I couldn't just stand there like lunch waiting to be eaten.

The dog stepped forward. Saliva foamed at the corners of its mouth. The growling got louder and I sensed it was about to attack.

The sound of the front door closing spurred me into action. I reached for the gun in my waistband and managed to get a grip on it. But as I pulled it out the dog threw itself at me with lightning speed.

It rammed into me with the force of an express train. I crashed against the door. The dog's jaws clamped over my arm, but I whipped it back before its teeth sank into the flesh. The gun fell from my hand and clattered onto the hardwood floor, but I somehow stayed on my feet.

As the dog tried to take a bite out of my thigh, I delivered a savage punch to its nose. It yelped like a human and one of its front legs gave way. It staggered sideways and I took the opportunity to jump clear and hurl myself across the room.

I wouldn't have made it if the door hadn't swung open at that point. The animal was momentarily distracted by the sudden appearance of its owner. It gave me the precious seconds I needed to reach the sink. Next to it I had spotted a knife rack.

I managed to pull a knife out just as the dog came charging at me. I heard Garcia cry out, but I wasn't sure if he was telling the dog to go for me or hold back.

I stood firm as the Rottweiler leapt at me. But in aiming for my face it left its broad, heavy chest exposed. And that's where I plunged the blade. Right up to the hilt.

It didn't stop the solid, grunting mass of fur and muscle from smashing into me. Its weight sent me sprawling backwards onto the floor and its teeth came to within an inch or so of my face. But thankfully death was instantaneous and it stifled even a final, pathetic whimper as the dog went limp and rolled onto its side.

A wave of relief and exhaustion washed over me. But there was no time to appreciate the fact that I hadn't been seriously hurt. I needed to brace myself for a new threat.

In the form of Raymond Garcia.

As I struggled to sit up he came into the room and stood over me, holding my gun. I couldn't tell from his expression if he was upset about the dog because he looked totally stunned. We shared a long moment of silence.

Then he mouthed a single word: 'Jordan?'

I didn't answer, just continued to stare up at him as my heart went wild in my chest.

'My God,' he said. 'You could almost be my twin brother.'

He was right. It was almost like looking in a mirror.

42

HE WASN'T EXACTLY my double. His eyes were blue and mine were brown. His lips were slightly thinner and his nose just a little wider.

There was also a bit more flesh below his chin. And his hairline had receded further back on his forehead. He was carrying a few more pounds than me and was at least two inches shorter.

But from a distance it would have been difficult to tell us apart. Especially given the fact that our hair matched and we both had a tan.

'You must be Garcia,' I said.

He studied me through squinting eyes, assessing something – maybe my level of desperation. Or maybe whether or not I was real.

I shook my head in bewilderment. My thoughts were coming too fast to articulate.

What did it mean? Was this guy my doppelganger? They say every-one has one – a man or woman who looks almost exactly like them. But if so, then what were the odds on me meeting mine in these circum-stances? A trillion to one maybe.

His eyes shifted from me to the dead dog and I felt a cold panic tighten in my throat. Had he been attached to the beast? Had it been a treasured pet as well as a guard dog? I hoped not.

His eyes moved back to me and I noticed them focus on the dog's blood that stained my T-shirt.

'I'm sorry about the dog,' I said.

His mouth tightened a little.

'No great loss,' he said. 'He stank and kept shitting. It means I won't have to pay a vet to put him down.'

I sat up straighter with my back against the cool surface of the fridge door. Garcia seemed unsure of himself. The hand that held the gun was trembling. His heavy breathing seemed to crackle in his throat.

'What are you doing here?' he said.

'Looking for answers,' I told him.

A knot appeared in his brow. 'How did you find out where I lived?'

'Your partner. I called in at your office at the same time he did. He took some persuading, but he eventually opened up.'

'What else did he tell you?'

'That you're probably stealing from the Texas Syndicate.'

He parted his lips in surprise.

'I don't give a damn if you're ripping off a good-for-nothing crime lord,' I said. 'That's not what I want.'

'Then what do you want?'

I held his gaze. 'I want to know why I'm not dead. Why the FBI took me to a restaurant to meet Martinez, but then set me up to be shot outside. Why your business card was in the pocket of the suit that Aaron Vance gave me to wear. And why my sister had to die.'

He took a deep breath through his nose.

'Your sister and the two agents should not have been killed,' he said. 'They would still be alive if the Feds had put a bullet in you outside the restaurant.'

'That much is obvious,' I said. 'It's the rest I'm interested in.'

I could see him turning it over in his mind, running through his options.

'On your feet,' he said.

I did as I was told. He motioned with the gun and stepped to one side.

'Into the hall. And then onto the living room. I have to call Vance. Let him handle this.'

I shuffled forward and canned the urge to turn around to try to wrest the gun from him. Any sudden movement was bound to spook him and cause him to squeeze the trigger even though he probably didn't want to.

In the living room he told me to stand with my back to a set of French windows. Beyond them was a large garden with a flat lawn and some trees. The room was L-shaped and sparsely furnished. Two sofas, a coffee table, a flat screen TV and a drinks cabinet. There was a house phone lying on the table. Garcia picked it up with his free hand.

'Look, before you call him will you tell me what's going on?' I said. 'I don't want to go to my grave not knowing.'

He ignored me and punched a number into the phone.

A moment later he cursed under his breath and I figured he'd got Vance's voice message.

'It's me,' he said into the phone. 'Call me straight back.'

Then he switched it off and licked his lips.

'Come on, Garcia,' I said. 'What does it matter if you come clean? I won't be telling anyone. Just start at the beginning. Tell me why they faked the execution.'

He thought about it some more, then shrugged.

'They did it because a few weeks earlier your picture was shown on the news,' he said. 'Aaron Vance saw it and realized that there was a striking resemblance between you and me. So he came up with a plan to fake the execution and make the world think you were dead. They knew it was possible because they'd done it before apparently. So guys like you could be experimented on.'

I felt the blood rush to my head. Could it be true that I'd been allowed to live because I looked like some crooked lawyer?

'They wanted to keep you alive so that they could kill you all over again,' he said. 'But the second time it had to be in front of Julio Martinez. That's why I arranged to meet him at the restaurant.'

I felt my heart rate spike as the penny dropped.

'They wanted Martinez to think it was me who was shot,' he said. 'That was the only way to convince the bastard I was really dead.'

43

'ABOUT TWO MONTHS ago I contacted Vance with a proposal,' Garcia explained. 'I told him I had a dossier full of incriminating information on the Texas Syndicate that would blow the organization apart.'

'Such as?' I asked.

'Bank records, offshore accounts, articles of association, the names of paid contacts within the state legislature, the police, the prison system and the media. Plus, details of their links with the Mexican drug cartels. Distribution routes, storage facilities, safe houses. Enough to put a lot of top people away for a long time.'

'What was the FBI's reaction?'

'They were keen. And why wouldn't they be? The Syndicate has become a major embarrassment to law enforcement agencies. It wields enormous power and influence, especially here in Texas. Nobody in my position has ever turned against it and so the Feds realized they couldn't pass it up.'

'So why have you decided to rat on them?'

'I want out and I need to do it before they realize I've been taking money that wasn't mine to pay off gambling debts.'

'Money that belonged to the Syndicate?'

He nodded. 'They trust me because we go back a long way. There are family connections down the line. So I have access to funds both here and abroad. About two months ago Martinez ordered the murders of four gang members who'd been feeding information to the cops. They were slaughtered and dumped in an alleyway not far from here. It was part of a crackdown on leaks and betrayal. It scared the hell out of me. So I moved a sizeable pile of cash into my own accounts and started planning for a new life far away.'

'But why fake your own death if you'll have to give evidence against the Syndicate eventually?'

'Because testifying in court was never part of the deal. I told Vance I wasn't prepared to do that. Or go into the witness protection programme. I know what would happen if I did. One day I'd be pulling out of my driveway and the car would explode. That's how it works. They'd eventually find me.'

'So the Feds went along with it?'

'They knew that what I had to give them made it worth their while. Everything is either documented on paper or on disc. It's all in a briefcase that's hidden upstairs. A briefcase full of dynamite. There's no need for me to testify against anyone.'

'So you told Vance that he had to convince the Syndicate you were dead so Martinez wouldn't look for you.'

'That's right. And Vance was tasked with coming up with a way to do it. He told me he was in his office when your photo appeared on the TV. He said he was struck by the likeness. He spent a week looking into it before outlining his proposal to the guys in Washington. They gave the go-ahead and then he told me how it would go down.'

'So these pants I'm wearing are part of a suit that belonged to you?'

He looked at them and nodded. 'Vance convinced me it would work. He said they had every angle covered. So I arranged to meet Martinez to go through some financial matters. While you were being taken to the restaurant in my place, I went to a safe house in Houston. But I had to come back here after you got away. I told Martinez I spent the night with a friend after the attempt on my life. He's been trying to find out who tried to kill me and why. But of course he's getting nowhere.'

I had to admit it was an ingenious plan. And it would have worked like a dream if the hooded guy hadn't missed me. But I felt the anger welling up inside me. My sister, two FBI agents and a San Antonio detective had died because of what this no good shyster had done.

I looked at the gun in his hand and tried to figure out if I could get it from him before he pulled the trigger.

And that's when I saw something that almost made me smile.

At that very moment the phone started ringing. He had placed it back on the coffee table, but as he reached for it I rushed him.

He jumped back and squeezed the trigger.

Click.

Before he could work out for himself why it hadn't fired I was on him. He tried to hit me with the pistol, but I grabbed his wrist with one hand and drove the other one into his stomach. As he doubled over I seized the gun from his grip and then brought it down hard on the back of his neck.

He collapsed in a heap, but remained conscious. I stepped away from him and said, 'You should never play with guns unless you know how to use them.'

He rolled on his side, clutching his stomach with one hand and the back of his head with the other.

'The safety catch,' I said, making a show of flicking it off. 'You left it on.'

The phone stopped ringing, and Garcia said, 'That was Vance. He'll think there's a problem and come over.'

I didn't think that Vance or any of his agents would press the panic button because Garcia hadn't answered the phone. So there was no rush to get going. Besides, I needed to consider my next move. An idea was taking shape in my mind, but it was risky and it might not work.

'What are you going to do?' Garcia asked.

There was a look of sheer terror in his eyes now that the tables had turned. He'd started to sweat and his face was devoid of colour. He started mumbling so I told him to be quiet. I wanted to think. My head was starting to ache. It felt like a giant bruise that was gently pulsating.

My mind dialled through what Garcia had told me. It was hard to believe that the most outrageous part of Vance's plan – the faked execution – had been so easy to pull off.

They knew it was possible because they'd done it before apparently. So guys like you could be experimented on.

Jesus.

Just how often had a death row inmate survived his own execution? And how many of them were still alive and hidden away in some grim government research facility? It was incredible and yet strangely plausible because lethal injection had become the accepted method of committing legalised murder. As Vance had pointed out to me, drugs could be used to make a person appear dead.

And it was easy to see why the government would want to do it. Why not make use of all those human guinea pigs? Far better to experiment with new drugs and dangerous chemical agents on real people than on rats or dogs or monkeys – especially people who are believed to be dead.

It means there are no concerned relatives, no financial liabilities in the event of death, no outcry over human rights issues, no worries about high mortality rates.

The debate over whether to use 'live' death row inmates for non-consensual clinical trials had been raging for years. Opposition to it was strong and I could see why the government had decided to start faking executions. Call me heartless, but I didn't actually have a problem with it. It was a way at least to make sure all those murderers and rapists paid their debts to society.

I wondered how many executions were faked each year and how inmates were selected. Maybe it depended on what drugs were being tested at any given time. Or perhaps, as in my case, one of the law enforcement agencies needed a corpse or someone to take a fall.

'You should go,' Garcia said. 'Just get as far away from here as you can. If you don't you'll end up dead. There can be no happy ending to this.'

'Tell me why I shouldn't kill you,' I said. 'It was you who sparked off the chain of events that led to my sister getting shot.'

'Don't lay that one on me,' he said. 'The only person who was supposed to die was you. But then you were going to die anyway. That's why I didn't feel bad. At least you got to live a while longer.'

In a perverse kind of way he had a point. In his place, given the circumstances, I might have done the same thing.

'How often have you been meeting with Vance?' I asked him.

'When we need to,' he said.

'Where?'

He swallowed. 'There's a small lake south of here close to the municipal airport. It's called Parson's Hollow. There's a parking area which hardly anyone uses.'

'How long would it take to get there?'

'Fifteen minutes or so.'

I pointed to the phone. 'Then I want you to call Vance back. Tell him to meet you there in an hour. If he asks what it's about tell him you want to talk over what's happened.'

'He'll smell a rat.'

'Not if you don't give him a reason to. If you do I'll blow your fucking head off.'

To make sure he got the message I waited for him to sit up and then pressed the muzzle of the gun against his forehead.

This time Vance answered and the lawyer told him he wanted to meet up.

'I just want a face to face conversation,' Garcia said. 'No it can't fucking wait. An hour at the lake. Be there.'

He severed the connection and handed me the phone. But in doing so he made a mistake that cost him his life.

He tried to grab the pistol from me. As I pulled my arm back his hand closed around mine and put pressure on my trigger finger.

The gun went off. The blast was muffled somewhat because it was pressed against his chest. He fell back, blood gushing from the wound. He started writhing in agony but I could tell from the damage that he would soon be dead. I knelt beside him, feeling a knife of guilt twist in my gut.

'Help me – please.' As he murmured these words bubbles of blood formed in his mouth. His face was scrunched up in pain.

For a fleeting moment I thought of doing as he asked, but instead, I said, 'The dossier. Tell me where it is and I'll get an ambulance for you.'

If I'd thought he had a chance I wouldn't have said it, but he didn't so I reckoned it was worth trying to salvage what I could from the situation.

He mumbled something that I didn't catch so I asked him again about the dossier, not really expecting him to give me a coherent answer. But then he opened his eyes, looked up at me, and mouthed a single word:

'Bath.'

Before I went in search of the bathroom I hurried into the kitchen to have a look out front. I wanted to know if the gunshot had attracted any attention. But the street was quiet and I saw no one out there. I reckoned if a neighbour had called 911 I would have soon heard the whoop of sirens.

The bathroom was upstairs, a large airy room with a corner tub. There was only one place to conceal a briefcase and that was behind the side panel which was made of plastic and easy to remove.

Sure enough, it was there. An ordinary black leather case. I took it out and thumbed it open, surprised that it wasn't locked. Inside were dozens of documents and three or four CDs.

I glanced at some of the paperwork and saw mention of several banks, including two in the Cayman Islands and one in Panama. There was also a list of names, among them a Judge Roy Sanders and a police detective named Dennis Cross. Next to the names a sum of money and what looked like a bank account number.

Garcia was right, I realized. This was dynamite.

I rushed back downstairs with the case, but by the time I got to the living room Garcia was already dead. I checked for a pulse and listened to his heart just to make sure.

I tried not to let it get to me. The guy had essentially got what had been coming to him. As a lawyer who represented some of the state's biggest criminals, there was always the strong possibility that his life would come to a violent end.

I forced myself to focus instead on the plan that was coming together in my head, a plan aimed at achieving the two objectives I'd now set myself. The first was to ensure that Kate came through this crazy mess in one piece.

And the second was to make someone pay for letting me spend ten years on death row for a murder I did not commit.

Before leaving Garcia's house I went to his study and fired up his computer. Having watched Kate surf the internet in the hotel I knew how to get online and use Google.

I was looking for a specific address and I thought it would take me an age to find it. But to my astonishment it took less than five minutes. In the new high-tech world nothing was private or secure anymore.

I wrote down the details on a sheet of paper. Then I raided Garcia's closet and took out one of his shirts and a sober grey suit. They were as good as new and probably made-to-measure. They were also a perfect fit.

I retrieved Garcia's keys from his pocket and took his wallet too. It contained credit cards and a hundred dollars in cash. Plus his driving license with the photo of a man who looked just like me, only younger.

A minute later I backed the Mercedes out onto the road. I left the engine running while I shut the garage door and went over to the SUV to get the holdall with the money.

As I drove away from Garcia's house I checked all around to see if anyone was watching me.

I saw no one.

44

THE SKY WAS a flawless blue when I got to the lake.

Vance was already there, standing at the water's edge next to a grey Honda Civic. He turned around as I drove towards him across the otherwise empty parking area. He gave me a little wave and I saw smoke from a cigarette curl above his head.

I brought the Mercedes to a halt on the black tarmac next to the Honda. Vance had returned his attention to the lake so when I got out he wasn't looking at me. I wondered how close I would have to get before he realized I wasn't Raymond Garcia.

I kept my head down as I approached him. The pistol was tucked into my waistband under the jacket.

On the way here I'd gone over what I was going to say to him and how I was going to play it. This was the only chance I was going to get to put things right for Kate. I couldn't afford to blow it.

He let me almost reach him before he turned around and the moment he did I drew out the pistol and pointed it at him. He froze with the cigarette in his mouth and two jets of smoke spewed out of his nostrils.

I don't think he realized it was me at first because his eyes were drawn to the gun. But as he looked up and registered my expression he suddenly knew. His mouth fell open and the cigarette dropped out onto the ground. He instinctively reached for his gun beneath the suit jacket.

'Don't do it,' I warned him. 'Not unless you want me to blow a hole in you.'

He stopped going for his gun and let his hand hang loose at his side.

'Raymond Garcia is dead,' I said. 'And before you start with the bullshit about you being my friend and saviour he told me everything.'

He ran the tip of his tongue across his upper lip.

'What do you mean?' he said. 'What is there to tell?

'Nice try,' I said. 'Now turn around.'

I gave him a hard stare to show that I meant business and he slowly turned. Then I held the gun against the back of his neck while I patted him down and removed his service pistol from its holster.

I pushed him up against the side of the Honda so that he was facing me again. Then with the gun still trained on him I told him what I knew. The deal he made with Garcia. How he came up with the plan to fake my execution. Why he wanted Julio Martinez to see me gunned down outside the restaurant. I then told him what I'd done with Michael Cruz and how Raymond Garcia had met his end. He listened to me in stupefied silence, his eyes suddenly bulbous with panic.

'You bastards have stepped over the line once too often,' I said. 'And because of that my sister is dead. Now I'm going to make you pay.'

I felt a wave of pure hot rage flow through me. It took a great deal of willpower not to pull the trigger.

'Your sister wasn't meant to die,' he said. 'And I'm really sorry that she did.'

'But you gave the order.'

'It wasn't like that. I sent our agents there to see if you'd turn up. They were meant to—'

I grabbed his jacket then and yanked it hard.

'Get on your knees,' I yelled.

When he was down I stood behind him and pressed the muzzle into the back of his head. My hand shook violently. I wanted to put the fear of God into him, make him believe that he was about to be executed.

'Don't kill me,' he pleaded. 'Just disappear. You've got a life now. I give you my word we won't try to find you. I'll tell Washington you're dead.'

I almost laughed.

'If you think you can save yourself by lying then you're a fool, Vance. I know you'll do whatever it takes to cover up what's happened. You can't afford not to.'

'But what good would it do to kill me?'

'It'll make me feel better. At least I'll know that I've got even for my sister.'

He started to speak but I cut him off and said, 'Where's Kate?'

He licked his lips and took a deep breath. 'She's at the safe house with her baby. The same place you spent the night.'

'Who's there with her?'

'Daniels.'

'Have you talked to her?'

'Briefly.'

'What has she told you?'

'Everything that happened to her after you abducted her in the parking lot,' he said. 'She said you stopped Larson from beating her up and then you took her to Mountain City. She said that by then she didn't think you would hurt her. That's why she picked you up after she heard the shots and saw you running away from the house.'

'What else did she say about me?'

Vance wiped a hand across his face. He knew what I was getting at.

'I want the truth,' I said.

He gave a slight nod. 'At first she tried to pretend she didn't know who you were. But I didn't believe her. So I pressed her on it and eventually she came clean and told me how she learned of your identity from the TV news report on the shootings.'

I wasn't surprised that Kate had opened up. She was scared and confused and would have found it hard not to buckle under the pressure of an FBI interrogation. Vance would have been firm, perhaps even rough. He would have used every trick in the Bureau's book to extract the relevant information from her.

'So you intend to kill her now to stop her talking,' I said.

He hesitated, which told me he was about to lie, so I kicked him hard in the back and he toppled forward onto his front.

'You bastard,' I said. 'You callous, fucking bastard.'

He lifted his face off the ground and said, 'What do you expect us to do? She knows you're alive. She's therefore a risk. And it's your fault for getting her involved.'

He was right about that. I was to blame. And that was why I couldn't just walk away. I owed her. She was an innocent victim in all of this just like my sister had been. I'd let Emily down, but I was determined to save Kate.

I told Vance to sit up. Then I stood in front of him. I stared hard into his face, as though seeing him for the first time. There was a hint of raw desperation in his eyes. Clearly he was a man who was not used to failure. To become a Special Agent in Charge he would have had to put in a lot of toil and commitment – and carried out his fair share of 'dirty jobs' no doubt. For despite its holier-than-thou image, the FBI had been a law unto itself since the reign of J Edgar Hoover. Everyone knew it and everyone ignored it. The Feds were experts at covering up their crimes and misdemeanours. They pulled out all the stops – including the elimination of people who they perceived to be threats or potential embarrassments. People like Kate and me.

'Here's the deal,' I said. 'I won't kill you if you have Kate and her baby brought to me here.'

He wrinkled his brow. 'Are you insane? I can't do that.'

'You can and you will,' I said. 'You'll call Daniels and get him to bring them. Just him. Nobody else. Tell him you've had orders from Washington to kill them both right away.'

'He won't believe me.'

'Why not? You're the boss and he'll know it's what you plan to do eventually anyway.'

He shook his head. 'It's not that simple. Something like that would have to be sanctioned.'

'Then sanction it or I'll kill you right now.'

He studied my expression for about fifteen seconds and he must have realized that I meant what I said because he agreed to do it. I told him to get his cellphone out slowly and to put it on speaker.

'Now make the call,' I said.

I was prepared to shoot him at that moment. But I didn't really want to. My thirst for revenge had been quenched by the realization that it would be cold-blooded murder. I'd killed the other men in self-defence. If I pulled the trigger now it would be an execution. And when it came down to it the primal instinct to kill wasn't in me.

Vance told Daniels he'd been ordered to neutralize the Pena woman and he wanted him to take her and the baby to the lakeside parking area where they'd had meetings with Garcia. He sounded convincing and Daniels did not even question the order.

'Tell the woman you're taking her to a hotel or something,' Vance said. 'Otherwise she might get worried.'

I took the phone from him and put it in my pocket. Then I got him to open the Honda's trunk and told him to get inside while I moved the Mercedes to the edge of the parking area where it couldn't be seen. He wasn't happy, but he complied because he knew he had no choice.

Five minutes later, after I'd parked the Mercedes amongst some bushes, I moved the Honda so that it was parallel with the side of the lake. That way I could position myself behind it when Daniels arrived.

I then let Vance out of the trunk.

'Give me your cuffs,' I said.

I knew he had a pair in his pocket because I'd felt them when I patted him down. I got him to lean forward over the Honda's hood and put his hands behind his back.

Then I attached them to his wrists.

'What now?' he asked.

'We wait,' I said. 'And when they get here I don't want you lying to Kate by telling her that you'll take care of her. If you won't tell her the truth, then keep your mouth shut.'

I looked up at the access road to the lake. There were no cars in sight. The sun was starting to go down, throwing shadows across the landscape.

I turned back to Vance and said, 'For your information Michael Cruz doesn't know who I am. My face was covered when I dropped in on his office. So there's no need to kill him. And one other thing. If I drive away from here with Kate then you can have Garcia's dossier. At least then it won't all have been for nothing.'

His eyes widened. 'You have it with you?'

'It's in the Merc,' I said. 'A briefcase full of documents and discs. Looks to me as though you could do a lot of damage with it.'

A smile almost touched his mouth. He began to say something but I told him to shut up because at that moment I saw a vehicle in the distance moving slowly down towards the lake.

45

I RECOGNIZED THE vehicle as it drew nearer. It was the Dodge that had pursued me through the city after the failed attempt on my life outside the restaurant.

I was crouched down behind the Honda next to Vance, peering through the front windows. I had the gun in one hand and held onto the cuffs with the other.

'If for any reason this doesn't go smoothly I swear I will put a bullet in you,' I said to Vance. 'Do you understand?'

He nodded.

The Dodge moved slowly towards us across the parking area. I couldn't see who was inside because of the tinted windows.

'Now just stay calm and don't try anything stupid,' I said. 'This could all be over in less than a minute and you'll get to see another day.'

The Dodge came to a stop. When nothing happened immediately I felt my whole body go stiff. The thought struck me suddenly that maybe Kate wasn't even inside.

But then the driver's door opened and a man stepped out. It was Daniels. I recognized him instantly. He opened the rear door and helped Kate out. She was holding Anna.

Seeing them caused an intense wave of relief to surge through me. Vance acknowledged their arrival with a curt nod. Daniels raised a hand in response. Then he took Kate by the arm and walked her towards the Honda.

When I jumped up I took them completely by surprise. Daniels stopped dead and glared at me. I aimed the gun at him and he looked from me to Vance.

'Just stay where you are,' I shouted. 'Don't move a muscle.'

But Daniels did what I feared he might do. He pulled Kate in front of him and whipped out his pistol. I couldn't risk taking a shot. So now there was a stand-off, and just to make things worse, the baby started to cry.

'Put your weapon down and step out from behind the vehicle,' Daniels yelled.

My response was to step behind Vance and hold the gun to his right temple.

'I suggest you talk some sense into your man,' I said to Vance. 'Before there's a bloodbath.'

Vance spoke with calm authority. He ordered Daniels to drop his pistol and let Kate go, explaining that they had no choice.

Daniels took a long time to do as he was instructed. His eyes kept shifting nervously between me and his boss. And all the time Anna kept crying. Finally he stepped away from Kate and tossed his gun onto the ground.

I shoved Vance forward and moved around the Honda. I asked Kate if she was OK. She looked petrified, but she nodded and started patting Anna on the back.

'What's going on?' she said.

I ignored her and told Daniels to get his cuffs out and warned him that if he resisted I'd shoot him.

'It's not an idle threat,' I said. 'I've got nothing to lose here.'

He didn't resist and a minute later his hands were cuffed and he was standing alongside Vance.

I stepped back from them and turned to Kate. Anna had stopped crying and was looking around curiously at her surroundings. When she saw me she smiled and I couldn't help but smile back.

'Please explain to me what's happening,' Kate said, her voice fragile.

'I couldn't let them kill you,' I said.

She was shocked. 'But they wouldn't do that.'

'So why do you think he brought you here?'

She looked at Daniels. 'He said he was taking me to a hotel.'

'Well there are no hotels here. You were brought here to be killed along with Anna.'

She looked at Vance and waited for him to tell her that I was lying. But he held his tongue and looked sheepishly down at the ground.

'Oh my God,' Kate said.

'They killed Larson,' I said. 'And they killed my sister. You'll be next

201

if you don't let me take you away from here.'

'The police,' she said. 'We have to go to the police.'

'If that's what you want to do then do it,' I said. 'But I can't. And be aware that without me to back up your claims they're unlikely to believe you. And there's a fair chance that while you're trying to convince them that your story is true you'll mysteriously disappear.'

She looked at me and I felt a smothering weight of guilt.

'I'm sorry I got you into this,' I said. 'But you've got to trust me now. You need to get away from here. I can help you start again.'

Her uncertain gaze lingered on me for a while longer and then she came to a decision.

'Very well,' she said in a tearful voice.

I got Vance and Daniels to give me their cellphones. I then flipped open the trunks of both vehicles and told them to climb in – Vance in the Honda and Daniels in the Dodge.

'Don't panic,' I said. 'As soon as we're away from here I'll put in a call to the cops to tell them where you are.'

'What about the dossier?' Vance said.

'It'll be under the Honda.'

He gave a slight nod. 'Thanks.'

A thought struck me and I said, 'I want you to make sure my sister is buried near our parents. The Green Pastures Cemetery in Houston.'

'Consider it done,' he said, before climbing into the trunk.

A few minutes later I stopped the Mercedes next to the Honda and slid Garcia's briefcase under the vehicle along with their cellphones and car keys.

I asked Kate to give me her cellphone and then tossed it in the lake.

'We'll get you a new one so that it can't be traced,' I said.

Then I drove away from the lake with Kate and her baby in the back seat.

46

KATE STARTED TO cry a few minutes after leaving the lake. Her sobs were pitiful and they reached deep inside me.

I said nothing because I knew she had to get it out of her system. She'd just discovered that she was going to have to embark on a new life and lose contact with her family and friends. Her name would have to change and she'd have to find somewhere else to live. It was devastating for her.

But I found a small crumb of comfort in the fact that her life had been shit before I arrived on the scene. She had told me so herself. And she'd been looking for a fresh start away from Texas and the man who had been violent towards her.

I could only hope that this new life would be a better one. And that one day she might even thank me for turning her world upside down.

It wasn't long before Anna was crying too, upset and confused by her mother's tears. I tried not to let it distract me as I drove east towards the interstate.

'Where are you taking me?'

'Houston,' I said. 'I'll check you into a hotel for the night. You can think about where you want to go. Then tomorrow I'll buy a car and take you there.'

'Can't we just keep driving? Put as much distance between us and Texas as we can?'

I shook my head. 'For one thing the car's stolen and the Feds will be looking for it. For another there's something I have to do tonight. It's why we're going to Houston.'

'What is it?'

'You don't need to know.'

She thought about that and thankfully chose not to press me.

'So how come you can buy a car?' she asked after a moment. 'I didn't think you had any money.'

'I got lucky,' I said. 'I've now got plenty of cash to help you get settled.'

'Why are you bothering,' she said. 'You could have been in Mexico by now. I didn't expect to ever see you again.'

I shrugged. 'You're in trouble because of me. It wouldn't be fair to leave you.'

She was silent for a spell, then said, 'I need things for the baby. I left everything back at the house.'

'No problem. We'll stop at a mall on the way. You can load up on essentials.'

Kate began whispering to Anna and then started humming a tune to try to get her to sleep. I felt tears pressing behind my eyes and I had to blink to keep them back.

'You'll be OK,' I said after a couple of beats. 'Things will work out.'

She stopped humming and said, 'I wish I could believe that.'

I wanted to say more to reassure her, but I wasn't convinced it would work so I said nothing and focused on the road ahead.

We stopped at a shopping mall just outside Houston. I called the cops from a pay phone and said I'd seen a man being forced into the trunk of a car at the lake close to the municipal airport in San Antonio. I hung up when they asked me for my name.

Then Kate went into a grocery store with $200 cash that I gave her. She came back out twenty minutes later with two bags filled with baby stuff.

We then drove to an upmarket hotel near the city centre, which had a large parking lot at the rear. I checked in under Garcia's name. I showed his driving license – which the desk clerk barely looked at – and then paid for a double room up front in cash.

The room was bigger and far more comfortable than the one we'd stayed in the previous night. There were two Queen-size beds, a plush en-suite bathroom and a large flat-screen TV. The hotel also supplied a crib for the baby and after Kate fed her she put her down for the night. We dimmed the lights and sat facing each other across a small occasional table with a fruit bowl on top. Kate looked gaunt and tired and her mouth was downcast.

'I suppose I ought to thank you for saving me,' she said. 'Seems like you're making a habit of it.'

'I'm sorry about Frank Larson,' I said. 'It wasn't good to see him like that.'

She looked up at the ceiling, her sad eyes glistening.

'Are you sure that he was killed by the FBI?' she said.

I nodded. 'Vance didn't deny it when I accused him. I can only assume that Larson recognized me and told them so, which was a big mistake.'

She thought about that and said, 'So how did you come to be at the lake with Vance?'

I filled her in then on everything that had happened to me since we had been separated and everything I'd learned from Garcia and Cruz. She listened without speaking and when I was finished I picked up the holdall and emptied the money on one of the beds.

Her eyes went saucer-wide.

'There's about eighty thousand dollars there,' I said. 'It'll make it possible for both of us to buy new identities and solve a lot of other problems.'

She stared at the money in stunned silence, her face pale and drawn, her eyes heavy and swollen. And then a tear trickled down her left cheek.

She got up suddenly and rushed into the bathroom where she broke down. She left the door open so I followed her in. She was leaning over the sink, crying.

I reached out, put a hand on her shoulder and found it impossible to suppress a shimmer of desire. *God, this woman would be easy to love,* I thought.

The next thing I knew she was in my arms and I was holding her close to me as she wept against my chest. The wave of emotion that swept through me was both powerful and unexpected. It made me realize that I cared for Kate even though we had only just met and I knew nothing about her. It was a strange yet exhilarating feeling. And scary too because it gave rise to the absurd idea that maybe fate had brought us together for a purpose.

She stopped crying and took a step back. I still had my hands on her shoulders and could feel the sweetness of her breath on my face. She gazed up at me and her sad eyes drew me in. Something passed between us then but I wasn't sure what it was or if it meant anything.

But I did know that I suddenly wanted to kiss her, to feel the taste of her lips against mine. I resisted, fearing that she would pull away or cringe at the prospect of kissing a convicted murderer.

Things were going to be tough enough in the days ahead, I thought. I didn't want her to suddenly become suspicious of my motives.

'I'm sorry about the tears,' she said. 'It's just too much to take in.'

I dropped my hands away from her shoulders and smiled.

'No need to apologize,' I said. 'I know this can't be easy.'

She turned to look at herself in the mirror above the sink and grimaced at her reflection. Then she pulled a tissue from the box beside it to wipe her eyes.

I had to fight the urge to take her in my arms again. It was so strong that I backed out of the bathroom so as not to make a fool of myself. I went straight to the mini-bar and took out a miniature whisky. I downed it in one long swallow and felt it burn its way through my gullet.

Kate emerged from the bathroom, her cheeks red and slightly puffy. She fixed me with a penetrating gaze and then walked over to me and took my face in her hands.

'I want you to know that I'm grateful for what you're doing, Lee,' she said. 'I know it would be easier for you if you just took off and didn't concern yourself with Anna and me. But you've chosen not to and it says a lot about you.

'And you can't blame yourself for what's happened. You've been an unwilling pawn in a dangerous game and we've both been swept along by a chain of events. But at least we're still alive and I'm beginning to think that maybe we should look at this as an opportunity. Not many people get the chance to start their lives all over again from scratch.'

I don't know who moved first, whether it was Kate or me, but suddenly we were locked in a tight embrace.

What happened next took me completely by surprise.

47

HER KISS WAS subtle at first, the merest brush of her lips against mine. But it set my body on fire and stole my breath away. Her tongue eased my lips apart, the kiss widening, growing, becoming more intense.

I felt a surge of testosterone as she ran her fingers through my hair. Her breath was coming in fast, high-pitched gasps and the heat from her body was making me dizzy. I could barely control my excitement as I realized where this was going.

I hadn't been with a woman for so long and if there had been time to think I'm sure I would have succumbed to an attack of anxiety. But Kate was taking the lead and it was all I could do to keep up.

She pulled off my jacket and then unbuttoned my shirt, all the time pressing her lips against mine and moaning like a hungry tigress. I fumbled with her belt and she must have sensed that I was out of practice because she undid it for me and then unzipped her jeans and pulled them down along with her panties. Before I knew it she was pulling at my belt and by the time I was naked from the waist down I felt I was going to explode.

I helped her off with her T-shirt and marvelled at her silky-smooth skin. She had wide, dark areolas on small breasts.

We fell onto the bed farthest away from the cot and a decade of involuntary celibacy meant I couldn't hold back. But she understood because she pushed me onto my back and lowered herself on top of me.

It was like I had died and gone to heaven. As she rode me, I clenched my eyes shut, but the tears found their way free, nonetheless.

I lasted longer than I thought was possible – maybe a whole minute – and I was pretty sure that when Kate cried out it wasn't just for my benefit.

Afterwards we rolled onto our sides and held on to each other. We were both panting and sweating and I found it hard to believe what had just happened.

'I've never made a man cry before,' she whispered.

'I hope it didn't put you off,' I said, embarrassed.

She laughed. 'I can tell there's a lot you've forgotten about women. I just had the most moving experience of my entire life.'

I wanted to tell her that I felt the same way but my throat was so thick with emotion that I couldn't form the words. She stroked my face and kissed me softly on the lips.

'I think we both needed that,' she said.

I grinned. 'I know I did. It's been a long time.'

We snuggled up to each other and I just wanted to savour the moment. But the feelings stirred up by what had just happened sparked a riot of thoughts in my head. I wondered if this was the beginning of something real. Or was it nothing more than two desperate people seeking a brief respite from a horrible reality?

And I wondered too if what I was planning to do later tonight would turn out to be a big mistake. I didn't have to do it, after all. And it was going to be a huge risk.

But then I was reminded of the promise I made to myself on death row – that, if I ever got released, I would seek out the person who had really murdered Kimberley Crane all those years ago. And then I'd make them suffer for what they did to her – and to me.

'Are you always this restless after sex?' Kate said.

'I can't remember,' I answered truthfully.

She laughed. 'What you need is another drink. And maybe some dinner.'

I kissed her on the neck and said, 'Let's check out the menu.'

There were hotel robes hanging on the bathroom door so we slipped them on. As I poured us each a glass of wine from the mini bar, Kate studied the room-service menu. She chose to have a pizza with a mound of trimmings and a bowl of fries. I ordered the same for me.

While we waited for the food to arrive I asked her where she wanted to begin her new life. She gave me a serious look. 'Before I can even contemplate that I want to know what you plan to do when we get there. I have to think about Anna. She's all I've got.'

I told her what I had in mind and explained that nothing was set in stone. I said we'd rent apartments for a short time and I'd set about finding someone who could supply us with false ID documents.

'It shouldn't be that difficult,' I said. 'The country is sinking under the weight of forged papers by all accounts.'

Our pizzas arrived then and we got stuck in. They were hot and delicious and I washed mine down with two glasses of wine. When we were done I told Kate I was going out.

'Do you have to?' she asked, a worried expression on her face.

I nodded. 'There's something I need to do. Something that's important to me. It's why we're here in Houston.'

'Will you be coming back?'

I smiled reassuringly. 'Of course I will. Later on.'

'But what if something happens to you?'

I pointed to the money that was still piled up on the bed.

'Then you've got enough cash there to get you wherever you want to go.'

She drew in a breath and said, 'Please be careful.'

'I will,' I told her.

48

GIDEON CRANE SAT at the table next to his swimming pool contaminating the air with cigar smoke.

It was a cold night, but the whisky swirling around inside him stopped him feeling it. He'd downed half a bottle already and he was determined to finish it before going to bed. And why not? It was the only way to blunt his senses and deal with this whole fucking nightmare.

Crane hadn't spoken to his wife since she'd stormed into his office to tell him that she knew about his affair with Beth. How long ago was it? Three? Four hours? He couldn't remember.

He'd tried to talk to her, but she'd retreated to their bedroom and had refused to come out. He'd heard her crying and it had infuriated him. *He* was the one who should be shedding tears. It was *his* life and *his* political aspirations that were under threat like never before.

He knew he faced a stark choice. Stay with Beth and try to weather the storm after Pauline filed for divorce and branded him a serial adulterer.

Or end it with Beth – the woman he loved – in the hope that Pauline would stick with him and not ruin his chances of becoming President. But how could he ever trust her? She was a manic depressive who had already tried to kill herself. She was unpredictable at best and was certain to make his life hell from now on.

He stared up at the stars, as though beseeching them to tell him what to do. But instead their cold indifference filled him with an intense rage.

Crane took a deep pull on his cigar and spun what was left of it into the pool. His eyes felt dry and heavy and his head was starting to swim a little.

He shouldn't have let it come to this. He should have dealt with Pauline a long time ago, when he first realized that she would never recover from finding out that she could not conceive. That was when she started to drift away from him and into her own tortured world.

Now he would suffer the consequences of standing by her out of self-pity and a misguided sense of duty. She was suddenly a woman scorned as well as a drug-dependent depressive. And that made her a lethal weapon.

He reached across the table for the whisky bottle and poured some into his empty glass. No half measures. He filled it to the brim and gulped down a mouthful before topping it up again.

His head thumped like a bass drum and blood pumped super-charged through his veins. He knew that in the morning he would have the mother of all hangovers. But he didn't care. This was a pivotal moment in his life and he needed help in dealing with it. Alcohol was the great comforter in times of crisis. That was why he had drowned himself in booze after that night ten years ago when everything changed.

Then, as now, he'd been confronted with an agonizing dilemma. His mind sucked him back and the images of the carnage pressed in on him.

When he'd woken up from the blows inflicted by Lee Jordan he'd found Kimberley lying on the floor with blood on her face and head. Jordan's gun was next to her. It was obvious he had attacked her before fleeing.

But she wasn't dead.

Crane knew that as soon as he knelt beside her and saw that she was still breathing. At first he tried to wake her, but then something stopped him – the sudden realization that he had been presented with an extraordinary opportunity to solve a problem. He saw a way to avoid a costly divorce and hold onto his fortune; a way to embark on a new life with Pauline, his then mistress.

In that moment of clarity he was seized by an impulse that was so strong he couldn't fight it. Probably because deep down he didn't want to.

So he'd picked up the gun with his handkerchief, careful not to smear Jordan's prints.

And then he'd shot his wife.

It had been as simple and as heartless as that.

The cops had never suspected a thing and the only person who knew the truth was Lee Jordan. But Jordan's story that he had hit Pauline in self-defence when she attacked him, but had not murdered her, was never believed.

Crane felt no guilt or sympathy for Jordan because the bastard should not have broken into their home. He'd found it almost as easy to live with what he'd done to Kimberley. The guilt was there, of course, a dull ache inside him, but he had always been able to supress it, even after he stopped drinking heavily.

Now, as a bitter taste settled in his mouth, he wondered if it had all been worth it. He was right back where he began – in a loveless marriage and with a difficult choice to make. Only now things were much worse. He was on the edge of a precipice. And whatever decision he made, the outcome – in respect of his political ambitions – would almost certainly be the same. He'd be ruined. The campaign would be over and he'd become a pariah. It would be the end of his lifelong dream and the start of an endless struggle with shame and disappointment.

Suddenly a thought wormed its way into his brain and he realized there *was* a way out for him. It sparked a surge of optimism. It was actually quite simple. He would do to Pauline what he'd done to Kimberley, only this time he'd make it look like suicide. It would be easy enough, considering her history.

All he had to do was go upstairs and get the gun he kept in the drawer beside the bed. He'd stick the muzzle in her mouth and blow the top of her head off. Then he'd put the gun into her hand and raise the alarm.

Sure, he would have to pull out of the race for the Republican nomination, but not for long. He'd stage a miraculous comeback before the Primaries, claiming it was what his troubled wife would have wanted.

As the idea grew in his head he felt his face flare with hope. This was his way out. He was sure of it. It was the solution to his problem, a way of getting both Beth and the Presidential nomination. Pauline's brother would be an issue, but he'd solve that by throwing money at him. He was sure that would work.

As he warmed to the idea he reached again for the whisky bottle, but this time he fumbled with it and it fell off the table. He tried to catch it, but in doing so he lost his balance and his chair toppled over, throwing him onto the patio. The bottle exploded next to him, the glass shattering into dozens of pieces, some of which rolled into the pool.

'Shit,' he yelled.

He tried to pull himself up, but he felt dizzy and disoriented. So he just lay there for about half a minute.

Then he struggled to a sitting position, closed his eyes and took a long, deep breath.

When he opened his eyes again he discovered he was no longer alone.

A figure loomed over him. A familiar figure.

It sent a chill through every fibre of his being. He was so stricken with terror that he couldn't even scream.

All he could do was stare.

At the ghost of Lee Jordan.

49

THE MAN WHO wanted to be the next US President looked absolutely terrified.

His eyes bulged out of their sockets as he stared up at me from where he sat on the glass-strewn patio. I pointed the gun at his chest but I don't think he even saw it. His gaze was locked on my face and it was clear that he thought I was an apparition.

His fear and confusion filled me with a heady sense of satisfaction. What he'd done had festered inside me for so many years. I'd had to accept that he had got away with murder by incriminating me. Nobody believed my story. In the face of all the evidence and Crane's emotional testimony it wasn't surprising.

That was why it had been impossible for me to resist the temptation to come here. Having been given the opportunity I knew I had to confront him and then to kill him. For what he had put me through and for what he had put Marissa and Emily through. Not to mention what he had done to his own wife.

I'd been watching him from the bushes at the edge of the lake before climbing the fence into his garden. Getting here had been relatively easy considering it was a gated community. A sign at the entrance had stated that the development was protected by a company called Security Inc., but I'd figured that even if the alarm was raised it would take them time to respond and then they'd have to find me. In the dark I'd been able to mount the perimeter fence without being seen and because the houses – all modern colonials – were so far apart, it'd taken only a few minutes to locate Crane's property.

Killing him was going to be easier than I thought. I hadn't expected him to be outside smoking a cigar and getting slowly drunk. And now that he was in front of me all I had to do was pull the trigger and leave.

'I know you killed your wife,' I said. 'I've always known. I didn't mean for her to get hurt. I hit out in a blind panic and the gun struck her on the head. But she was alive when I ran from the house. I made sure of it. I didn't shoot her so it must have been you.'

He clasped his hands together as though in prayer and said, 'Oh God, I'm so sorry.'

And there it was. An admission. Given willingly because he was drunk and thought I was a ghost that had come back to haunt him. It was almost laughable.

'You let me rot in a cell for ten years,' I said. 'All the time you knew I was innocent.'

'Forgive me,' he said, his voice pleading. 'Please.'

'My wife died because of what you did, Crane. And so did my sister. You've destroyed so many lives.'

He was sobbing now. The high-flying, powerful politician who cut a sharp and authoritative figure on TV was now a whimpering wreck. It made me want to drag this out, to watch him suffer, to wallow in his pain. But there was no time.

'You're a piece of shit, Crane,' I said. 'You don't deserve to live.'

A frown creased his brow suddenly and he leaned his head to one side.

'You're not a ghost,' he said. 'You're real.'

I grinned sardonically. 'Of course I'm real, you idiot.'

He was stunned. 'But I was there in the death chamber. I saw them kill you.'

'You *thought* that's what you saw,' I said. 'But it didn't happen. And now I'm here to kill you.'

'This is not possible,' he said. 'It can't be.'

'Why did you kill your wife?' I asked him.

Crane unclasped his hands and raked his fingers through his hair. His body shuddered with an involuntary spasm.

'Answer the fucking question,' I yelled. 'Why did you kill your wife?'

A sudden panic overcame his features and he said, 'It was too good a chance to pass up. I had an opportunity to get rid of her. It was a way out of the marriage.'

'You bastard,' I said.

I raised the gun and thought about the woman he had killed and all the years I'd spent on death row waiting to die.

And then I thought what a tragedy it would be if this vile man ever became President of the United States.

I started to squeeze the trigger.

But just then a voice behind me said, 'Don't shoot, Mr Jordan. If you do I will kill you.'

50

I turned my head slowly. Pauline Crane was standing there in a light-coloured dressing gown aiming a pistol at me.

I recognized her immediately from the TV and from the witness room in the execution chamber. She looked pale and dishevelled and her body was ramrod stiff.

The light from the pool danced in her eyes and her face was taut and serious.

'Please put the gun down,' she said. 'I promise I'll shoot if I have to.'

Her husky voice contained a controlled determination that left me in no doubt that she would.

I lowered my arm, placed the gun gently on the table, and cursed under my breath. I should have been more careful. Seeing Crane outside by the pool had caused me to drop my guard.

'Thank God,' Crane said, getting quickly to his feet. 'This bastard was going to kill me.'

But his relief was short-lived. As he took an unsteady step towards his wife she shifted the gun away from me and pointed it at him.

'That's far enough, Gideon,' she said.

He stopped dead and stared at her.

'What the fuck is this?' he hissed.

She regarded him with utter contempt and said, 'When I was upstairs I heard breaking glass. Then I heard voices. Just before I came outside I heard what you said about Kimberley. What you did to her.'

The sudden silence was electrifying. I watched the blood drain from Crane's face. Then he curled his lip and shook his head.

'I made it up, sweetheart,' he said. 'It's not true. None of it.'

His wife's eyes lit up with a sudden fury.

'You're a liar. You murdered Kimberley. And likely as not you'll do the same to me so you can be with your whore.'

'Don't be ridiculous,' he said. 'Please, Pauline. Stop this.'

She turned to me and said, 'I'll apologize on his behalf, Mr Jordan. I honestly had no idea.'

Crane snorted, a phlegmy back-of-the-throat noise.

'Are you crazy?' he ranted, slurring his words. 'This guy has come back from the fucking dead. He wants to kill me and he'll kill you too. So wise up and shoot him.'

But she kept the pistol trained on Crane. His anger mounted, fuelled by shock and whisky.

'Pauline, listen to me,' he said. 'I love you. I'd never hurt you. And I didn't kill Kimberley. You have to believe me.'

'I know what I heard,' she said. 'And right now it's all I can do just to look at you.'

'If you pull the trigger you'll be making a terrible mistake,' he said. 'We need to talk.'

'There's nothing to talk about. I'm going to kill you because I don't want the world to know what you did. People will think I was a party to it.'

Crane snapped his eyes on me and said, 'This is a dream, right? It's the whisky. I'm hallucinating.'

For just a split second I thought of pleading with Pauline to spare him so that he could face a trial and clear my name. But of course there was no guarantee it would work out that way. He would simply deny what he'd said and there would be no way to prove it.

So I kept my mouth firmly closed.

'You're a despicable man, Gideon,' Pauline said. 'It shames me that I actually fell in love with you.'

Crane turned back to his wife and then suddenly lunged at her. But with all the whisky inside him there was no way he was going to reach her in time.

She squeezed the trigger and the gun went off with a sharp retort.

51

THE BULLET HIT Gideon Crane in the chest and the force of it sent him sprawling backwards into the pool with a loud splash.

Blood from the wound immediately poured into the bright blue water like leaking oil from a stricken ship.

I stared, mesmerized, as his body floated on the surface, a shocked expression frozen on his face. His dead eyes stayed open and his limbs drifted out from his torso to form the shape of a star.

I looked anxiously at his wife, expecting her to turn the gun on me. But she'd already dropped her arm and the weapon was hanging at her side.

She turned to me and I was surprised to see that she appeared so calm and unruffled despite the fact that she had just murdered her own husband. I could see tears in her eyes but they didn't fall.

'You need to go, Mr Jordan,' she said wearily. 'Someone will have heard the shot. The police and security teams will be here soon.'

'Are you all right?' I said.

She nodded. 'I will be. In time.'

'What are you going to say to the cops?'

'I'm going to tell them that he was shot by an intruder.' Then she held out the pistol. 'That's why I want you to take this with you, along with your own gun.'

'But if it's registered they'll know its missing.'

'This is not my husband's revolver,' she said. 'It's mine and we've never bothered to register it. So please take it.'

I stepped up to her and took the gun.

'He got what he deserved,' she said. 'I'm sorry I denied you the pleasure of killing him. You must hate him even more than I do.'

'At least he's dead,' I said.

She took a deep breath. 'I was there you know. At the execution. I saw you die.'

'The execution was faked,' I said.

She creased her brow into a dark V. 'And the authorities just let you go? That makes no sense.'

I shook my head. 'I got away from them. They want me dead. I'm on the run. For your own sake don't tell anyone I was here.'

'It'll be our secret,' she said. 'But would you tell me why they let you live?'

'It's a long story. There's no time.'

She thought about it a moment and said, 'If you're still able to get in touch by phone in the weeks ahead then call me. You'll have no trouble finding the house number, I'm sure.'

'So you can satisfy your curiosity?'

'That's partly the reason,' she said. 'But I also want to send you some of my husband's money. You lost ten years of your life because of him. He owes you big time. And I feel that I do too.'

I heard the distant shriek of a siren.

'I'd better go,' I said, picking up the gun.

'Good luck, Mr Jordan,' she said. 'I think you're going to need it.'

Epilogue

I CAME AWAKE to the shrill sound of a child's laughter. I had no idea how long I'd been asleep. I'd probably dozed off shortly after we finished our picnic. Hardly surprising since I'd downed two glasses of sangria with the sandwiches that Kate had made.

Thankfully I was still wearing my shades so they protected my eyes from the fierce glare of the sun. It was still high in the sky and full of strength.

I sat up, pressing my hands into the soft white sand. Beneath me the multi-coloured towel was wet with my perspiration.

The beach was still pretty crowded and there were lots of people in the sea. They were swimming, splashing, messing around in rubber dinghies.

Kate was at the water's edge playing with Anna. The sight of them filled me with a deep sense of joy. I stroked my new beard and shoved out a grateful sigh. We were ten weeks into our new lives and there was every reason to believe we had a future.

My name is now Edward Riley. Kate's name is Cheryl Fuller, and her daughter is Bella.

I bought our new identities from a guy I sought out during two weeks we spent in Mexico City after leaving Texas. It cost me ten thousand dollars and for that I obtained ID cards, passports and even social security numbers.

I was confident that the FBI didn't know where we were. How could they? We'd been careful not to leave a trail.

Our apartment was here in Cancun, with a terrific view of the Gulf of Mexico. We'd leased it for six months – long enough to decide where we wanted to spend the rest of our lives.

And if we wanted to spend them together.

It was the one good thing to come out of all that had happened. I'd found love again. At least I thought so. Put it this way – I couldn't imagine a future without Kate, and I was pretty sure she felt the same way about me.

Money was not a problem. With our new IDs we were able to open a joint account with a Mexican bank and deposit fifty thousand dollars of the money I took from Garcia and Cruz. The rest I spent on a car and the apartment.

Plus, I called Pauline Crane from Mexico City as requested and told her about the faked execution and why the Feds did it. True to her word she quickly arranged for the sum of three hundred thousand dollars of her late husband's money to be paid into an offshore account to which I was given sole access.

Which meant I was rolling in cash!

The story of how an intruder murdered Pauline's husband dominated the media for weeks afterwards. Pauline described how Gideon Crane was outside by their pool enjoying a drink and a cigar when the attack happened. She told the police that she saw the killer from her bedroom window and described him as a black man in his early twenties. The cops were still looking for him.

Meanwhile, the FBI had announced that they had identified the man who murdered my sister and two of their agents as well as Frank Larson. According to the Feds the killer was one Raymond Garcia, a San Antonio-based lawyer whose company was under investigation for alleged links with organized crime.

Garcia was conveniently found shot dead in his home but the Feds said there was plenty of evidence linking him to the murders.

It was a smart move by Aaron Vance. He managed to clear up much of the mess he'd created in one fell swoop.

In fact he was still the man of the moment, following the arrests of a dozen or more senior members of the Texas Syndicate. His team had also seized many of the gang's assets and frozen some of their bank accounts in Panama and the Cayman Islands. According to reports the Feds had been given a ton of incriminating evidence by someone on the inside.

There had been so many big stories around since we fled from Texas

This one is for my good friend Ken Jacobs
who has sadly moved away and taken his bar with him

that the flow of news from Huntsville during the past couple of months had attracted very little attention.

But in that time no fewer than five inmates had been executed at the Walls prison. I remembered each of them from my time on death row, along with all the gory details of their crimes. As far as I was concerned they'd all deserved to die. The world was a better and safer place without them.

I just prayed that none of them was actually still alive – courtesy of the federal government.

'So you're awake at last,' Kate said as she walked up the beach towards me with Anna in her arms.

'You should have woken me,' I said.

She laughed. 'You were out to the world.'

She looked beautiful in her bikini. Her slender body was tanned and her dyed blonde hair made a striking contrast.

She sat down beside me and Anna immediately pointed back at the sea.

'She can't get enough of it,' Kate said. 'She loves it here.'

'Me too,' I said.

Kate looked at me and smiled. 'Do you really think we can make this work, Lee?'

I smiled back at her. 'Absolutely. Everyone deserves a second chance and this is ours.'

She leaned forward and gave me a long, lingering kiss.

'What was that for?' I said.

'That was for abducting me at gunpoint. If you hadn't I'd still be living in fear of losing my child – and maybe even my life.'

'But you're on the run from the federal government,' I said. 'You're with a guy who's wanted by the FBI and you've been forced to adopt a new identity.'

She laughed again. 'Exactly. So how did I ever get to be so lucky?'